KU-270-336

The
Silver Ladies
of Penny
Lane

BOOKS BY DEE MACDONALD

The Runaway Wife
The Getaway Girls

The
Silver Ladies
of Penny
Lane

Dee MacDonald

Bookouture

Published by Bookouture in 2019

An imprint of StoryFire Ltd.

Carmelite House
50 Victoria Embankment
London EC4Y 0DZ

www.bookouture.com

Copyright © Dee MacDonald, 2019

Dee MacDonald has asserted her right to be identified
as the author of this work.

All rights reserved. No part of this publication may be reproduced,
stored in any retrieval system, or transmitted, in any form or by
any means, electronic, mechanical, photocopying, recording or
otherwise, without the prior written permission of the publishers.

ISBN: 978-1-78681-984-0
eBook ISBN: 978-1-78681-983-3

This book is a work of fiction. Names, characters, businesses,
organizations, places and events other than those clearly in the
public domain, are either the product of the author's imagination
or are used fictitiously. Any resemblance to actual persons, living or
dead, events or locales is entirely coincidental.

For all Silver Ladies everywhere.

CHAPTER ONE

NEW BEGINNINGS

It was the tenth of January, one of those dull, dismal days when you thought the sun would never shine again. A day when Tess Templar stared at her less than svelte self in the full-length mirror that she and Orla had positioned with great care in the shop, to ensure it gave the most flattering reflection to the larger ladies who'd be pirouetting in front of it. It certainly wasn't doing much to flatter her. At this rate she'd be her own best customer.

She took a deep breath as the first customer of the morning squeezed through the door of Curvaceous, Tess's boutique, specialising in made-to-measure outfits for the larger lady.

'Good morning, Mrs Byron-Sommers!' she said brightly.

'Not a lot good about it,' muttered Mrs Byron-Sommers. 'It's freezing cold and wet out there.' She glared at Tess as if the weather were her fault.

'Oh dear,' said Tess. 'Well, never mind. Let's get you measured up then, shall we?'

Orla, her best friend and business partner, rolled her eyes and said, 'I'm just going to pop out for a couple of minutes.' And, grabbing her purse, she headed out of the shop.

She's going to buy buns, thought Tess as she got out her tape measure, and that's the *last* thing I need. She was still in shock after weighing herself that very morning for a post-Christmas reality check. And there it was – black on white – fourteen stone! *Fourteen* stone! One hundred and ninety-six pounds! Tess had even moved the scales around to three other places on the bathroom floor, hoping for a lower reading because fourteen stone just could *not* be right. But four positions out of four informed her that it *was* right. The New Year was a time for resolutions. And Tess knew she needed to do something about her weight. But more important than that, she needed to drag herself out of the rut that she'd got herself into. Because since David had died she'd lost the will for self-improvement. She had no one to feel special for. There was no man in her life now. She never met any, of course, because she never went anywhere to meet them. For that matter, where *did* you meet a man these days? Certainly not in a shop specialising in larger ladies' outfits.

And now she faced a very long morning with Mrs Byron-Sommers, a demanding woman, to put it mildly, who was finding it impossible to stand still due to sneezing every few seconds.

'I know you have a nasty cold, Mrs Byron-Sommers,' Tess said, her patience waning, 'but I really need you to stay as still as possible for just a minute, while I try once more for an accurate bust measurement.'

Mrs Byron-Sommers sighed noisily. 'I can't stand around here all day; I should be in my *bed*, you know, and I made a special effort to come here.' She clearly thought she was doing Tess an enormous favour by being here at all, and spraying the place liberally with her germs.

At that moment Orla came back through the door, clutching a paper bag after her morning pilgrimage to the bakery. She deposited the bag on the desk. 'Here, let me hold one end of that tape,' she said to Tess, rolling her eyes again. Between them they succeeded in encircling the woman, and Tess finally noted the measurement.

'Sure you'll be pleased as punch with the lovely outfit our Tess'll be making for you,' Orla said to their voluptuous customer, who was struggling back into her polyester dress.

'I certainly hope so,' Mrs Byron-Sommers replied, in a manner that indicated she had her doubts.

'See you next week then for the fitting,' Tess called, as the woman strode away without so much as a thank you.

'I'll put the kettle on,' Orla said, disappearing into the back of the shop. 'You'll be in need of refreshment. That woman is bloody impossible.'

'All I need now,' Tess said wearily, 'is to catch her damned germs.'

'You'll feel better with one of Pastry Parker's doughnuts inside you,' Orla said, rustling in the bag. 'And would you believe they're still *warm*!'

So it was doughnuts today.

'I won't have a doughnut,' she said firmly.

'Ah well, I'll just have to have them both,' said Orla. 'Anyway, I don't know what you're worrying about; you're quite happy as you are, aren't you?'

No, thought Tess, I'm not. I've let myself go, I feel old and unattractive. She hadn't felt like this when David was alive, but she wasn't as fat then either. Her years with David had been so special. She'd enjoyed being part of a couple again after five years of being divorced from the father of her children, Gerry. Now, almost three years without David, she felt she was drifting aimlessly into some sort of abyss. Was it too late at sixty-two to contemplate finding happiness once more? Trying something new? Perhaps even having an adventure of some kind? Probably not, with the shape she was in now. But she'd bust a gut before she admitted as much to Orla. Orla, of course, was equally rotund, but far less bothered by it. Her mantra was that large ladies did not want to come into this specialist shop to be served by two waif-like women. Orla was still very much on the lookout for a man again, but didn't think they were worth dieting for.

'I trust you'll still be coming to Boulters for an all-you-can-eat lunch on Wednesday?' Orla asked, as she tackled the second doughnut.

Tess sighed. Well, perhaps just one last time…

Tess and Orla had been friends for nigh on thirty years, ever since they lived next door to each other on Hawthorn Road; Orla and Gavin Regan from Dublin, and Tess from Scotland with Gerry Templar, her then husband, *very* Home Counties – Surbiton born and bred. Then, fifteen years after they'd first moved in, Gavin had a massive heart attack and departed Hawthorn Road, and this earth, at only forty-five years old. And Gerry, five years later, at fifty-five, left Hawthorn Road too, but Gerry left for Ursula, twenty years his junior. And Ursula was thin as a wafer.

The Hawthorn Road house was sold, and Tess had moved into a small three-bedroom cottage in Temple Terrace on the far side of Milbury with her two children. The name had tickled her; Tess Templar of Temple Terrace! There appeared to be no trace of any temple in the area, and Tess was to find out later that the builder of these cottages, back in 1834, was one Joshua Temple, who had erected them as two-up-two-downs in the traditional way, with a tiny garden at the front and a long straggling one at the rear. Over the years these semi-detached cottages had all had generous extensions added at the back to provide a larger kitchen downstairs and, in Tess's case, a tiny extra bedroom and a bathroom upstairs as well. The two original downstairs rooms had been knocked into one, and she'd added French doors to the large kitchen extension to access what remained of the back garden, along with a log burner in the sitting room before her money ran out.

The second bedroom, first occupied by Amber, had become Tess's workroom, although she did keep a single bed pushed against one wall. The tiny bedroom at the back, which was once Matt's, had become a general dumping ground, as tiny bedrooms are wont to be. But she kept a single bed in there too, although it was extremely unlikely either of her children would be returning. Recently she'd redecorated this bedroom à la Peppa Pig, because little Ellie sometimes liked a sleepover with her nana. There were times when she longed for a little more space, but then she considered the extra heating bills and the council tax and all the rest, and thought better of it.

About the same time as she moved into Temple Terrace, Tess and Orla had got together and opened the boutique; Tess the designer and dressmaker, Orla the persuasive saleslady. The shop, down a narrow lane just off the High Street, had originally been a greengrocer's. Because people were reluctant to navigate the cobbles down Penny Lane, and because there was little chance of bumping into Paul McCartney, the old greengrocer was unable to compete with the supermarkets on the main street. Their boutique wasn't huge but they only displayed a limited stock, most of the outfits being made to measure, and Tess worked mostly from home. They'd felt sure that, once their reputation was established, the ladies would seek them out, cobbles or not. And this was exactly what happened.

They called the shop 'Curvaceous', to reflect the shape of the ladies they were catering for. Orla reckoned size and shape should be no obstacle to elegance. And this became their business's unique selling point. Self-conscious ladies would pay handsomely for large outfits, tailor-made to their hefty measurements, which made them look as if they'd lost at least a stone. Tess had the gift of being able to minimise their girth with clever cutting and tailoring. Word got around and large ladies arrived in large numbers, heading through the door of Curvaceous in their quests for special outfits to wear at special occasions. 'Don't you look lovely!' and 'Gosh, you've lost some weight!' were, apparently, standard reactions, sending further customers scurrying to Curvaceous. Tess still had to buy her own clothes off the peg, because she was far too busy to make anything for herself. They'd done well, considering Milbury wasn't a very big place.

Tess and Orla had lunch at Boulters every Wednesday. Boulters was one of the main reasons Tess had ended up at fourteen stone. The building had once been a brewery, and some redundant brass pipework had been left in place to add a sense of authenticity and provenance. It was one of their very favourite places – 'All you can eat for just six quid!' You could go back and fill up your plate time and time again. There was a long, long counter loaded with a range of delicious specialities from around the world, from hot, spicy delights to creamy curries and wonderful pasta. Each dish was complete with its own little label telling you what it was. But in case you needed further information, there were a couple of chefs in attendance – mainly to refill the containers, looking discreetly the other way as most customers overloaded their plates and then glanced guiltily around to see if they were being watched. Tess liked the Indian and the Italian, whereas Orla favoured the Chinese and the Mexican. They had become experts at getting through at least £12 worth each, and sometimes they even managed a whole £18 worth. The place was always crowded but, nevertheless, they managed to elbow their way across to the serving counter.

'It's a wonder to me how Boulters manage to make any profit at all,' Tess said.

'There'll always be some eejit who only dabbles with their food,' Orla said dismissively.

On this particular Wednesday, Tess hesitated as she loaded her plate, when a sudden vision of the super-slim Ursula drifted into her head. Ursula, who had usurped Tess's place as Mrs Templar, would be swanning into the church, no doubt clad in some Victoria Beckham rip-off, on the arm of *her* ex-husband. And there Tess would be, the poor old ex-wife, in a double-X-sized shift, very overweight and all alone.

So, with this thought in mind, Tess said, 'I'm not going back for seconds.'

Orla, fork in mid-air, stared at her. 'Are you ill or something?'

'No,' said Tess, 'I'm just bloody fat, and I want to get this weight shifted before Amber's wedding in July.' And maybe men will start to look at me again, she thought. And of course it was completely the wrong thing to do, but here she was taking comfort from the creamy chicken masala and seriously considering the gnocchi *alla Romana* to follow. 'So this weight *has* to come off.'

'You're always saying that,' Orla said.

'Well, I'm saying it again.'

'Since you've just scoffed one heaped plateful of calories you might as well have a few more. Start the diet tomorrow.'

Tess groaned. 'I'm *always* starting the diet tomorrow!'

'Me too,' Orla said, glancing down at her flabby tummy.

'Perhaps we should join a slimming club?' Tess suggested, as they returned to their table with reloaded plates. 'I just don't seem to have the willpower to go it alone.'

'These people make their money by taking a fiver off you every week, just to tell you you've lost a whole pound, or gained two,' Orla said. 'For sure you know that yourself?'

'Well, I expect you're right,' Tess conceded. 'But if you're weighed each week and spending money you expect to see results, right?'

'It's all psychological,' said Orla.

'Psychology matters because surely that's where you get your willpower from,' Tess said. 'So I'm going to join one anyway.'

'OK, OK, I'll come with you.' Orla sighed as she surveyed her empty plate. 'Too late to start today though, so shall we just go back for another refill?'

'I suppose we might as well,' Tess agreed, thinking of the gnocchi.

*

The following morning, Tess stared in the mirror at her sixty-two-year-old self, at her fat tummy and chunky thighs, and sighed despondently. Half the clothes in her wardrobe were about four sizes too small. She was going to have to do something about all this flab before her lovely daughter got married in July. She was very proud of Amber, who, by sheer hard work, had become a much sought-after make-up artist, and who often brought back little tubes of this and pots of that for her mother. And Tess badly wanted Amber to be proud of her too. One of the reasons she wanted to find a new man, of course, was so that she'd have a partner to accompany her to the wedding and not look like the sad old ex-wife. But if she *had* to go alone to face her ex-husband, Gerry, and her smug slim younger replacement, Ursula, then she just had to get this weight off and make some attempt to look really good. And it wasn't just for Gerry and Ursula, or even for Amber; it was for *herself.* To restore her confidence, which had taken a bashing over the years. She knew she'd let herself go after David died, when it seemed just too much trouble to bother about her looks. And then there was the chemotherapy for the breast cancer eighteen months ago, which had taken her hair and her remaining confidence with it. Her hair had grown back, but not her confidence. It was high time to do something about it all.

Tomorrow, though; she'd start tomorrow. Tonight she'd just chomp her way through the rest of that packet of Pringles while watching *EastEnders*. But Tess knew things had to change, because kneeling on the floor, cutting out dresses and skirts and coats, and then sitting at the sewing machine stitching the things together, was not conducive to keeping slim. All you got were sore knees, chunky thighs and a fat bottom. And she was constantly reminded by the quote on the fridge magnet Orla had given her at Christmas, which said: *Dear Lord, if you can't make me thin then please give me fat friends!*

And then, just the other day, when Matt and Lisa had visited, her four-year-old granddaughter, Ellie, had cuddled up to her on the settee and said, 'I love you, Nana, 'cos there's *lots* of you!' Everyone laughed – so cute and hilarious! But when Tess thought about it afterwards, she decided that, cute and hilarious as it might be, it was a timely reminder that there was indeed an awful lot of her.

There were no two ways about it: it was about time she made some changes.

CHAPTER TWO

'STONE' WORK

Later that day Tess googled slimming clubs in Milbury and discovered that the nearest, Slim Chance, met every Tuesday morning in the Women's Institute hall. She decided that she and Orla should join up at the very next session.

It was a grey, damp morning and Orla moaned the entire way there about what a waste of time all this was. She'd been to a slimming club before and, guess what, she'd only lost one stone in the whole damned year! 'It'll be a waste of money,' she informed Tess.

There were times when Tess was sorely tried by her friend. 'So why are you coming then?'

'Well, I suppose this one might be miraculous. But I shan't be sticking around for a year to only lose a stone. Anyway, I thought you'd like my company.'

Tess wasn't at all sure that she did. Orla could be very negative if she didn't particularly want to do something, and this was a typical example. They'd left early because Tess wasn't too sure of the location, and she wanted to get there first to avoid the embarrassment of being weighed in front of a load of people she didn't know.

'And we're far too early,' Orla moaned. 'We'll have to sit around for hours now.'

Tess pulled into the car park of the Women's Institute hall a mere fifteen minutes early.

'The door will still be locked,' said Orla, plainly looking for an escape.

It wasn't, of course. Tess led the way cautiously inside. It was a long, dark, narrow building, the windows along one wall facing straight onto the brickwork of the storage depot next door. It had a wooden floor with a platform at one end, on which was positioned a desk and, alongside it, the dreaded weighing machine. There was a smell of stale bodies in the air, and a middle-aged woman was busy opening up the windows.

'Hello!' she said. 'You're nice and early! I'm Judy.'

Tess and Orla introduced themselves and listened with interest as Judy explained that she had to arrive early to cover over any Women's Institute material referring to jam-making or cake-baking with her large posters of 'before and after' slimming successes. Judy was stockily built but not fat, probably in her forties, Tess reckoned. She had blonde hair tied back in a ponytail and a lot of mascara, and wore black leggings with a vivid orange tunic proclaiming, across her ample chest, 'Slim is Sexy!' She also had a very loud voice, with a strong Geordie accent.

'I'll be with you in a minute. I've still got to cover up this poster about the cake-baking competition. And you need to be filling out these forms,' she said, as she handed out the paperwork to them both. As she spoke, the hall was beginning to fill up with an assortment of women.

'Right, everyone!' she bellowed, picking up her clipboard and motioning them all to plonk their overweight bottoms on the plastic chairs arranged in a large semicircle. 'We've got some flesh to move here, have we not!' Tess looked round at the owners of the aforementioned flesh. There must be at least forty of us women, she thought, and only two men. She'd felt distinctly podgy when she arrived but, as she looked around, she began to feel positively svelte.

'Judy's really good,' the woman beside her said. 'She *cares*, you see.'

'Have you been coming long?' Tess asked.

'Oh, just a year. But I've managed to lose a stone. Do you know, she's got some of these people reduced to *half* their original size! I think it's her mission in life.'

Orla, on Tess's other side, snorted and gave Tess an 'I told you so' look. 'A bloody *year*!' she muttered.

'But,' the woman continued, 'I feel so much better and I've got myself out and about again. My partner had gone off with another woman, you see, and I blamed myself. I was fat and tired all the time, so I suppose I couldn't blame him. But I've met someone else now and it's given me the incentive to get some more weight off.'

'Good for you,' said Tess, wondering where she'd met the 'someone else'.

The woman sitting directly opposite her, whose name was Mabel, was seriously overlapping her plastic chair with both buttocks.

'It's good for the morale to come here,' Orla muttered, 'if nothing else.' She'd taken the opportunity to leave a heap of their business cards on the central table: CURVACEOUS – *the best bespoke boutique for larger ladies.*

'I'm not sure you should have done that,' Tess said. 'These women are trying to lose weight, not cover it up.'

'Well, if it's going to take them a year to lose a stone they're going to need something to wear in the meantime, aren't they?'

Judy was scrupulously fair. Anyone who'd lost any weight at all was praised to the skies, and even those who'd gained were encouraged to do better with phrases like: 'Don't let this put you off' and 'We all get weeks like this, don't we, girls?' The 'girls' nodded enthusiastically. Recipes were exchanged, sympathy was extended to all those with selfish husbands who continued to demand fry-ups and takeaways, and stars were distributed to everyone who'd hit their target weight. Mabel with the buttocks had lost four whole pounds! Wow! Wild applause all round.

'There are only two blokes here,' Orla observed.

'You're only looking for one.'

'Well, neither of these two would fit the bill.'

'Don't tell me,' Tess sighed, 'that you only came here in the hope of finding a man?'

'It's the only place I haven't tried already,' Orla replied, grinning.

'Shh! Shh!' Everyone was ordered to quieten down so that Judy could commence her lengthy diatribe, the gist of which was that, if you did as Judy told you, by next week everyone should have lost at least two pounds and possibly more.

'Some of you,' she added, looking directly at Orla, 'have more to lose than others. Would you believe that when I started here I weighed *twenty stone*!' Everyone gasped. Judy did a little twirl. 'And just look at me *now*!'

As they walked away from Slim Chance, Tess said, 'We are *not* going to Boulters tomorrow.'

Orla grimaced. 'Could we not have just one teeny-weeny plateful?'

'No, we couldn't. We either do this diet properly or we don't do it at all.'

'Oh, all right, all right! But tell me this: how are you going to get through *EastEnders* without a packet of crisps or something?'

'I'll just think about how damned fantastic I'm going to look at Amber's wedding and the slinky outfit I'm going to be wearing. And, since it's more than likely you'll be invited too, you should bear that in mind.'

Tess had thought it would be so much easier if Amber and Peter would just pop into the local registry office and get the deed done in a matter of minutes. Particularly after all the time they'd been living together. But Amber was determined to have a stage-set wedding and Tess had no intention of being the frumpy character in the scene.

But she was cheered after her visit to Slim Chance; there was hope on the horizon. Perhaps she might widen these horizons , get out of her comfortable rut, and perhaps she too might meet somebody else – but where? He certainly wouldn't come knocking at her door.

As she rounded the corner into Temple Terrace there *was* someone at her door, but not exactly the someone she had in mind. There, for no accountable reason, stood Lisa and Ellie.

When her son, Matt, had married six years previously, Tess had been somewhat in awe of her new daughter-in-law, and still was for that matter. Lisa was one of those small wiry women, always immaculate, always frantically busy, always in control. She was the polar opposite to tall, scruffy Matt, but she'd succeeded in tidying him up along with everything else in her path. She then decided she'd like her first child to be born in April the next year, because she needed to be at a very important sales conference in Zurich at the end of May in connection with her job as a hotel manager. So, naturally, Ellie duly arrived in April. And now Lisa had discovered she was pregnant again, which was planned, of course, and just fine with the baby due in mid-July, so as not to interfere with her frenetic autumn work schedule. You did not argue with Lisa or her hormones.

However, she had not been best pleased when Amber announced her wedding was to be at the end of July, just days after Lisa was due to give birth. Amber had landed herself the prestigious job of chief make-up artist for a high-budget film that was due to begin shooting in the middle of August. Amber's refusal to alter the wedding date had resulted in a certain froideur between the two sisters-in-law.

So Tess was mildly surprised to find Lisa and Ellie on her doorstep, because her daughter-in-law rarely did anything without an appointment.

'Really sorry to bother you, Tess,' Lisa said, clutching her jaw. 'But I've got the most hellish toothache. I've managed to get an emergency appointment with that guy on Milbury High Street and I don't really want to drag Ellie in there with me.' She sighed. 'It's Freya's day off, wouldn't you know?' Freya was their latest au pair. 'I'll only be an hour or so. I was *sure* you'd be home on a Tuesday morning.' She looked at Tess with a hint of annoyance. 'I was just about to *go*.'

Tess had to stop herself from apologising for having been out.

'That's fine, Lisa,' she said. 'Toothache's awful. Off you go. Leave Ellie with me.'

As Lisa set off with a brisk wave and Tess opened the front door, Ellie was already delving into her pink bag. 'I've brought my mouse family for you to see, Nana.'

'A mouse family?'

'Yes.' Ellie withdrew a collection of tiny furry mice, all conventionally clad: Mum in a pink apron (what would the women's libbers make of *that*?), Dad in blue trousers, and two even tinier mice, one in pink, one in blue. All so politically incorrect. Never mind, Tess thought in amusement, if anyone cared you could always swap them all around.

'There's a mummy and a daddy and two babies,' Ellie explained. 'That's a *family*.'

'Yes, of course it is,' Tess said absently, heading into the kitchen and filling the kettle for a much-needed cup of tea. *Sans* sugar, of course; she must remember to buy some sweeteners.

'If Mummy has another baby, we'll be a family too,' Ellie continued.

Tess wasn't altogether sure if she'd been told of the pregnancy yet, so decided to say nothing on the subject. 'But you're a family *now*,' she said. 'You'd just be a *bigger* family.'

Ellie looked confused.

'You can have really tiny families,' Tess went on. 'One mummy and one baby, for instance.'

'What about the daddy?'

'Well, sometimes the daddy goes away.' Tess wondered how far she should go with this conversation. 'Not all families have a daddy and a mummy, Ellie. Now, shall we have a cup of tea?'

'Are you a mummy?' Ellie persisted.

'Yes, I'm your daddy's mummy and Auntie Amber's mummy.'

'So where's the daddy?'

'Well, Grandpa Gerry's the daddy, but he's a daddy who went away.' Tess racked her brains for a way to change the subject; how could she explain Ursula?

'When I'm a mummy I shan't let the daddy go away,' Ellie said firmly, making Tess feel she'd been somewhat careless.

'Good luck then,' Tess said with feeling as she sipped her sugarless tea, trying not to think about the daddies she'd let slip through her fingers. Not that David had been a daddy, and he had, of course, brought about his own departure. Ellie, fortunately, was too young to remember him, thus avoiding the need for further explanations. Thank goodness the subject of Ursula hadn't come up.

As Ellie fussed about with her mice and her mug of tea, Tess wondered if she'd ever regain the confidence Ursula had drained from her. David had helped, but that feeling of inadequacy still lingered. Then she wondered if she'd ever again be able to attract anyone at all of the opposite sex and, if she did, where she could possibly meet him.

All of a sudden she felt desperately lonely.

CHAPTER THREE

MAN HUNT

'So, now I've made a start on my weight problem, do you think I should start looking for a nice man?' Tess asked. She knew Orla was an expert on this matter, since she was forever in search of a man. They were in the shop dressing up Dolly, the window dummy, in springtime yellow – with weddings in mind.

'Well, poor David's been gone a couple of years now, and it's time you had some fun,' Orla said. 'And just think how nice it would be to have someone to go to the wedding with!'

'That's what I was thinking,' Tess said. Orla's thoughts were coinciding with her own; it would be wonderful to have someone to escort her, and Tess imagined herself arriving at the church on the arm of a good-looking man.

'I suppose I should get out more,' she replied pensively.

Orla was hell-bent on finding herself another partner, although she wasn't keen on the idea of marriage. And, although Tess valued her independence in some ways, deep down she'd like to be one of a couple again. She'd missed the warmth of a close relationship after Gerry had taken off. Food had become a substitute and it was then she gained that first stone. Then she'd had a few years with David; poor David, who met such an untimely demise. As Tess added a row of pearls round Dolly's neck she thought about David again.

David, who fancied himself as a Jamie Oliver type, cooked with butter and cream and all things delicious. He also drove a red Jaguar E-Type like a bat out of hell. He, too, had been married but had no children. Tess often thought that, if she'd met David instead of Gerry all those years ago, the marriage would have survived. He was a kind, friendly man, and she'd loved him deeply. He was a soulmate as Gerry had never really been. And he was such an excellent cook! She'd gained the second stone around that time. But they'd had only three years together before David had the massive heart attack, whilst navigating that hairpin bend at seventy miles an hour, which hailed the end of both man and machine. Tess was devastated. He had meant so much to her. She'd been desperate to find some comfort somewhere, and had found it in Jaffa Cakes and a little glass of something with which to wash them down. A packet every evening, and another half stone.

There had been no one since, but now Tess felt she was ready for a close relationship again. Was that because Amber was getting married shortly? Well, that didn't make sense because Amber had been living with Peter for years, so why did she suddenly feel this need, this feeling of being incomplete? All she knew was that it would be very nice to have a soulmate once more. Or, if not a soulmate, then even someone to go out with occasionally, or to go on holiday with. She hadn't been on a proper holiday for three whole years; only a few days in Edinburgh for a friend's wedding, when it had rained the whole time, and a spa weekend with Orla. Now she longed to feel the sun on her face once again! And perhaps with a nice male companion. But she'd never quite been brave enough to do anything about it. And she had no intention of admitting this to Amber, because she knew Amber would say something like, 'You're fine as you are, Mum.' Her daughter, like most young people, reckoned that once you were over sixty there was no need whatsoever for love and romance, since you'd got one foot firmly in the grave. But like it or not, life was still designed for twosomes. And she didn't want to be forever one of that motley collection of divorcees and widows huddling together at social events.

'So, where are all these widowers and divorced men?' Tess asked.

'We outlive them,' Orla said. 'So there's not many around and they're difficult to find.'

Orla should know; she'd been trying for long enough.

As Tess pondered over the problem, Amber breezed into the shop.

Tess gazed at her long-limbed daughter and thought, I used to look like that! But Tess's body had taken more than its fair share of punishment: the pregnancies, the hysterectomy, the menopause, the breast cancer. In theory, she thought, I should surely be one hell of a lot thinner… but nature had other ideas.

'I know you're busy, Mum,' Amber said, pecking her mother on the cheek. 'But I've come to ask you a big favour.'

Tess wondered what was coming.

'I'd love it if you could make me my wedding dress.'

For a moment, Tess felt tears pricking her eyes. She took a deep breath. 'I'd *love* to,' she said.

'Thing is, Mum, I've seen this dress in Harrods which is absolutely stunning. And so is the price – we're talking telephone numbers here.

So I took a couple of photos of it when no one was looking and I've made some sketches.' Amber produced a folder from the depths of her shoulder bag. 'Here we are! As you can see, it's absolutely plain, elegant, understated, classic…'

Tess studied Amber's sketch. The dress was slim-fitting, full-length and boat-necked with elbow-length sleeves. Tess knew only too well that something that looked so simple wasn't at all simple; it would require intricate cutting, seaming and finishing. One wrong stitch would stand out a mile on such a classic design, and that was why Harrods were charging a fortune. But she knew she could do it. And how wonderful it would be to make something so beautiful for her slim, lovely daughter, instead of the marquee-like creations she was normally asked to produce.

'It's a beautiful design, Amber.'

'Isn't it? And of course I'll pay you, Mum, but not as much as Harrods are asking!'

'No, darling, it will be my gift to you. But we need to talk about the fabric – silk, probably.'

'Mum, you're an angel!'

When Gerry had made his exit almost eleven years previously Amber was twenty-three and Matt twenty-one, both old enough to know that 'these things happen'. But nevertheless they were both shattered and Matt had rarely spoken to his father since, while it took nearly four years of Gerry's cajoling before Amber agreed to make contact with him again. And now even Ursula, unaffectionately known as 'Arsula', or even 'the Arse' to both Amber and her mother, had used her considerable charm to persuade Amber that it was *only right* that Gerry should walk his daughter down the aisle.

Tess felt a little resentful because she'd been prepared to give Amber away herself if necessary, and Matt too had offered to do the deed, even if it was traditional for the father of the bride to take on this role. Furthermore, it would have given her something to do, instead of sitting there by herself, sandwiched between Matt, Lisa and Ellie. And probably Orla. And, of course, there was always the chance that Barbara, her sister, just *might* show up.

At the end of her first week's dieting at Slim Chance, Tess had lost four pounds, twice the recommended target, and Orla had lost only one.

'Well, it's better than gaining one, I suppose. But all that effort for one bloody pound!' Orla muttered. But she brightened up visibly when a new man joined the group. He was called Barney and, apart from a bit of a tummy, didn't appear to be very overweight. He had a friendly face and a good head of hair, so Orla wasted no time.

'Look,' she murmured to Tess, 'there's a spare seat over there beside that Barney, so I think I ought to go across and make him welcome.' With that, she was gone. And, thought Tess, he seemed pleased enough with Orla's company.

The woman sitting next to Tess looked particularly worried.

'Have you been coming here for long?' she asked Tess.

'This is only my second week,' Tess replied. 'But I'm really thrilled to have lost four pounds.'

The woman sighed. 'I'm going to visit my son in Canada this September. I haven't seen him for three years and I can't let them all see me like this!' She patted her tummy. 'I had breast cancer last year and ate for England.'

Tess turned to face her. 'So did I! Have breast cancer, I mean. I was told to keep strong and not to even *contemplate* losing weight. I took that as a cue to eat anything I liked, any time I liked.'

'Well, you need comfort, don't you?' The two women nodded in their shared understanding. 'My name's Shirley, by the way.'

'Hi, Shirley, I'm Tess. Good to meet someone else who's been through the mill.'

'How much weight are you hoping to lose?' Shirley asked.

'Two and a half stone, so I've got my work cut out. What about you?'

Shirley sighed. 'Well, two stone would be terrific. But it's so difficult when you spend evenings on your own in front of the telly. Are you married, Tess?'

'Divorced,' Tess replied. 'And then I had a lovely partner for a few years but he died. You?'

'I'm a widow,' Shirley said. 'My husband died a couple of years ago. And it's so easy to eat rubbish when you're alone, isn't it?'

'*Tell* me about it! I suppose it's a form of loneliness or something. I really miss David – that was my partner, as opposed to my ex-husband. I sometimes think I got the timing of my relationships wrong!'

'Well, Tess, I think I know how you feel, so perhaps we can chivvy each other along.'

'I'm up for that!' Tess said. 'For the first time in years I'm feeling positive, and determined to improve my looks, my health and my life. It'll be a tough journey though, as I'm not over-endowed with willpower!'

When Tess and Orla came out onto the street later, Orla said, 'That Barney is a really nice guy. I could *so* fancy him!'

You could fancy Frankenstein's monster, Tess thought. 'Is he married?' she asked.

'Well, I didn't ask him *that*. But have no fear, I shall find out.'

As the weeks progressed, on a good week Orla managed to lose a pound or two, and on a bad week she gained a pound or two, the result of which was that she stayed more or less the same. Tess had been delighted to lose seven pounds in just two sessions. But she fully intended to lose a further two stone in the coming months, though she was aware that the weekly weight loss would become smaller as time passed. Shirley was doing well too, and they'd become quite competitive, which was a help because Tess was aware that Orla was only really there in the hope of snaring the unsuspecting Barney. It was on the fourth week that Barney brought his wife along with him, and she was even bigger than Orla. Orla was devastated. Apparently she'd tried several times, she said, to ask him about his marital status in as subtle a way as possible; so subtle that he plainly had no idea what she was getting at.

'I'm not paying out any more money to that damned slimming club,' Orla announced as they headed home. 'It doesn't suit my metabolism.'

'It suits mine,' Tess said cheerfully, pleased with her progress. 'I'm not sure you were here for quite the right reason, Orla.'

Orla didn't reply.

Tess had taken to eating an apple while she watched *East-Enders* and she'd also started walking a couple of miles each day, unless the weather was particularly inclement. And it was having results. She'd started looking in the mirror more often and wasn't cringing quite so much as before. Not only that, she was pleased she'd managed to summon up some willpower and was finally doing something about herself *for* herself. Already she felt healthier and happier. But she was no nearer at all to finding a soulmate, or even a male friend for social outings or Amber's wedding. She constantly dreamed of arriving at the church, slim and stylish, with a gorgeous man on her arm. Well, a half-decent one would do.

'Slimming clubs aren't the right place to find a man,' Orla said as they were driving home, 'but I have discovered a great online dating agency.'

Tess sniffed. 'I'm not *that* desperate.'

'Yes, you are. Anyway, it's not a case of being desperate; how else do you meet the opposite sex these days? Everyone meets online now, Tess. And this one sounds good. Meetings for the More Mature – MMM, it's called.'

Tess laughed. 'MMM! Mmm…!'

'Don't mock! I think it would be ideal for us; for instance, there's a great-sounding fellow on there called Darren, who lives in South Wales and owns a bookshop. A *bookshop*! Now wouldn't he be perfect for you, when you're always reading?'

'It doesn't quite follow that this could be a match made in heaven,' Tess retorted. 'He might have rotten teeth and bow legs.'

'Why are you so fussy? You're no oil painting yourself!'

'I have my standards,' Tess said drily. 'And you wouldn't be winning any beauty contests either.'

'In that case I'll just have to rely on my magnetic personality. Now, here's something: you can be on MMM for free, but if you pay £150, you can join their *elite* section, which is called the Hearts Club and entitles you to six introductions which, they say, is *guaranteed* to find you the love of your life – the "Ace of Hearts" – and if you don't, they refund your money. And, it also entitles you to join one of their singles' cruises round the Greek islands at a twenty-five per cent discount. C'mon, Tess, what's not to like? You can afford £150!'

'I don't know, Orla. Why don't you give it a go and I'll see if I fancy it?'

'It would be more fun if we could join MMM together,' Orla said pleadingly.

'What, go out in foursomes or something?'

'No, but we could compare notes and we could maybe do that cruise together. We are, after all, what's known as the Silver Singles these days,' Orla added, 'and we should be very sought after.'

'We should?'

'Not,' Orla continued, 'that many of us emerge from the hairdresser these days looking very silvery, buy you know what I mean.'

'If you say so. And I fancy the Greek islands,' said Tess wistfully.

The Greek islands! She and David had booked, almost three years ago, that cruise round the Greek islands for the middle of May, and it was on 29 April that he met his untimely end. On the day they should have commenced sailing she was bidding him a tearful farewell in the crematorium. But she was beginning to come round to the idea again, so perhaps this was an omen? Perhaps it was a sign that David was telling her she had mourned long enough and she should go? It was time to move on. He had had a lovely romantic streak, but he was also very down to earth and practical, and she had a feeling he would approve. *You can't avoid the Greek islands or anywhere else just because I've gone, Tess; for God's sake, get out there, meet people!* Yes, she could almost hear him saying that.

It took twenty more minutes of Orla's wheedling before Tess finally agreed to join MMM but held off on paying for the privilege of signing up to the Hearts Club. Even then she was none too sure she was doing the right thing. But there was a tiny chance she might meet her soulmate, or at least someone nice to accompany her to the wedding. The idea of the cruise was appealing, but it was the thought of smug, skinny Ursula that finally spurred her into action.

*

Ursula had joined Gerry's advertising agency eleven years earlier, at the exact time Tess was in hospital undergoing a hysterectomy. The thing about hysterectomies is that, apart from the pain and discomfort, you're not exactly in the mood for sexual shenanigans for some time afterwards. But of course Gerry had never been a patient man, and Ursula, Tess was told later, had set her sights on him from Day One. She liked older men, apparently, but why she should fancy Gerry Templar quite so much would forever be an unsolved mystery, as far as Tess was concerned.

She, of course, was the last to know about the affair. And, at a time when she felt unattractive and particularly vulnerable, she found out purely by accident. Lipstick on Gerry's collar or perfume on his shirt? Oh no, it was the packet of condoms nestling in his briefcase between the *Financial Times* and the *Advertising Gazette*. Tess had only looked in there because Gerry had, as usual, mislaid a set of keys, and he never looked properly among the detritus that lined the bottom of the briefcase. And Tess had stared in shock and disbelief at the offending packet in her hand. What on earth…?

He was carrying them *for a friend*, Gerry explained. As you do, of course. At that time she had no idea that the 'friend' was Ursula, but she did know that he was lying. In the end it was Brenda, Gerry's long-suffering secretary, who'd enlightened her after Tess, furious about her encounter with the condoms and aware that he was never home until late these days, had stormed into the office to ask why Gerry was having so many meetings and business trips lately.

'Meetings? Business trips?' Brenda looked mystified.

There was the mother and father of all rows when Gerry finally made it home and admitted that perhaps, yes, he was having a mid-life crisis, but nevertheless he was madly, passionately and deeply in love. With Ursula. Sorry, and all that.

After Tess had the locks changed, she concentrated hard on her tailoring and dressmaking, but the hurt and the feeling of inadequacy persisted. She'd never had an abundance of self-confidence, and now she felt unattractive and completely lacking in any sex appeal. She consoled herself as many lonely ladies did, turning to the nibbles every evening, followed by a glass or three of Chardonnay.

*

Orla had asked Tess round so they could study the MMM website together. She made her famous lamb curry. Orla lived in a ground-floor flat in an Edwardian house about a ten-minute walk from

Temple Terrace, which meant that, wherever they were dining together, they could safely be wining as well, and totter home afterwards. Orla's flat was, as always, in a state of chaos, which fortunately didn't bother Orla at all. She had some nice pieces of antique furniture, generally covered in piles of newspapers, half-dead plants, wayward cups and saucers, and old editions of *Vogue*. Orla was passionately interested in fashion and seemed to buy these magazines as an excuse to spit venom at their 'far too thin' models.

When they'd finished eating, Orla topped up their glasses of wine and said, 'Come and look at these men I've discovered.'

Orla wanted Tess's approval before she committed herself to her first date. She showed Tess the selection of males she'd downloaded. They all appeared to be suspiciously handsome and ultra-successful.

Tess studied the selection. 'How can you be sure they really look like that? And can that one *really* be a film director? With looks like that, surely he'd have his pick of the ladies?'

'You're always so suspicious!'

'Well, I've learnt to be. And what sort of description did you give yourself?'

'Just told it as it is,' Orla replied shortly.

Tess doubted that. 'Let's see what you've written about yourself then.'

Unwillingly Orla clicked away, and then handed over her phone.

'That's not *you*!' Tess exclaimed, staring at a youthful, smiling, bikini-clad lady.

'Well, it was taken a few years back,' Orla grudgingly admitted.

'And what's this about being a *successful entrepreneur*?'

'We started up the shop, didn't we? And don't forget that I started that cleaning business too.'

'What, you mean you and Maeve O'Connor? Mopping up a few office floors? How long did that last – a month?'

'Oh, for goodness' sake, Tess, don't nit-pick! Let a little light into your life!'

'OK, OK, so you've selected the best bits about yourself. And so have these guys. Just don't be disappointed when they're not all they're cracked up to be.'

But Orla *was* disappointed. The three guys she met were shorter, less attractive and considerably less successful than they'd made themselves out to be.

'Right, that's it,' Orla said. 'I'm going to pay the £150 and join the Hearts Club. These guys are vetted so they should all be above board.'

'And you'll be vetted too,' Tess reminded her.

After much discussion Tess finally agreed to follow Orla's example, paid her £150, and wrote as honest a description of herself as possible. The photograph she chose had been taken on holiday in Sardinia three years before. OK, it was flattering, but at least it *looked* like her. She wasn't sure how MMM went about checking her out, but they must have done something because it was twenty-four hours before they confirmed her membership. Later she was to wonder what exactly it was they *did* do...

Because her first 'heart' was Benedict.

CHAPTER FOUR

WHERE THERE'S A WILL...

'He's very good-looking,' Orla said, looking at the photo of Benedict with approval. 'I wonder why he's chosen you?'

'Well, thanks a bunch!' Tess said. 'You *really* know how to boost my confidence!'

'But you know what I mean, don't you? Of course, we might just be the two best-looking women on the site, mightn't we? Anyway, if you don't fancy him, tell him you have a lovely friend.'

'He must already have seen your photograph,' Tess said. 'And he's chosen *me*. Now what am I going to wear?' What *was* she going to wear? Knowing what to wear had been a life-long problem for Tess, which was ironic since she always knew what suited everyone else.

'Since it's a lunchtime date I'd ditch the tiara,' said Orla.

'I might wear that royal blue dress I bought for Christmas, if I can still get into it.' Would that dress be all right or would everyone be in jeans? It was yet another thing to worry about because; she was so unused to meeting new men and going to smart restaurants.

*

Now, squeezed into the royal blue dress, Tess looked across the table in Pelligrini's (the most upmarket Italian *ristorante* for miles around) at her first 'heart', and reckoned he was even better looking than his photograph.

At that moment Benedict leaned forward and, gazing at her with his beautiful hazel eyes, said, 'I'd like to take you to meet my mother.'

Tess nearly choked on her *timballini tricolore* (which was definitely *not* diet-appropriate) and said, 'I beg your pardon?'

'I think she'd like you,' Benedict said.

'She *would*?' This was moving far too fast. MMM had described this man as single, good-looking and successful, which sounded like an unbeatable combination as far as Tess was concerned. Benedict, in the flesh, did not disappoint. But there had to be a snag because it just couldn't be this easy.

'But you hardly know me,' she protested, laying down her fork.

'That doesn't matter, Tess. I can tell by your appearance and listening to the way you speak that any man would be honoured to have you by his side.'

Tess wasn't sure she could eat another mouthful. That she, Tess Templar, sixty-two years old, overweight and average in appearance, could be considered in any way attractive by this gorgeous man, beggared belief. There he sat, silver-haired, suave, charming and smiling with what she was sure were his own teeth. In fact, he could easily have been George Clooney's older brother. What an amazing dating site this was! Were *all* the men as gorgeous as this?

'Here,' he said, 'let me top up your glass.' He'd even chosen the most expensive wine on offer, and she knew she was drinking it far too quickly. But she couldn't believe she'd found this Adonis on the very first date! It was, she decided, £150 well spent. Orla would be green with envy. Absolutely *green*.

'I hardly know what to say,' Tess said, gulping the wine. She decided against telling him that nobody, not even her ex-husband, had ever said they'd be *honoured* to have her by their side. She began to wonder about his eyesight; he wasn't wearing glasses but his velvety brown eyes appeared quite normal. And she wasn't aware of having said anything particularly groundbreaking. Of course, she still had a trace of a Scottish accent, so perhaps he liked that.

He'd never married, Benedict told her. 'Just never found the right person, but I've had a few partners over the years.'

They chatted generally for a bit and she was halfway through her *zabaglione* with bitter chocolate sauce (she was going to bitterly regret this at the next weigh-in), when he repeated, 'So, *would* you be prepared to come with me to visit my mother? Just for an hour or so?'

Tess stared at him. 'What, *now*?'

'Well, after we've had some coffee. I trust you'd like some coffee?'

'Um, yes please.' She polished off her dessert. 'I have to ask: *why*?'

'Why what?'

'Why do you want me to go with you to visit your mother when we've only just met?'

'The thing is, she's ninety-three today and I always visit her on her birthday. And, do you know what? She always asks me the same thing. "Benedict," she says, "when are you ever going to settle down with a nice lady?" She says she'll die happy when she knows I've found someone.'

'She's dying?' Was this some kind of joke? Tess wondered. He's *found* someone? *Me?*

'Well, she can't last a lot longer, I suppose.' Benedict summoned the waiter and ordered coffee. Then, smiling winningly, he continued, 'You don't have to marry me or anything, Tess!' He laughed heartily at such a possibility. 'But if you could just give the appearance of being a devoted friend – and I hope we *will* be friends – it would make her very happy. Could you manage that for half an hour or so? She doesn't stay awake very long and I'll do most of the talking. I'd be so grateful, Tess.'

The coffee arrived and Tess played for time, fiddling with her teaspoon and a sugar lump. Then she replaced the sugar lump in the bowl and felt a little more saintly. Why, she wondered, was a man as gorgeous as this not inundated with ladies falling over themselves to be his devoted friend? Why did he have to go online to find someone in the first place? None of this was making any sense at all. However, he had insisted on paying for an extremely expensive lunch in this renowned restaurant, so she supposed the least she could do was accompany him to see his old mother on her birthday. Particularly as she'd be *more* than happy to become his friend.

Tess pictured herself arriving at Amber's wedding with this dishy man in tow! Oh, to see her ex-husband's smug face! And that bloody Arsula!

Benedict settled the bill with his gold Amex card, then shepherded her out to the car park where she'd left her old Ford Focus earlier.

'I'll bring you back here afterwards,' he told her, as he aimed his key at a beautiful dark green Aston Martin. This was getting better and better! He then opened the passenger door for her to lower herself into the sumptuous cream leather interior. Tess wondered if it would be very naff to take a picture, because no one would believe this.

The engine purred to life and they set off towards the city, Tess feeling more and more apprehensive. What had she let herself in for? This whole experience was becoming quite unbelievable. He didn't talk much when he was driving, other than to mutter about the traffic. It didn't matter how gorgeous your car might be – you couldn't move any faster than anyone else in London.

Benedict parked outside a tall, terraced Georgian townhouse in Kensington.

As he opened the door for Tess to get out of the car, he said, 'Such a waste! She's only been using a couple of rooms for years.' He then picked up a small gift-wrapped box from the rear seat before locking the car.

As they entered by the elegant black-painted door, Tess felt her mouth dry up with nerves. What on earth was she supposed to say to a ninety-three-year-old lady whom she knew nothing about?

'What do I call her?' she asked Benedict anxiously.

'Oh, best just to call her Mrs de Vere,' Benedict replied. 'That was her final surname – I think. She was married three times, or was it four? No, one of them she never bothered to marry. Yes, stick with Mrs de Vere. And don't worry, because we won't be staying long. She's very frail so she'll probably fall asleep halfway through our visit anyway.'

At that moment a short, tubby woman emerged from a doorway on the left.

'Ah, Mr Benedict!' she said. 'Your mother hoped you'd call this afternoon. She's awake at the moment.' She stared openly at Tess.

'Thanks, Peg.' He turned to Tess. 'Peg looks after Mother. Peg, this is Tess.'

'Pleased to meet you,' said Peg, still gawping at Tess.

Feeling distinctly uncomfortable, Tess was led up the imposing central staircase towards one of at least half a dozen doors, where she was ushered into a large room with dark, heavily embossed wallpaper, and dark green velvet swag curtains framing French windows which, Tess could see, led out onto a small Juliet balcony. There was a huge open fire burning in the Adam fireplace and a distinct smell of mothballs. In the middle of the room was an enormous oak four-poster, on which reclined a tiny, ancient lady in a ruffled white nightgown. At first Tess thought she was asleep but, as they approached the bed, her eyes flew open.

'Benedict, dear boy!' she said in a surprisingly strong voice.

'How are you, Mother?' Benedict asked as he bent to kiss her. 'And happy birthday! Just a little something from us!' He handed her the box.

His mother laid the box to one side without even glancing at it. 'And who,' she asked, 'is *this*?'

'This, Mother, is Tess,' he replied, propelling Tess forward.

Tess held out her hand to grasp the old lady's birdlike claw. 'Happy birthday, Mrs de Vere,' she said dutifully. She was aware of being studied again, and very thoroughly.

'Have you known Benedict long?' Mrs de Vere asked, never taking her eyes off Tess.

'Not long, Mother,' Benedict got in quickly. 'But at last I've met someone special! I knew you'd be pleased! Now, what have *you* been up to?'

'What have *I* been up to?' She turned her attention back to her son. 'There's not a lot I can get up to, lying here. Your brother's coming over later.'

'Aren't you going to open your present?' Benedict asked.

'Later,' she said, turning her attention back to Tess. 'And what do *you* do for a living?'

'I'm a dressmaker,' Tess replied.

'A dressmaker!' Mrs de Vere digested this information for a minute. 'And who exactly do you make dresses for?'

'Well, anyone who wants one. I run a small boutique with my friend.'

'How charming! And how did you meet Benedict?'

Tess gulped. Benedict said, 'Oh, friend of a friend – you know how it is!'

'No, I don't,' said his mother. 'Tell me.'

'I knew straight away she was the one for me,' said Benedict, ignoring her question.

Tess looked at him in astonishment. *What* was going on and what was she supposed to say?

The old lady looked at Benedict, then at Tess, and then back to Benedict again.

'You know his history?' she asked, turning her attention back to Tess. 'I can scarcely believe you've brought about this miraculous change at such a late stage in his life. It wouldn't have anything to do with the will, would it, Benedict?'

'Tess is a very special woman,' Benedict replied. 'And of course it's nothing to do with the will! I've just come to my senses at long last.'

'And you're prepared to take him on?' she asked Tess.

Tess thought quickly. 'I like a challenge,' she said.

'You've certainly got one there,' his mother replied.

Tess noticed the old lady's eyelids beginning to droop, and prayed for an escape.

'Anyway,' said Benedict, 'we don't want to tire you, Mother, so I'll pop in again later in the week.'

She peered at her son again. 'I've no idea what took you so long to find a wife. But thank God for that!' She closed her eyes. 'I can die happy now, knowing both you and your brother are settled and I can divide things up the way they should be – half to you, half to him.'

'Thank you,' said Benedict, 'but you aren't going to be dying for a long time yet.'

Apparently satisfied, his mother succumbed to sleep, emitting gentle snores.

'Time to go,' said Benedict. 'Let's get you back to your car.'

Thoroughly confused, Tess let herself sink into the Aston Martin again and be driven back to Pelligrini's car park in Surrey, Benedict strangely silent all the while. She couldn't imagine what might happen next. Would he make a date there and then or would he phone her? Or was there something not quite right about this entire episode?

As Benedict parked and helped Tess out of the car, he said, 'Thank you *so* much, Tess. You were terrific! Any time I can do you a favour in return… *oh!* His attention was diverted towards a very attractive young man advancing at speed in their direction. 'Oh, *Maurice!*' he exclaimed, his whole face lighting up.

'*Darling!*' exclaimed Maurice in a very pronounced French accent. 'How did it go? I thought you were *never* coming back!' And with that he embraced Benedict fiercely. As an afterthought he turned to Tess and said, 'Bonjour, you are Tess?'

Tess was at a loss for words.

Maurice wasn't. He said, 'Do you think it worked, mon cher?'

'I think so,' Benedict said. 'Tess was really great and Mother appeared convinced.'

'Très bien!' said Maurice, putting an arm round Benedict's waist. 'Merci, Tess.'

'Like I said, any time I can do you a favour, Tess,' said Benedict, pecking her on the cheek, 'just you let me know.'

'Thank you for a lovely lunch,' she said, before turning and walking quickly towards her car.

Tess didn't know whether to laugh or cry. She'd been well and truly 'used'. Used to fool an old lady. Then again, perhaps it was kinder that the old lady should die happy in the knowledge that her son had finally become heterosexual.

Later, the more Tess thought about the afternoon's encounter, the more she wondered how Benedict's mother, who seemed a wily old bird, could be so easily convinced that her son was about to settle down with a suitable woman. Perhaps she was happier being able to deceive herself into believing what she needed to believe. Perhaps Tess had done her a favour after all. But plainly, Benedict had not suddenly become heterosexual; it was all something to do with the conditions of the will. She'd never know and she never wanted to know. She herself had been taken for a fool, hadn't she?

'Any time I can do you a favour, Tess,' were his parting words. Perhaps she should take him at his word and make a date with him for Amber's wedding, because she was unlikely to find another man as good-looking and elegant. But no, Tess couldn't do that. She owed it to Amber, and to herself, to attend the wedding with a genuine companion. Showing up with Benedict would be purely an act, tempting as it would be to see the look on Ursula's face.

What a farce her first MMM date had been! Why on earth had she ever let Orla talk her into wasting £150? Still, it had been an experience and she'd probably had that amount spent on her at lunch. And she doubted she'd ever get to ride in an Aston Martin again.

At least the story had Orla in hoots of laughter a few hours later, as Tess descended a ladder, having placed some frothy hats above the wedding outfits on display.

'Well,' Orla said, wiping her eyes, 'he might have been using you but, come *on*, you were planning to use him too – mainly to escort you to the wedding if nothing else, weren't you?'

'But I wanted him to be a little *more* than that, Orla. And he couldn't have been more than a *very* occasional friend, could he?'

'There are plenty of heterosexual fish in the sea, so you'll just have to keep looking.'

'But how come Benedict wasn't listed as looking for a *male* partner?'

'Because he *wasn't*,' Orla explained with mock patience. 'He obviously already has a partner. He was after a wholesome-looking woman to act the part of a possible wife in order to fool his poor old mother.'

'*Wholesome!*' Tess glared at Orla.

'Well, you'd prefer to look wholesome rather than debauched, wouldn't you?'

Tess wasn't at all sure she preferred to look wholesome. Was that how people viewed her, as *wholesome*? She sighed; she certainly had her work cut out if she was going to achieve this slim glamorous image she had in mind. Did wholesome equal dull? Is that why Benedict really chose her?

'How can I be sure these guys haven't all got an ulterior motive?' she asked.

'You can only find out by meeting them. Anyway, you got a nice lunch out of it and no harm done. Let's have a look on MMM and see who else there is.'

CHAPTER FIVE

HAPPY FAMILIES

It couldn't be postponed any longer. She and Gerry had to discuss Amber's wedding; who was paying for what, who had to be invited and who didn't.

'I'm not having him coming to *my* house,' Tess informed Orla. 'We need to meet on neutral territory. Probably Amber's place. Trouble is, trying to get everyone free on the same day.'

They chose the following Thursday, although at the last minute Amber's fiancé Peter was summoned to a conference in Marseilles. They decided to proceed without him: at least Gerry was back from his annual fortnight in Madeira, Amber had a rare day off, Matt had already agreed to pay for the wedding cars, and anyway, he'd be in Hong Kong that day, and Tess was greatly relieved to have a break from making a dress for the dreaded Mrs Byron-Sommers, who appeared to have a lot more money than taste. The woman wasn't just obese, she was elephantine. And, with her insistence on a mauve synthetic fabric, she was a nightmare as far as Tess was concerned, and probably her greatest challenge yet.

Tess felt weary and wintry when they convened at Amber's flat, which was a showpiece of open-plan minimalism with white leather sofas grouped on polished concrete floors, and adorned with a large abstract canvas which, Amber had admitted, had cost the equivalent of their annual holiday. Tess wondered how they'd cope with messy little children if they ever had any.

And that particular day she was also feeling a little depressed at her lack of compatibility with the first 'heart' she'd met. Amber, who'd been working long hours, was yawning even before the meeting began. Gerry, of course, was suntanned and smiling with what looked suspiciously like whitened or veneered teeth. And he'd brought Ursula along. She was also deeply tanned, with sun-kissed hair and a blindingly white smile, which Tess knew was due, in part anyway, to implants, because she'd apparently had problems with receding gums and wobbly teeth. Amber had gleefully reported this fact some years previously. And Ursula hadn't put on an ounce from the last time Tess had seen her. She was wearing a cream cashmere roll-neck sweater and jeans that appeared to have been sprayed on. Tess wasn't sure what she resented most: the hair, the clothes, the figure, or just Ursula in general.

'I didn't expect you to come, Ursula,' Tess said through her gritted, rather imperfect teeth.

'You don't mind, I hope?' Ursula said, plonking herself down on one of the leather settees and crossing one skinny leg over the other.

'No, of course not,' Tess lied, feeling more lumpy and colourless than usual, as Gerry dutifully pecked her on the cheek.

'You look like you could do with a holiday yourself, Tess,' he said. 'We all need a break to get through the winter.' He then sat down on the settee next to Ursula.

'The fact is,' Tess said, 'I can't afford any kind of break at the moment, not until I know exactly how much I'm going to be contributing towards the cost of this wedding.'

'Well, she *is* your daughter,' said Ursula with a tight smile.

'And she isn't *yours*,' Tess snapped, feeling her hackles rising.

'Let's not get off on the wrong foot,' Gerry said calmly, withdrawing some paperwork from his briefcase. Tess wondered what lurked in there these days. 'Let's start with the venue for the reception,' he continued. 'Ashley Grange is not cheap, but *so* luxurious and with that terrific river frontage… I'm footing the bill for that, of course.' He looked around with a smug expression. 'Deposit already paid. Now, we must talk about the food and the booze. What's the final guest total – anyone know?'

'Definitely one hundred,' Amber said, placing a cafetière of coffee and four mugs on the table. 'And you know that Peter's family are paying for the booze and we're paying for the food.'

Tess sighed. A hundred! At the last count, when they'd sent out the 'save the dates', it had been eighty, which she reckoned was about thirty too many anyway. She knew that most of the 'extras' would be business colleagues of Gerry's. He was never one to miss an opportunity to impress and do some networking.

She recalled their own modest nuptials in the austere little church in Strathcoy; she in a short day dress she'd made herself, Gerry in a rented Moss Bros suit. Her one and only bridesmaid was Jessie, her best friend (in the absence of her errant sister), who'd provided her own dress. Then lunch in the Strathcoy Hotel and a three-day honeymoon in York because Gerry had a contact there, after which he was keen to get back to 'civilisation', as he put it, because he said he wasn't 'designed' to be north of Watford for too long. Tess sighed at the memory.

'What about Barbara?' Gerry turned to Tess. 'Has anyone heard if she's coming or not?'

Tess shrugged. 'You know my sister. I'll email her again to see if I can get a definite answer. But she hates coming back to the UK, as you know, so it's anyone's guess.'

'And you, Tess, are you coming alone or bringing someone?'

Here was the million-dollar question. 'Probably bringing someone,' she said. Well, she could always change that, if she had to. Which she most likely would.

'We'll count that as another possible space at the top table then,' Gerry said, looking at her quizzically.

'Flowers!' Ursula piped up. 'What about flowers?'

'Done and dusted!' said Amber. 'I've found a fantastic place in Chelsea!'

There followed some discussion about how much the church was going to cost, how much the vicar was going to cost, and whether they should offer to pay the bill for the bridesmaid's dress.

'Well, I certainly can't make it,' Tess said firmly, as all eyes swivelled in her direction. 'I'm working round the clock at the moment.'

'Well, at least you'll have plenty of money coming in,' said Ursula cattily.

Tess's hackles had reached new heights. 'Just about enough to cover my community tax, my electricity, my gas, my water, my share of renting the shop – but not quite enough for a couple of weeks in Madeira!'

'Whoa, whoa! Easy, easy!' said Gerry the arbiter.

Tess noticed he'd aged considerably in the few months since she'd last seen him, and he was definitely paunchier. There were folds of flesh over those blue eyes she'd once so adored.

Amber rolled her eyes at her mother and then turned to Ursula. 'Er, Ursula, I think it might be best if you keep out of this. And, as regards to a bridesmaid, I've decided against that. I'll just have Ellie as my flower girl.'

'Well, I only said that because Gerry's having to foot the lion's share of the bill,' said Ursula, smiling brightly.

Tess wondered if implants ever fell out. She hoped these would.

'Anyway, I think we've covered pretty well everything,' Amber said. 'Mum is paying her share by making me a beautiful dress, copied from a designer model, saving me thousands.'

Ursula wasn't finished yet. 'Surely there's a copyright on that?' she asked.

Even Gerry had had enough at this point. 'Will you keep out of this!' he snapped at his paramour.

'I was only trying to *help*,' she replied sulkily.

'Well, you aren't damn well helping!' Gerry snapped. He turned his attention back to Tess. 'That's fine, Tess, and I think we've covered everything.'

'I doubt it,' Tess replied. 'There's bound to be something we haven't thought of. Probably best if I email you.'

'Probably,' Gerry agreed, glancing at Ursula.

As they prepared to go their separate ways and Ursula was 'paying a call to nature', Gerry rested his hand on Tess's arm. 'Are you OK for money?' he asked quietly.

Tess stared at him. 'Yes, I'm fine. Why do you ask?'

'I just worry about you sometimes,' he said.

'Well, you've no need to,' she said. 'I'm managing quite well, thank you.'

'I'm sure you are, but you look so tired, and you seem to be a bit short on holidays and your social life.'

As if he knew or cared! Tess was astounded. Why on earth was he suddenly so solicitous about her wellbeing?

She gave a little laugh. 'Not at all,' she said. 'I belong to a very exclusive little social club, have met some *wonderful* men friends, and my social life is quite *exhausting* at times! And I'll be doing a cruise round the Greek islands in a couple of months' time.'

Gerry looked surprised. 'Well, that's all right then…' And he was about to say something else when Ursula reappeared.

There was no way Tess was going to let him see how she was really feeling. And now she really did have to find someone.

CHAPTER SIX

SPECIALITY OF THE DAY

Someone called James fancied meeting her. Not Jim, or Jimmy, but James. And James was a solicitor, which was all very respectable, and he lived in Chalfont St Giles, which was even more respectable.

'I bet he'll bore the socks off you,' Orla predicted.

'Just as long as he leaves my knickers on,' Tess replied, wondering what sort of outfit she should wear this time. What was appropriate for lunching with a solicitor in a country pub near Windsor? She'd try for the smart 'county' look. She only possessed one cashmere sweater so she'd better wear that, with her new wool trousers and sensible loafers. And pearls. A discreet double row of pearls round her neck and studs in her ears.

Deciding what she should wear on special occasions had always been a minor trauma for Tess.

Not for the first time, she wondered if she'd spent most of her life trying to fit in; not to stand out in the crowd, always to wear the right thing and say the right thing, not to upset anyone. Was that her fairly strict Scottish Presbyterian upbringing or her own eager-to-please nature? Heaven knows, but she'd always tried to please Gerry and look where that had got her. David, though, had loved her just as she was. So perhaps now it was time to stop trying to please other people and start trying to please herself.

'I've seen the Queen look more exciting,' Orla commented when Tess popped into the shop en route to her date.

'Off you go then to meet your plumber, or whatever he is, in your tatty jeans,' Tess said.

'I'll have you know he runs a sanitation company.'

'So, he's a plumber.'

'Well, there's nothing wrong with that.'

'I didn't say there was.' But I'd rather be meeting my solicitor, Tess thought. What a boost to my confidence this would be! I could do with coming up in the world, and he's bound to go to nice places; I bet this pub is really something.

And so Tess got into her car and headed towards Windsor. It was a cold, wet late February morning and, as she peered through the overworked windscreen wipers, she dreamed of a country pub with a huge inglenook and a blazing fire. She was to meet James at midday, and she arrived in the pub car park five minutes early, so she sat in the car and wondered which of the smart vehicles parked alongside might belong to James. The Porsche, perhaps? Or the Merc, or the Alfa Sport?

Just then an enormous motorbike snarled into the car park and a black-leathered giant dismounted. Tess watched as he removed his helmet, exposing a bald head adorned only with one large silver earring. This was no youthful rocker, more like an elderly thug. Where *did* these people come from?

She watched him go into the pub and consulted her watch. She'd give it another five minutes and then she'd go in. James had said he'd be waiting for her at the bar, at the far end, next to the board advertising 'Speciality of the Day'. 'Let's hope you'll consider *me* the speciality of the day!' he'd quipped, so at least the man appeared to have some sense of humour.

But Tess felt nervous. What if he hadn't arrived? Was she going to have to stand next to 'Speciality of the Day' and wait for him? She supposed she'd better get used to this sort of thing, because it was most likely to be the only way she was going to meet up with these 'hearts'. She certainly wasn't going to have any of them come to pick her up from home. In fact, even MMM advised against that. *Meet on neutral territory*, they advised. *We can't guarantee you're going to love all your 'hearts' and, if you found a persistent or obsessive one, you certainly wouldn't want him knowing where you live.* Persistent? Obsessive? *That* hadn't featured in their marketing blurb.

Tess pushed the door open to an already crowded bar. It was well supplied with artificial beams, and on every wall were pictures of motorbikes and detailed diagrams of engines. Not exactly what she'd envisaged. She peered past the chatting customers, looking for today's 'Specials' sign. No one likely to be James was standing by the blackboard, only Motorbike Man, still clutching his helmet. It was just as she feared; she must have got there before him. Surely he should have made a point of getting there first if he was any kind of gentleman? Well, there was nothing for it but to share the space with Motorbike Man so that James could spot her when he finally arrived.

She reached the sign and wondered if she should order a drink, when Motorbike Man said, 'Tess?'

Tess jumped. 'Yes?'

He held out his hand. 'James.'

For a split second she stared at him in astonishment, then remembered her manners.

'Well, this is a surprise,' she said lamely.

'Let's find a table,' said James. 'Then I'll pop into the loo and remove these leathers.'

They squeezed past table after table before finally finding a vacant one next to a mock fireplace, minus the roaring fire. Or any kind of fire. It was bitterly cold.

'I'll just get these off,' he said, 'and then I'll get us a drink.' And with that he disappeared round the corner. Tess decided to keep her coat on but unbuttoned it to expose her cashmered bosom. Everyone in here was clad in jeans and trainers and leather jackets. When James reappeared, he too was wearing faded jeans and a less than pristine grey fleece. He reminded her very slightly of Grant Mitchell in *EastEnders*.

'What's your poison?' he asked.

'I'm driving,' Tess replied. 'So I'd better have a lime soda or something.'

'Aw, live dangerously!' he said. 'One glass of something isn't going to hurt.'

'Just a small white wine then, please.'

He came back with a large glass of wine and a pint of beer for himself. 'Pinot Grigio OK?'

'Yes, fine.' Tess cleared her throat. 'Did you say you were a solicitor, James?'

'Correct,' he replied, raising his glass. 'And *you* make dresses?'

'And other things. I run a little boutique with my friend.'

'And what else do you like to do, Tess?'

'Well, I enjoy a bit of gardening and—'

'You're not into biking then?' he interrupted.

'Not really.'

'Bikes are my passion. Did you see my Fat Boy out there?'

'Fat boy?' Tess was confused. 'I didn't see any fat boys.'

He roared with laughter. 'No, no, that's the name of the bike! You must have seen my Harley? You know what? Riding that's the nearest I get to an orgasm these days!' He poked her playfully on the arm, perilously close to her left breast. 'But I'm open to offers!'

Tess was beginning to feel distinctly uncomfortable as well as somewhat overdressed. She twiddled nervously with her pearls. 'Have you been on your own for long?'

'Ever since my other half took off with her Spanish night-class teacher a year and a half ago. I *ask* you!'

'I'm sorry to hear that,' Tess said. 'Mine took off with a woman young enough to be his daughter eleven years ago.'

'Eleven years!' He regarded her with amazement. 'You must be a bit short of orgasms too!' He roared with laughter again.

'I *have* had a relationship,' Tess said, 'with a lovely man who died in an accident a couple of years back.' She didn't like the way this conversation was going.

'You're so very ladylike!' said James. 'But I'm living in hope that there's still some hot blood coursing around in these veins of yours, underneath that jumper!' He gave her another playful poke.

Tess sipped her drink. 'I've never met a solicitor like you before.'

He laughed. 'They all say that! Anyway, I specialise in company law, not all those messy divorces and stuff. I have a mate who does all that though, and he'll sort me out when I divorce the bitch – make sure she gets next to nothing.'

Tess wondered how quickly she could escape. She gulped her wine. I *wanted* to like him, she thought, but I don't. I want to go home.

'Stay there while I get us another drink,' he ordered, and with that he was up and heading towards the bar.

He returned with another glass of wine and another pint.

'I can't drink this,' Tess said. 'I'll get arrested.'

'Of course you won't! Not enough police round here to catch a cold. If they can't catch me with my Milwaukee-Eight engine, they aren't going to catch you in your – let me guess – Micra? Focus?'

'I still don't think—'

'Thing is, you've got to out-race them. See, this Harley is so much lighter than the old softail. It's 1,868cc.'

'Oh, really?'

'Did you see the movie *Terminator 2*? It featured in that. Great bike!'

Slowly Tess buttoned up her coat.

'Aren't you going to drink that? No? Never mind! Fancy coming back to my place?'

She shook her head. 'No, thank you.'

'Or I could come to yours? You're somewhere near Kingston, aren't you?'

'No thanks, James.' Tess was standing up. 'I don't think there's much point. I'm not looking for instant sex, or motorbikes for that matter. And I really should be getting back.'

'Why? We're supposed to be getting to *know* each other!'

She sighed. 'Somehow I just don't think we're likely to be compatible. Sorry, James.'

'You don't know anything about me,' James snapped. 'And you could be quite attractive if you loosened up a little. Let your hair down.'

Tess picked up her shoulder bag.

'Off you go then! Get into your little 1200cc or 1400cc Micra or Focus or whatever it is, and head back to your sewing machine! I bet the car's silver and you listen to Classic FM when you're driving.'

'Thanks for the wine.'

Tess headed for the door, hoping he wouldn't see her getting into her 1400cc silver Ford Focus. Not that she was ashamed of it; David had found it for her and it was a great car. But she knew James would have a self-satisfied smirk on his face; he was that type. As she turned the key in the ignition, Classic FM was playing some soothing Beethoven. She sat quietly for a moment and let the music drift over her. What was wrong with driving a Focus and listening to Classic FM? She didn't like his sneering superiority and she didn't like being typecast as some mediocre sort of woman. Perhaps the problem was his. Perhaps he wasn't attracting the women he hoped he would, and it had made him bolshie and bitter. She was trying very hard to give him the benefit of the doubt. Or was the problem *hers*? Did she need to loosen up, as he suggested? Had she become a narrow-minded old prune? As well as being *wholesome*? Could you be both? But she had to be honest with herself; she did not like the insinuations he was making and his manner of speaking.

Damn the man! She'd spent one hundred and fifty hard-earned pounds to meet men like Benedict and James. She should never have listened to Orla. And, come to think of it, that bullish James looked nothing at all like the lovely Ross Kemp who played the part of Grant Mitchell.

But Tess knew it was partly her own fault. She'd probably felt self-conscious and vulnerable by wearing the wrong gear. But how was she to know it was a pub for motor enthusiasts? She'd given James an easy excuse to mock her. After all these years she still got it wrong. And she cringed as, yet again, she remembered Marilyn Ford's birthday party…

*

It was the summer of her seventeenth year and Marilyn Ford was the most popular girl in Tess's class. Everyone wanted to be in Marilyn's select little group, including Tess, but she was not one of the chosen few. Marilyn was not only pretty but she also lived in a big house where, it was rumoured, they had a *swimming pool*. Nobody, but nobody in Strathcoy had a swimming pool. And she was greatly revered by her less fortunate classmates. Tess never knew why – having been ignored by this girl for years – she'd been invited to Marilyn's birthday party. Perhaps it had been some sort of mistake, or perhaps it was because she'd recently won a dressmaking competition and had her photo in the local paper, thereby qualifying, however temporarily, to be included in the exalted circle. More likely it was because her sister, Barbara, who was three years older, had recently shocked Strathcoy to the core by eloping with an *Egyptian*. Barbara had spent most of her nineteen years scheming about how to get away from Strathcoy and see the world, and her passport had come in the shape of Omar, who was handsome but considered feckless by their parents. Not only was he a wheeler-dealer, her mother said, but who knew what sort of background he had? And worst of all, he was *thirty-seven*! Their father had forbidden her to see him. So Barbara did what Tess suspected she'd do, and took off with him. Yes, that would be why she was invited; everyone loved a scandal and they'd want to know about Barbara.

It was August and Tess, as usual, panicked about what to wear. It was bound to be a posh do. There was no money, her mother said, to go buying party dresses. But Tess had a Saturday job in Woolworths and had saved just enough money to buy some material and make a dress: something summery and pretty and full-skirted. She eventually found some cotton, adorned with pretty pink roses against a background of honeysuckle. Tess loved it and wasted no time in shaping it into a party dress. It took four evenings, after school and homework, to get it exactly right. Finally, the day before the party, she could pirouette in front of the bedroom mirror in her finery.

On the afternoon of the party, which was due to start at 6 p.m., she donned the dress, brushed her hair out of its usual ponytail, applied her one and only lipstick which, by chance, was an exact match for the roses, slipped her feet into her white sandals, and sprayed herself liberally with her mother's L'Aimant perfume. She'd got a little box of bath salts and talcum powder from Woolworths and hoped it would make an acceptable present.

Tess set off on her bicycle for the ten-minute ride to Strathcoy's poshest suburb, which was set high above the town and so required some energetic pedalling.

It was a beautiful day with not a cloud in the sky. Tess felt increasingly nervous as she made her way up the Fords' immaculate drive, since she was ten minutes late and could hear voices and laughter coming from somewhere at the back of the imposing double-fronted house. She hoped she could slip in unnoticed.

Marilyn's mother answered the door. 'Just go through, dear,' she said to a breathless Tess. 'They're all in the back garden by the pool.' By the *pool!* Oh, *wow*, so the rumours were correct: they had a pool!

Anxiously Tess wandered across an enormous lounge and through the French windows to where she could hear the laughter and splashing outside. There were around ten girls and three boys, all either in swimsuits in the pool or in shorts, shirts tied at the waist, feet bare.

There was a moment's silence as Tess came into sight.

'Didn't Marilyn *tell* you it was a pool party?' one of the girls asked, emerging from the water, dripping and grabbing a towel.

'No,' Tess replied. 'She didn't.'

She felt overdressed and out of place. She wasn't a great swimmer, but at least she could have worn a shirt and the shorts she'd remodelled from an old pair of jeans. Instead, she sat sipping lemonade, isolated in a sea of the rose-patterned fabric, the full skirt of which had bunched up all around her, while everyone else splashed and swam and danced to The Mamas & the Papas and The Beach Boys. And, on top of that, Marilyn hadn't looked wildly impressed with the bath salts and the talcum powder either. But at least she had had the decency to apologise for not mentioning that it was to be a pool party. Thank goodness for Alan Muir, who'd come to rescue her, refilling her glass with lemonade and accompanying her to the cold buffet. He was a nice lad, and had asked her to the pictures the following week. Her meagre ration of self-confidence shattered, Tess felt sure he only asked her because he felt sorry for her. It was never destined to be a big romance and Tess, although grateful, didn't fancy him, so that was that.

In later years she wished she'd had the confidence to jump straight into the pool, pink roses and all, saying something witty like, 'If you can't beat them, join them!' Everyone would have laughed and she wouldn't have minded wearing a dripping-wet dress for the remainder of the party. Instead, wearing the right thing, and not standing out in the crowd, had become something of an obsession.

*

'That's it,' Tess said, 'I'm not doing this any more. You can stuff your MMM.'

She emerged from the shop window, where she'd been positioning a wrap dress in dark blue wool on Dolly the dummy. It was late February, a quiet time of year; people were still paying off Christmas, the main winter sales were over, and it was too early and too cold to contemplate spring.

'You were just unlucky. Anyway, you're not going to love them all, for God's sake,' Orla retorted from the cupboard-like office at the rear of the shop, where she was supposedly doing the monthly accounts.

'He didn't look or act like any solicitor I've ever met,' Tess went on. 'I got the impression that he was only interested in his precious motorbike. And sex, of course. He was quite blatant about that.'

'Aw, never mind. Perhaps he was just trying to shock you out of your Conservative tea party look!'

'I don't look anything like someone at a Conservative tea party,' Tess snapped.

'Well, you did yesterday. Now, ask me about Paul.'

'Paul?'

'The sanitation man. Lovely guy and *loaded*! He bought me a fantastic meal and we never stopped talking. And then I asked him back for a coffee.'

'Orla! You know you're not supposed to do *that*!'

'Maybe not, but he fixed that dripping tap in my bathroom. And he's coming back tomorrow to check the kitchen waste disposal; you know I told you the water takes forever to drain away? Paul thinks it's the U-bend.'

'Apart from his plumbing skills, do you like him?'

'Actually, I do. He makes me laugh. And I can just be myself with him. And he doesn't mind a bit of excess flesh. He said, "the more there is of a woman, the more of a woman there is". You can't argue about that, can you?'

'I suppose not.'

CHAPTER SEVEN

REMINISCING

Tess had to agree with Orla that she might have overdone the 'Shires lady' look yesterday, particularly the pearls. Not that it mattered much, because she'd never have fancied James or his damned bike in a month of Sundays. And she wished she wasn't forever trying to please; she'd spent years trying to please Gerry, and look where that had got her. She must now concentrate on pleasing herself.

As Tess sat down behind the little counter in Curvaceous she recalled that first meeting with Gerry. Thirty-nine years ago, when she fell off the bus! It was an unusual first encounter to say the least.

She'd been honing her dressmaking skills in an East End warehouse that supplied outfits for most of the West End stores and, on this particular occasion, she'd taken the bus up to Oxford Street for a late shopping night. It was pouring with rain and she wanted to go to John Lewis, so when the bus was held up in heavy traffic directly opposite the store, she took the opportunity to jump off. Unfortunately, just as she started to jump the bus lurched forwards; she lost her balance, and fell in an undignified heap into a giant puddle. People stopped in their tracks to gawp at this bedraggled woman, but only one extended a hand and asked, 'Are you all right?'

Tess wasn't sure if she was all right or not as she hobbled onto the pavement. She only knew she was wet and cold, and she'd injured her ankle. She certainly did not want to draw attention to herself.

'Have you hurt your foot?'

For the first time she looked into the blue eyes of her rescuer, and liked what she saw.

'I'm OK, really!' she said. 'But thank you.'

'No, you're not,' retorted the good-looking stranger, who, as well as the blue eyes, had blond hair and a very winning smile. 'You're limping, and you're wet. Let me buy you a coffee.'

'No, really, I—'

'I insist! Come on, there's a great place just round the corner. Think you can hobble that far?'

And Tess let herself be led into a warm, steamy coffee bar, just off Oxford Street, by this handsome stranger.

As they sat down he extended his hand. 'Gerry Templar.'

'Hello, Gerry,' she said. 'I'm Tess. Tess MacKenzie.'

He grinned. 'Not often do pretty Scottish ladies fall into my arms from the back of buses. But I've been living in hope!'

Then he bought them each a frothy coffee and pulled over a chair from a nearby table. 'Your ankle's swollen,' he said. 'You need to keep your foot up.'

Tess was aware that she must look an absolute mess, with her wet hair and muddy coat. And probably her mascara had run all over the place. This guy must be a really kind and diplomatic soul, because no one in their right mind could possibly fancy her at the moment.

'So, Tess, what do you do when you're not falling off buses?'

'I'm training to be a dressmaker,' she told him. 'I'm doing tailoring at the moment. And one day I'd like to set up my own business.'

'Good for you! And when I have my own advertising agency I'll be sure to promote your designs.'

'When is that likely to be?' Tess asked, sipping her coffee.

Gerry Templar lit a cigarette, blew out some smoke, narrowed his eyes and said, 'By the time I'm thirty. Which gives me four years.'

He was, at that time, working for a large prestigious agency, but Gerry had even bigger ideas. And what Gerry wanted he usually got. She found out some time later that he'd also had a fiancée at the time. People did, back then, promise to marry each other, buy engagement rings, set the date. But Gerry was instantly smitten with Tess, and the rest was history. Tess was later to learn that when Gerry fancied something, or someone, that was it. In retrospect she'd never been quite sure if there had been others, until that fateful day when she discovered Gerry had transferred his affections to Ursula. Their marriage did not survive the younger woman.

Ursula's lower half was solely dedicated to pleasure and hadn't suffered the indignities of reproduction or, heaven forbid, a hysterectomy. Not only that: she made great cocktails and great contacts, and Gerry's agency thrived as a result.

It had taken Tess a very long time to trust any man again. Until dear David came along years later.

Tess was woken from her daydreaming as a woman came in through the shop door. This lady was not one of their regulars. As always, Tess made a mental assessment of how difficult she might be to dress; she was probably around five foot seven and sixteen stone, so not too much of a challenge.

'I've been recommended to come here by Mrs Byron-Sommers. I've lost four stone and I've decided I need a completely new wardrobe.'

'Well, you've come to exactly the right place,' said Orla. 'What did you have in mind?'

What she had in mind was a skirt suit, a trouser suit, two skirts and two dresses.

When Tess arrived home that evening she was still thinking about the new customer and the half-dozen new outfits she wanted. It prompted Tess to have a look at her own wardrobe. She'd completely forgotten about some of these clothes that she hadn't worn in years. She did what most women do, wearing only about a quarter of what was hanging in there, and she'd read somewhere that if you hadn't worn a garment for a year – or was it two? – you should get rid of it. But Tess still liked some of these things, if only she could get into them. Well, she was trying to do something about that, but now it was time for a wardrobe cull. A great idea, but not that easy. She'd really loved most of these items in the first place, and some of them had cost a lot of money, or they had a special association with someone or somewhere.

Tess spent the evening hauling stuff out that she wasn't likely to wear again. Some went straight into a black bin liner – like the waterfall cardigans and flared trousers, destined for the charity shop – and some were thrown across the bed in a haze of indecision, much to the disgust of Dylan, her large tabby cat, who'd been asleep on the duvet. The remainder she was keeping. OK, so she couldn't get into some of it, but it was stuff she couldn't bear to part with and, most importantly, *it was all going to fit again.* Definitely.

Tess's excess weight wasn't all due to gluttony. Not *all.* She shuddered, thinking of her shock and disbelief when, two years before and not long after David's death, having attended a routine mammogram she'd been told she had breast cancer. She could remember saying, 'There must be some mistake – I haven't felt a lump!' Nevertheless, breast cancer it was, and there followed those eighteen months of gruelling treatment: chemotherapy, radiotherapy and the loss of her hair. It had all grown back quickly, and better than before, but she'd never forget the horror of seeing herself in the mirror, robbed not only of the hair on her head but the eyebrows and eyelashes as well. She'd never realised before how much her hair defined her.

She'd worn a wig and lots of eye make-up, but was full of admiration for some of the women she'd befriended in the oncology department who'd worn their baldness with pride. She'd never had that kind of confidence. And, as the weight piled on, so her confidence dropped even further.

Everyone had meant well. 'Go on, have that cream cake/ice cream sundae/sticky toffee pudding – you need to keep your strength up!' No, she didn't, and she didn't need to keep her strength up with a double portion of cheesy chips either. But oh, it was all so very comforting! It had taken months to get back to where she was now. And there was still a very long way to go. It would take months more. Amber's wedding may have been the catalyst for her decision but she really needed to do this for herself, to restore her confidence and to feel attractive again.

Now, in a moment of determination, Tess chucked all the 'doubtfuls' strewn across the bed into the bin liner. She'd take that bag straight down to the charity shop before she changed her mind.

The new customer wasn't the only one who was going to need new outfits. Tess had her cruise to think about.

CHAPTER EIGHT

WEIGHING IT UP

The following day was quieter than usual, and Tess took the opportunity to look up some patterns for her new customer. Despite her best intentions, after a few minutes she found herself drawn to the MMM site, hoping to discover whether she'd merely been unlucky or if perhaps the problem had something to do with her.

'I thought that the whole point of paying this money and being a "heart" was that you were guaranteed to meet a decent sort of person. Someone who's been *vetted*.' Tess was still recovering from her encounter with James.

'Well, there was nothing *wrong* with him, was there? Just because he was a motorbike fanatic. You can hardly blame him for that.' Orla sniffed. 'See, if you'd gone for that guy with the bookshop, the one I told you about in the first place, you'd probably be living with him in Wales by now.'

'It's all right for *you* with your plumber,' Tess said.

'If you hadn't been so high and mighty about the sort of bloke you wanted to meet, you'd probably have met someone great by now.'

'I was *not* being high and mighty!' Tess snapped.

Orla had started giggling again. 'Never mind, only another four to go and you can get your money back.'

Tess started giggling too. 'I'm not sure I'm strong enough to meet any more! But that's why I'm determined to do this damned cruise – because I might as well get *something* out of it, even if it's only a suntan. And those Greek islands must be so beautiful.'

'Talking of which,' Orla said, 'I've booked Lauren to look after the shop while we're away.'

Lauren was the wife of Orla's elder son, Jack. She was rarely in Orla's good books; Lauren was never at home, the house was a tip, the kids had no manners, and apparently she never put a decent meal on the table. However, apart from all that, Lauren was very obliging and very useful when Orla wanted time off. Not only that, Lauren was popular with the customers too, and usually sold more outfits than her mother-in-law did.

It was exciting to think of the cruise. Lauren would be looking after the shop, her neighbour had promised to look after the cat and, for a whole glorious week, Tess would only need to look after herself.

There was to be one night in Athens, with just enough time to see the Parthenon before heading to Piraeus to board the *White Rose* for the cruise to Mykonos, Santorini, Rhodes and Crete. It would be very hot and Tess was already wondering what to pack. The minimum of stuff probably: a couple of swimsuits and sundresses, some trousers, a nice evening dress or two.

'I've put on a pound this week,' she said. 'The months are passing, Orla, and I still have twenty-one pounds to lose, so I've a long way to go.'

'You're fine,' Orla said. 'Stop worrying – men like a bit of flesh!'

'Well, Gerry didn't,' Tess said. 'So, how's Paul?'

'He's great. He's talking now about updating my bathroom, because he can get some really trendy stuff for a song, and he'd fit it himself of course. All he asks for is a nice meal on the table and a bit of nookie now and again.'

Tess was yet to meet Paul. She wondered if he could be persuaded to have a look at her leaking radiator, without her having to provide the nookie.

The queue for the weigh-in at Slim Chance seemed to get longer each week, as the number of slimmers increased. 'Pre-holiday panic' was how Judy described it: the removal of layers, the baring of the body. Realisation, revulsion, reparation! As usual the group mainly consisted of women, with only three males: Phil, who was so obese he required two plastic chairs to accommodate his enormous bottom; Barney, whom Orla had once fancied and now came every week accompanied by his wife; and Kevin, who was merely chubby and not bad-looking, but appeared reclusive and non-conversational. Tess looked around for an empty seat and saw one next to Shirley.

'How's it going?' Shirley asked.

'Could do better,' Tess replied with a grin. 'My social life is making things difficult.'

'I don't have much of a social life,' Shirley said sadly. 'I lost touch with quite a few people when I was having my treatment, so I'm a bit out of the loop.'

Tess thought for a minute. 'Why don't you come round to my place one evening and I'll do us a Slim Chance dinner?'

'That would be fabulous! Thanks so much! And we can exchange recipes. Thing is, I'm going to be away for a couple of weeks up in Manchester. My younger son and his wife have won a holiday in South Africa, would you believe, and guess who's got to keep an eye on the kids?'

'You're a saint! How old are they?'

'It's not too bad – they're both boys, twelve and fifteen, so not babies or anything. And they'll be at school all day. It'll just be the usual ritual of making sure they do their homework, prising them away from their phones occasionally, and getting them fed.'

'Well, let's set a date for when you get back,' Tess said, taking out her diary.

They arranged a date and Shirley said, 'I'll look forward to it. Where do you live?'

As Tess gave her the address, she decided it would be a far more pleasant evening than having another disastrous encounter with some ridiculous 'heart'.

Shirley had already been weighed and wasn't interested in waiting for Judy's lecture.

Now, as Tess stood in line to be weighed, she compared herself to the other slimmers. She knew she was tall enough to be able to carry her extra weight without it showing too much, and she was very careful to dress in a way that concealed the worst bits. In fact, seeing so much flab on display all round, she was beginning to feel positively normal. Tess was pleased not to stand out (memories of Marilyn's birthday party again!) although she wouldn't mind so much standing out for the right reasons, of course. *Just look at that Tess Templar – doesn't she look amazing!*

'That first day by the pool, or on the beach!' Judy sighed as she began her lecture. 'Particularly by the pool, because it's a confined area with everybody watching everybody else. Go on, *admit* it! You say to yourself, "is she fatter than me?" or "are her thighs bigger than mine?" or "God, I'm glad I don't look like *that*!" only to discover that you do, in fact, look *exactly* like that, because you hadn't realised there was a full-length mirror on the *outside* of the changing room door as well! And you weren't wearing your specs.' Judy paused for effect. 'Ladies, and you gentlemen as well, you have time to do something about it if you start *now*!'

The ladies murmured their assent and headed home, full of good intentions, to queue up again the following Tuesday morning to face the dreaded weighing machine. Most, of course, had weighed themselves when they first got out of bed, naked, and then mentally added a couple of pounds for clothing. This was particularly tricky in winter when they wore heavier clothing, and so the hall was littered with discarded coats, scarves, sweaters and boots.

On this occasion the woman in front of Tess had removed her watch, her belt and even her socks. She turned to face Tess with a sheepish grin. 'I don't even wear a bra on Tuesdays,' she admitted, cupping her boobs up into a perkier position. 'At home I only ever weigh myself with my wedding ring and my glasses on, otherwise I can't see the bloody number on the scales.' She looked frozen, standing there barefoot in a T-shirt and summer jeans.

Tess hadn't lost any weight this week either.

When they were all seated in what by now was a double semi-circle, Judy commenced her speech. 'I need to know,' she said, 'how much weight each of you want to lose, and,' she tapped her nose, 'exactly *why* you want to lose it.'

The braless woman had got most of her clothes on again and had produced a pot of some sort of mush. 'Breakfast,' she explained to Tess, who was sitting next to her. 'Daren't have it until after the weigh-in!'

Tess nodded. She sympathised, having only had a banana for breakfast. The mush looked almost enticing. Almost.

Apparently Mabel, the woman with the huge buttocks, was going to New Zealand to see her sister. 'I haven't seen her for ten years,' she said, 'and I was thin as a rake then.' She sniffed. 'And now I'm going to have to sit in a plane for twenty-odd hours with an extension seat belt!'

'And that worries you?' Judy asked.

'Yeah, it's kind of humiliating.'

'And bloody uncomfortable for whoever's sitting next to you, wedged into half a seat!' Judy didn't mince her words. 'So, what are you aiming for?'

'Well,' said Mabel, 'I'm not expecting miracles or anything, but I'd just like not to have to have the extension belt.' This remark warranted a round of applause.

'I want you to visualise sitting there comfortably with a *normal* seat belt,' said Judy, 'and having an interesting conversation with whoever's next to you, who's sitting squarely in his or her own seat. I want you to imagine this every waking moment, particularly when you're looking at the buy one get one free offer for custard creams in Tesco. Got it?'

'Yeah,' Mabel replied meekly.

'Who's next?' Judy hollered.

Next was Phyllis. 'I don't eat that much,' she wailed. 'I'm sure it's genetic with me; doesn't matter what I do.'

'Yes, it does matter, Phyllis!' Judy rolled her eyes. 'If I had a pound sterling for every person who informed me that their fat was genetic, I'd be a bloody rich woman by now. And on my yacht in the Caribbean or somewhere, not sorting out you lot!'

There were a few nervous titters before Judy started lecturing the group about people who deluded themselves and were hoping for sympathy more than weight loss.

'Now you, Myra!' She directed her stare at the braless lady who was finishing off the last of her breakfast. 'Remind me, Myra, why you want to lose weight.'

Myra looked uncomfortable. She wasn't overly large, just tubby round her middle like the majority of older women.

She cleared her throat. 'I need to improve my appearance,' she said, 'because my husband has gone to live with another woman.'

There was an embarrassed silence.

'And this woman,' Myra went on, 'is thin as a rake. No belly at all.'

I know this feeling only too well, Tess thought.

'And, naturally enough, you want your husband back,' Judy stated.

'No,' said Myra, 'I don't. I'm glad to see the back of him. I just want a flat belly, like hers. It's become a sort of obsession, I suppose.'

'Have you considered exercising?' another woman asked, breaking the awkward silence.

'Or finding a guy who likes bellies?' someone else suggested, which lightened the mood and caused some giggling.

'You're doing this for *you*, Myra, and you alone.' Judy stared hard. 'You *can* have a flat belly! And, although exercise helps, exercise alone won't do it. That's why we're all here.' She shifted her gaze. 'Tess!'

Tess jumped involuntarily.

'You've not lost this week but you've been doing really well up to now. What went wrong?'

'I'm not too sure,' she said.

'And tell us why you want to lose weight, Tess.'

'For my daughter's wedding at the end of July, and to feel better about myself.'

Judy closed her eyes and appeared to make some mental calculations. 'That's just over four months away,' she said. 'Have you bought your outfit yet?'

'No,' said Tess. She was aware that, what with making Amber's dress plus the orders for Curvaceous, there would definitely be no time to make her own.

'Right!' said Judy. 'I suggest you buy it one size smaller, hang it on the outside of your wardrobe door, look at it every single day, and damned well fit into it by July! OK, who's next?'

There was a strange kind of fervour about Judy. She had this fanatical enthusiasm for spreading the word.

Never mind – I *will* lose that weight before July, Tess thought.

CHAPTER NINE

FAT CHANCE

Tess shoved open the door, entered the hall, hung her coat on her grandmother's treasured Edwardian coat stand, and took a long hard look at herself in the age-stained mirror. Gerry was right, she did look tired and worn out, and she *was* worn out, damn it. She'd been working hard and there was still a backlog of orders to get through. The thing about working from home was that you never really stopped; no leaving it behind at five or six o'clock until nine the next morning. Even as she watched television, she was aware of the fabrics waiting to be cut out in the bedroom, which had become her workroom too. More often than not, there was a pattern pinned onto a fabric, spread across her cutting table, or on the floor, which took up half the room. It was too tempting to go back in there and cut the thing out, if only to fold up the table and clear the floor space. Then she'd make something fast, filling and fattening to eat late in the evening, washing it down with wine. But she'd been trying hard to change all that of late.

Now it was time to get started on Amber's dress. And then she needed to find a nice, normal and hopefully not-bad-looking guy to bring to the wedding. She wondered if there was some way to check on these prospective MMM escorts before meeting up with them. MMM did not, of course, divulge any addresses, but considering she'd specified the 'hearts' had to live within a fifty-mile radius, it might be possible to vet at least some of them beforehand by checking the telephone directory or the business directory.

Tess wondered why she hadn't thought before of checking up and doing some background research on some of her matches. One William Appleton of Appleton Catering Services, described by MMM as a go-getter and head of a catering empire, would like to meet her. She studied his photograph. He was thin-faced, slightly foxy-looking, with a pronounced Adam's apple, but not unattractive. Pity about the catering empire though, when she was trying so hard not to think about food. Then again, perhaps he did diet meals. Most big companies did these days.

William Appleton lived in a house called 'Maybill' on Chestnut Avenue – which sounded leafy and respectable – in a London suburb only about ten miles away. They'd arranged to meet at the Blackbird, a well-known pub about halfway between their respective residences. But, pleased with her decision to be more thorough, at 11 a.m. on the day, Tess decided to have a look at where this William Appleton lived.

She'd always thought of avenues as wide and tree-lined, which this one wasn't. There was a noticeable lack of chestnuts, or any greenery for that matter; only a row of drab grey pebble-dashed semi-detached houses. She decided for sure she must have got the address wrong, as William Appleton, with his catering empire, would surely live in a large, detached house on a leafy street. She drove along slowly, studying the houses on her left – few of which displayed a number, let alone a name. At the end of the road she turned around and drove back, studying the houses on the other side. Then halfway along she saw it: a crudely painted sign saying 'Maybill', dangling from a ramshackle garden gate and partially obscured by a large, luridly painted van parked outside. Unable to believe what she was seeing, Tess decided she had to have a look – if she could find a parking space. She eventually found one some way down the road, and walked back to Maybill, edging her way around the van, which proclaimed in enormous red lettering on both sides: 'Bill's Burgers and Hot Dogs!' Beneath, in smaller lettering, was written 'Appleton Catering'.

Tess opened the gate at the exact moment an elderly woman, in a grubby dressing gown and bleached hair adorned with giant rollers, opened the door and stooped down to pick up a bottle of milk. Nice to know milk was still being delivered in Chestnut Avenue.

'You looking for someone, love?' she called out.

Tess cleared her throat. 'Is this where William Appleton lives?'

'William!' she snorted. 'That's *posh*! You after some burgers or somefink?' Without waiting for a reply she shouted, 'Bill-ee!' before disappearing inside, clutching the milk bottle.

Tess stood mesmerised inside the gate as a scrawny man, a cigarette dangling from his lips and with an enormous gut, limped to the door. 'The missus says you want somefink.'

She tried to think of something to say. 'Do you only do burgers and hot dogs?' she asked after a moment.

'Yeah, that's about it, darlin'.'

'Oh well, never mind,' Tess said lamely. She thought quickly. 'I understand, Mr Appleton, that you have an appointment at six o'clock this evening?'

He had the grace to look surprised. 'So wot if I 'ave? Wot's it to do with you?'

'I thought I should tell you that the person you're hoping to meet will *not* be there,' Tess said, edging back through the gate. 'And I don't think your description of yourself was entirely accurate.'

'I don't know what the hell you're talking about,' he snapped, as he went in and slammed the door behind him.

Tess closed the gate, edged back round the van, and headed towards where she'd parked her car.

'You cannot believe *anything* you read in these descriptions,' Tess ranted to Orla in the shop that afternoon. 'Just as well I went to check him out.'

'I wonder if he'd have turned up in his hot-dog van,' Orla said when she finished laughing.

'There must be some normal, nice men around somewhere on this planet,' Tess sighed. 'But I somehow doubt I'm going to meet any kind of "heart" through MMM. How's the plumber, by the way?'

'He's absolutely fine. Very successful guy. You can keep all these so-called executives and the like. And I bet he's as financially secure as any of them. Plumbers are like gold dust these days, you know. You'll have to wait weeks for someone to come round to fix your leaking pipes because they're so in demand. And they can charge what they like because people are so desperate to get things fixed. Certainly a whole lot better than some dodgy bloke flogging hot dogs.'

'You're right,' Tess agreed. 'Has he got any friends?'

She was making light of her strange dates but, deep inside, she wondered if there was something wrong with *her*. Why was she attracting all the wrong kinds of men? Apart from Orla she didn't know anyone else who was Internet dating, so she couldn't compare. But she'd read in the papers about couples who'd met online and were deliriously happy, accompanied by photos of them beaming ear to ear, arms entwined. Was MMM not the right site for her? However, she'd paid her money now and she might as well see it through.

At that moment the door opened to herald the arrival of Mrs Byron-Sommers. She waddled slowly into the shop.

'Those cobbles will be the death of me,' she gasped. 'Anyway, I thought I'd come in for my fitting.' She hung on to the counter while she tried to get her breath back.

Tess had been dreading this moment. Because of the nasty shiny mauve synthetic fabric Mrs Byron-Sommers had insisted on choosing for her dress and jacket, there was little she could do to minimise the woman's enormous girth. And she would doubtless be expecting miracles.

'I'm doing the best I can with this,' Tess said, emerging from the workroom at the rear, carrying the hanger bearing the huge dress. 'If you'd like to pop into the changing room, Mrs Byron-Sommers?'

There was a great deal of huffing and puffing before the woman finally emerged, like a galleon in full sail, and headed towards the mirror.

'Can't say it's very flattering,' she muttered.

'I've done exactly what you asked me to do,' Tess said. 'Unfortunately that fabric is never going to hang well, and the colour is unforgiving.'

'Are you saying it's all my fault?'

Yes, Tess thought, that's exactly what I'm saying. 'Well, it was your choice, and, if you remember, I recommended the midnight blue silk, which would have been beautiful on you.'

'But mauve's my favourite colour!' Mrs Byron-Summers did a slow, wobbly turn in front of the mirror. 'I don't like this. Can you do me something else? I've got my holiday in May, you know.'

'Sorry, no. I'm up to my eyes in work. Perhaps later in the year? But why don't I finish this one off for you? You may get to like it.'

Mrs Byron-Sommers waddled her way back to the changing room.

'I'm never going to like this,' she snapped. 'And I doubt my Reg will agree to pay for it.'

All Tess wanted to do was get rid of her, go home, soak in the bath and pour herself a giant glass of Pinot Grigio. She felt exhausted after her visit to Appleton Catering Services and then this wretched woman. On top of that, she was now thinking that she wasn't even a very good dressmaker. And if she ever found a nice man, chances were he wouldn't fancy her anyway. She could see herself being a Silver Single for ever.

Her confidence severely dented, Tess headed home when Mrs Byron-Sommers eventually left the shop. As she opened the door her phone was ringing. It was Lisa, her daughter-in-law. 'Matt's on a trip to Dubai, and I've been asked to an amateur dramatic production of *Abigail's Party*. My younger sister's playing Abigail, would you believe! And my babysitter's gone down with the flu, the au pair is on her day off, so is there any chance you could have Ellie for the night?'

Ellie duly arrived, hugging a large blue furry rabbit.

'He's called Baxter,' said Ellie. 'He's my friend.'

'He's replaced Teddy as Ellie's new best friend,' Lisa explained, as she handed Ellie's pink overnight bag to Tess. 'And she chose the name.'

'Why is he called Baxter, Ellie?' Tess asked, as her granddaughter propped him up on the settee with great care.

''Cos that's his name, Nana.'

'Yes, but why is that his name?'

'Because I like it,' said Ellie, looking around. 'Where's Dylan?'

'He's outside somewhere,' Tess replied.

'Does he catch mice?'

'Yes, I'm afraid sometimes he does,' Tess said. 'That's what cats do. He probably reckons he's doing me a great favour since I'm so useless at catching mice for myself.'

Ellie thought for a moment. 'You should try, Nana; Dylan could show you.'

Tess couldn't fault Ellie's thinking. That settled, CBeebies was selected on the television and Ellie, thumb in mouth and clutching Baxter tightly, proceeded to watch *In the Night Garden*.

Because she'd spent half the morning checking out Appleton Catering Services and all afternoon in the shop, Tess had missed her daily walk. In fact, she hadn't walked for several days, and she was feeling stiff and out of condition. As she prepared supper in the kitchen she did a few shaky knee bends and squats, which she'd been told were good for toning the thighs. Heaven only knows, her thighs certainly needed toning. She groaned as she straightened up.

'Why are you making funny noises, Nana?' Ellie, still clutching Baxter, had appeared in the doorway.

'Just trying to do some exercises, Ellie.'

'Mummy does exercises,' Ellie said, ''cos she's having a baby. Are you having a baby, Nana?'

'No, no, Ellie, I most definitely am not having a baby.'

Ellie looked doubtful. 'You might be though,' she said, staring at Tess's tummy. Then, before Tess could come up with a suitable reply, she asked, 'Can I sleep in Daddy's bedroom tonight?'

'Of course you can,' Tess replied. 'You know it's your bedroom now whenever you come to stay.'

'And Baxter's?'

'Oh yes, Baxter's too.'

It was after supper as Ellie was getting ready for bed that she asked, 'Where's my dress?'

'Your dress?'

'For Auntie Amber's wedding.'

Tess tried to think if and when there might possibly have been any reference whatsoever to a dress for Ellie to wear at Amber's wedding, where she was to be a flower girl.

'Well, Mummy hasn't actually asked me to make it yet,' she said.

'Silly Mummy. And it has to be pink. That's my very most favourite colour.'

*

It was the end of April, the wedding a mere three months away, and Tess still had a further sixteen pounds of weight to lose and a man to find. Could that possibly be achieved? Since her brief encounter with the hot-dog man she'd done nothing further about finding an escort. But as Orla constantly reminded her, she'd paid her money to MMM and there were another three or four possibilities out there. Not to mention the cruise, which Orla had already booked for them both.

It was while she was entering some measurements in her diary that she noticed the date: 29 April, the anniversary of David's death. She recalled the day she'd first met David, when her old VW Beetle had come to a grinding halt right in front of what she took to be a garage. And wouldn't you know, that was the day she'd left her mobile on charge at home. Well, if you're going to break down, she thought, you might as well do it right in front of a garage.

Then, as she emerged from the car, Tess became aware that it wasn't exactly the sort of garage she'd had in mind. It was a rather smart showroom, selling all manner of sports cars and classic motors. Her heart sank. Well, never mind – perhaps they could recommend a garage or at least let her phone for the breakdown service.

When she walked into the glossy showroom, a stockily built man, who'd been sitting behind the highly polished mahogany desk, stood up and walked towards her. He had a friendly face.

'Can I help you?'

'I'm not sure you can,' Tess replied, and then recounted her tale of woe. 'And I forgot to bring my mobile with me…'

He smiled reassuringly. 'What type of car is it?'

'Oh, it's just an old Beetle. It's right outside.'

'Great cars, Beetles. I'll get Nick to have a look at it. Unless, of course, you'd prefer to call your breakdown service?'

'Oh, no, no, I'd be happy for you to look at it. But I don't want to be any trouble…'

'That's settled then,' he said firmly, picking up the phone.

He had lovely blue eyes and a mischievous smile, but Tess felt instinctively that she could trust him.

Nick, who was obviously the mechanic, duly appeared.

'Would you have a look at this lady's Beetle out the front there? See if we can be of any help?'

Nick looked curiously at Tess. 'You got the keys?'

As he headed out of the door she said, 'This is so kind of you!'

Her benefactor smiled disarmingly. 'It's quiet here today, so no problem. Now, how about I make you a cup of coffee? And what do I call you?'

Within minutes he was calling her Tess and she was calling him David, and he was telling her that he owned this business because he had such a passion for vintage and classic cars. And she was telling him about Curvaceous and measuring up larger ladies. They were chatting and laughing like old friends when Nick reappeared, spanner in hand, shaking his head sadly. The car was old, he said; *this* had gone wrong, *that* was broken beyond repair, and everything else appeared to be on the point of collapse. In his opinion it would cost more than the car was worth to put it all right. He suggested she had it towed to her own garage for a second opinion, and then he disappeared.

'Not a great prognosis,' said David.

'I've known for a while it was on its last legs,' Tess admitted. 'I've been saving up for something newer. I fancy a Ford Focus.'

David appeared to be deep in thought. Then he said, 'Would you consider letting me buy it from you? It's a classic, you know, and I could give it new innards.'

And so, on that spring day Tess found herself a new lover, who gave a generous price for her old Beetle and, with his trade connections, succeeded in finding her the almost new silver Ford Focus that she was still driving today.

David was a gentleman. He was the kind of man she'd love to meet again, but they weren't exactly thick on the ground. Perhaps the next man she'd meet would restore her faith in the opposite sex.

The next man happened to be one Andy Barrymore.

Andy Barrymore was, according to MMM, the owner of the prestigious 'Beeches' at nearby Ferndale. The Beeches was a boutique hotel with a famous cocktail bar, gourmet restaurant and spa. How could such a successful man be looking for companionship on the Internet? He looked handsome too. In his MMM photo he appeared silver-haired, dark-eyed and had nice teeth which, hopefully, were his own. With thoughts of Benedict entering her mind, Tess wondered for a moment if this Andy might be gay. Surely not? Why would he be seeking a lady 'for companionship, outings, and sharing a cocktail or two' if he were? In the next paragraph he explained that he was so busy with the Beeches that there was never time to meet nice ladies and, if anyone cared to contact him, he'd be delighted to introduce himself properly and show off his hotel, his cocktails and his gourmet restaurant. This, Tess reckoned, was her kind of man. But with memories of Appleton Catering Services, she decided to investigate the venue.

The Beeches – surprise, surprise! – was actually surrounded by beech trees at the end of the village and, according to the sign at the gate, had a four-star rating. From what she could see through the trees it was a large Edwardian building, but she decided to go no further in case Andy Barrymore himself should see her checking him out. Then again, perhaps an astute businessman would be impressed by her thoroughness.

Well satisfied, Tess set off for home, hoping she'd be successful in getting a date. There must be a long queue of women hoping for the cocktails, the gourmet meal and, not least, the man himself. She suspected he would not be alone for long, so she drove straight home, got onto her laptop, and requested a meeting. Two hours later Andy Barrymore replied, saying he'd be delighted to meet up with her next Thursday evening, at the Beeches at 6 p.m. Would that suit? And why didn't she bring along an overnight bag so that she could enjoy his hospitality without having to drive home afterwards? He could arrange a room for one night – would that be OK? That seemed very OK to Tess, although she wondered if she'd be expected to pay for the room, which would most likely be very expensive, thanks to all those stars. But what the heck!

Tess decided not to tell Orla. At the mere mention of cocktails and the rest, Orla was very likely to put the plumber on hold and head for the Beeches herself. In fact, Tess suspected that Orla was beginning to tire of her lover. She still hadn't got the new bathroom he'd promised, and Tess noticed that she was often connected to MMM when it was quiet in the shop. And the fact that she was so keen to go on this cruise did not tally with her being madly in love. It was a wonder that she hadn't come across Andy Barrymore herself. Perhaps she had, and wasn't letting on? So she didn't tell Orla anything. Not that she was going on a date with someone who owned a hotel, or that she'd checked the place out in preparation. If she told Orla she'd researched the place, and mentioned the gourmet restaurant and the cocktails, Orla would be *green*. And not only would she be envious, she'd probably apply to meet him herself. And this guy was not for sharing!

CHAPTER TEN

COCKTAILS AND CAJOLERY

Tess spent the next couple of days in preparation. She paid a visit to the hairdresser for some highlights and lowlights, she shaved her wintry legs (not that he'd see them, of course, but simply knowing her legs were hairless made her feel more attractive), and she covered her pallor with some St Tropez. Then she delved into her underwear drawer for some tummy-toning knickers to compress the flab. Better take two pairs: one for going and one for coming back. That's if she decided to stay, which was by no means a foregone conclusion because, should Andy be anything like her previous encounters, she'd be leaving promptly, cocktails or not. Then she wondered what to wear on top. Trousers? A dress? In the end she chose her smart new black trousers with a cream silk top and her cream tweed Chanel-type jacket. She packed the spare knickers, a nightie and a warm sweater for the journey home, along with her toiletries.

It was just after six when Tess drove through the gates of the Beeches and up the long drive, feeling very apprehensive and a little out of her comfort zone. The approach was bordered by the beeches, through which she could see immaculate lawns and a beautiful magnolia tree on the left. The car park was hidden round the back and, after a lot of manoeuvring, she finally found one available parking space. Then she wondered whether to take in the overnight bag or whether to leave it in the car in case she had to make a speedy getaway. After a few minutes' lip chewing she decided it would appear presumptuous, to say the least, to meet Andy with a suitcase in hand. Feeling nervous, she walked into the reception area and gave her name to the pretty blonde receptionist at the desk. Mr Barrymore, she was told, would be with her in just a moment.

Tess settled herself into the corner of a leather Chesterfield sofa under a potted palm, and looked around at the chic decor, which was completely in keeping with the traditional exterior. She looked at the well-dressed group of people chatting quietly next to a collection of suitcases and wondered if they were coming or going.

'Tess?'

She jumped. He'd approached her from behind. Now she could see that Andy Barrymore was tall and every bit as attractive as his photograph. Tess gulped as she stood up and shook his outstretched hand.

'I hope I haven't kept you waiting too long?'

'No, no, not at all.' Tess noted his beautiful dark grey suit and pristine white shirt, with just enough cuff on display. What a smoothie! And he bore more than a passing resemblance to the lovely late Cary Grant, whom she had swooned over in the cinema during her teenage years.

'I've been looking forward to meeting you,' he said, giving her a winning smile. Then, glancing at his watch: 'I'm sure the sun's over the yardarm by now, so why don't we have a little drink and get to know one another?'

'Thank you, Andy,' Tess murmured. 'That would be great.'

He shepherded her into the long bar, people sitting or standing in groups. Pale polished floorboards matching the pale, polished clientele. This minimalist look was completely at odds with the Edwardian reception area, and certainly made a change from a pub. At the far end the bi-fold doors led onto a lawn, and could that be a lake? Not a copper kettle in sight! No open fire either.

'You must have one of our cocktails,' said Andy, pulling out a chair for her at a small table. 'Our barman's a real expert.'

The barman was putting on a well-rehearsed routine of bottle tossing and shaker rattling, playing to the audience who had gathered round to admire his expertise.

'May I recommend one of our specialities, Tess?'

'Oh, please do,' she replied, unable to remember when she'd last had a cocktail. As he headed towards the bar, Tess had a brief image of Amber's wedding reception here in the summer, with the doors open to the garden and guests strolling towards the lake. (*Tess's new man owns this lot*, Gerry would inform an open-mouthed Ursula. *Amazing, isn't it? So much classier than Ashley Grange!*)

'Here we are!' Andy said, as Tess returned to reality. He placed down on the table two tall glasses filled with a cream-coloured concoction, loaded with crushed ice and orange and lemon slices on top. 'Sarasota Sunset,' he informed her, sitting down opposite.

As he spoke, a waiter appeared with bowls of olives, pistachios and macadamia nuts.

Tess took a sip. It was delicious, but didn't taste particularly strong. 'Oh, wow!' she said.

He smiled at her as he pushed the olives in her direction. 'Tell me about yourself, Tess.'

Another sip and Tess felt her tension dissipating, along with her lack of confidence. She told him about her family, about the dressmaking and Curvaceous.

Andy told her he was divorced, had two daughters – both married with teenage kids – and about how he'd started as a humble trainee chef forty-five years earlier. He'd worked his way up, saved every penny, and it hadn't been easy. Dedication and determination were the only road to success, he said.

'Gosh!' he added. 'I've been so busy talking that I hadn't noticed our glasses are empty. Did you enjoy that? Shall we have another Sarasota Sunset?'

Tess hadn't realised that she'd drunk it so quickly – it was sweet and delicious, with just a tiny bit of a kick. She detected a liqueur base; was that Cointreau? And there was something else – a creamier liqueur of some sort – topped up with champagne?

'Oh well, perhaps just one more,' she said.

Andy clicked his fingers. 'Dino!' Dino appeared as if by magic. 'More of the same, please.'

The barman got busy and Dino reappeared, brandishing two more Sarasota Sunsets, giving Tess a dazzling Latin smile.

Tess could imagine summer days and sultry evenings in this place. The muted grey walls, the naked bulb lighting and the floor-to-ceiling mirrors weren't her normal taste, but they were growing on her fast. Andy was a very attractive man indeed, and a real charmer to boot. Now he wanted to know what she might like to eat and what her favourite wine was. Did she like fish? Absolutely fresh, caught this very morning and delivered straight to his kitchen.

She told him about her childhood in Scotland, about her sister Barbara, who'd eloped with Omar, and about her parents' disapproval. 'She's widowed now but lives in Nice and never comes back to the UK. God only knows if she'll come to my daughter's wedding.'

'Another Sarasota Sunset?' he asked.

Perhaps not, she thought. I'm already feeling a little dreamy.

'Or how about some champagne then?' he persisted. 'Bollinger be OK?'

'Oh, I shouldn't really,' she said. Then Tess thought, Why the hell *shouldn't* I! 'Well, perhaps just one wee glass then.'

One glass of champagne later and they'd covered the details of his rise to fame and fortune. It was now nearly eight o'clock. 'Time for dinner,' Andy announced.

Tess stood up, aware of being none too steady on her feet. He led the way into the adjoining dining room, to a sea of white tablecloths, crystal glasses, silver tableware and real flowers on each table. She noticed the tasteful, muted colours, the expensive prints on the walls, and the soft classical music coming from somewhere as an accompaniment to the low hum of conversation and the clinking of knives and forks. She sat down at the table for two overlooking the garden, and felt warm and happy and hungry. She hadn't had time for lunch as she'd been intent on making a pattern for Amber's dress. After that she'd varnished her nails and they'd taken forever to dry, so she couldn't risk grabbing a snack in case she smudged them.

Andy handed her an enormous menu, most of which was written in French. It was obviously the ladies' version, with not a price in sight.

'What would you recommend, Andy?'

'Shall we plump for the fish?' he suggested again.

That, she felt, would be a wise choice; after two creamy cocktails and a glass of champagne, rich sauces were a definite no-no. She had to think about Slim Chance next week and the lecture she might get from Judy. She settled for a seafood starter and sea bass for her main.

The waiter appeared to take their order. 'May I recommend the Côtes de Gascogne Colombard, Mr Barrymore?'

'Do you have a particular favourite, Tess?' Andy asked.

'Well, I like Sauvignon Blanc and Chablis,' she replied. 'I really don't mind.'

'We'll have the Chablis then, Dino,' said Andy, snapping shut the wine list with a flourish.

The wine arrived; the food arrived, each plate artistically presented. Sauces were drizzled, vegetables were layered, wine glasses were topped up. Tess was aware that her speech was slightly slurred because her mouth wasn't quite shaping the words the way she wanted it to. She didn't want him to think she couldn't carry her drink – of course she could! And he was such an attractive man!

Would she like dessert? She had to be weighed again next Tuesday, so no, she wouldn't.

'Just a few fresh strawberries then?' he persisted.

She thought for a moment. 'Oh, that would be lovely!' Had she pronounced the 'v'? Never mind, strawberries were fine. They arrived with a little pot of clotted cream on the side, and a glass of champagne as a final flourish.

'Oh, I shouldn't!' Tess said guiltily.

'Of course you should!' said Andy.

Well, she thought, just one wee spoonful of cream perhaps. She gulped some champagne.

'We'll take coffee in the lounge,' he said.

Tess hoped she could stand up without wobbling. She rose a little shakily from her chair and accepted his proffered arm as they walked out of the dining room.

'I think I might be a wee bit tipsy,' Tess murmured. Good heavens, she thought, it must be years since I've let loose like this!

'Of course you're not! But would you prefer to have coffee in your room, Tess? And have you brought an overnight bag? If you give me your keys I'll get Dino to fetch the bag for you. What's the registration number?'

Tess thought for a moment or two. 'It's a silver Focus,' she said at last.

'Ah yes,' said Andy, 'but there's a lot of them around, so we'll need the registration.'

The registration? Tess thought hard. She'd had the car for five years, so of *course* she knew the registration! There was a four in there somewhere, and an eight.

'There's a four and an eight in it,' she said at last, then hiccupped.

'Tell you what,' Andy said, 'we'll go to the car together, shall we?'

As they emerged into the cool night air, Tess tried to remember where she'd parked the car. There were fewer cars now than earlier, but they all looked silver in the artificial light.

'I've got to focus on the Focus!' Tess giggled.

It took a little time to locate it, and then Andy unlocked the door and withdrew her bag.

'Let's get to your room and we'll order some coffee,' he said, one hand holding the bag and the other supporting Tess's elbow. Then, up they went in the lift to the second floor where she was ushered into Room 206, a large bedroom with a king-sized bed, all in a sea of taupe and cream with chocolate-coloured accents. Tess suspected Kelly Hoppen might have been summoned to perform some of her magic here. She looked longingly at the bed and hoped Andy wouldn't hang around for too long. He was very fanciable and who knew what might happen on subsequent meetings? Anyway, there was no way he could possibly be allowed to view these big knickers, which were currently having to work extra hard. But it would be rude to shove him out of the door after his generosity this evening. She wouldn't mind a kiss! And she would, of course, offer to pay for this room.

'I think,' said Andy, 'that we should round off the evening with a nice little liqueur. What say *you*, Tess?'

'Perhaps a Scots lass like yourself would like Drambuie?'

'No, really, Andy—'

'Nonsense!' He was already on the phone.

She sat down on a low cream sofa and looked around the bedroom. Didn't he have any single rooms? Perhaps they were all taken. All she really *really* wanted was to go to bed; she didn't think she could last much longer. But within minutes, the ever-obliging Dino appeared bearing a tray of coffee, plus cups, milk and sugar, and a bottle of Drambuie with two tiny glasses.

'Won't do you any harm,' declared her host with a twinkle in his eye, as he filled both glasses up to the brim.

Tess hadn't drunk liqueurs in years. And she most certainly should not be having one now... but she'd quite forgotten how very nice Drambuie was. The taste warmed her up and she noticed again quite how attractive Andy was.

'Tess, I think you should lie down,' said Andy.

'Yes, I must,' she agreed, gazing longingly at the bed. And for the first time in years her thoughts were not just about sleep.

He helped her to stand up and guided her across the room to the bed, deftly removed the mountain of cushions and the bedcover, and turned back the duvet.

'I'd like to kiss you, Tess,' he murmured, looking into her eyes. 'You're a very attractive lady.'

And he was a very attractive man. How could she refuse after his generosity? After all, you only lived once...

When Tess awoke it was dark. For a minute she hadn't the faintest idea where she was. She tried to recall getting into bed. And why wasn't she wearing her nightie? She had no recollection of undressing but, nevertheless, she should have remembered to put on her nightie. Was there a lamp somewhere? She stretched out her hand in the hope of finding a light, and instead found another naked body. *Dear God!*

The body came to life. 'Are you all right?' it asked sleepily.

'No,' said Tess, trying to sit up. 'What are *you* doing here?'

'I'm afraid we both had a little too much to drink,' he said. 'But, come! Lie down, it's way too early.'

And Tess felt herself being enveloped in two warm arms, pressed against a manly chest, and aware – for the first time in years – of a virile protuberance. And, also for the first time in years, she felt herself responding.

The next time Tess woke up it was daylight, and she was alone. She rubbed her eyes and looked around. She could hear a blackbird singing outside her window, but otherwise all was quiet. She checked the time: seven o'clock.

Tess tried to collect her chaotic thoughts together and groaned. He'd been here, in this bed, and they'd made love. And she seemed to remember that she'd enjoyed it. But she had no recollection of getting into bed with him, or of him getting into bed with her. God, she must have been three sheets to the wind! Had she washed? Had she cleaned her teeth?

She got up gingerly, and crossed the room to open the curtains and look around. Was he in the bathroom, perhaps? No, he wasn't. In fact, there was no trace of him anywhere. Had she dreamed it? Then she noticed her trousers and jacket on a hanger, dangling on the outside of the wardrobe door. Had she taken the time to do that? And then she saw the rest of her clothes folded neatly on the chair and, on the top, the knickers, folded lengthwise. She'd *never* have folded her knickers!

With realisation came horror. Oh no! Oh, please God, *no!*

Feeling sick, she wandered into the bathroom and looked closely in the mirror at the smudged make-up and tangled hair. *I can never face him again*, she thought, *never*. It was as she wandered back into the bedroom that she saw the note on the bedside table.

Sorry to have abandoned you, but I have to be on duty and you need your sleep! It was a wonderful evening – and night! Just leave when you're ready and I'll hope to see you in reception, but I have a group of Japanese guests to look after, so forgive me if I don't. Will be in touch.

Andy X

Tess read it again. He probably reckoned he'd had a lucky escape from this drunken woman, make-up smudged all over her face, with big, ugly knickers. But the lovemaking had been rather nice, if speedy. Tess groaned. She'd have a shower, get dressed and get out of here. Then she looked at her overnight bag. It had never been opened.

She felt marginally better after she'd showered and made herself some tea from the hospitality tray. She donned the spare pair of knickers and got dressed, hoping she could slink out of the hotel without seeing anyone. Tess repacked her bag, opened the door a tiny chink and, furtively, looked both ways along the corridor. She was in Room 206 but she'd little idea of how she'd got here. Where was the lift? She could hear the sound of a service trolley and the housekeeping maids chattering round the corner. And she stopped dead in her tracks when she heard one of them say, 'Who had he got in 206 *last* night?'

The other one snorted. '*God* only knows! How many's that he's had this week?'

'Not so many,' said her companion. 'Only a couple, but last week must have broken the record!'

'Randy bugger!' said the other.

Tess closed the door again. She felt sick. How could she pass these women to get to the lift? She looked cautiously round the door again and noticed, with great relief, an exit sign pointing in the opposite direction.

She picked up her bag and headed for the lift. There were several people in reception, but no Japanese tourists, and no Andy. Come to think of it, he hadn't looked *that* much like the lovely Cary Grant.

Tess walked quickly through the door and headed towards her car, eager to be home.

CHAPTER ELEVEN

SCHOOL FOR THOUGHT

'That's another week without losing any weight,' Judy said, frowning, as Tess stepped down from the scales. 'Why do you think that is?'

Why? Where do I *begin*, Tess wondered.

'You've been naughty again, haven't you?' Judy said.

'I'm afraid so.' Tess felt hot blood coursing up her face. I've been very, very naughty.

'And the wedding's in July?'

'Yes,' Tess replied.

'Hmm,' said Judy. 'Have you bought that outfit yet?'

'No, I was wanting to lose some more weight.'

'You said that two weeks ago.' Judy consulted her file. 'And time is running out. You only have a few months in which to lose another stone.'

Tess felt ashamed. Not only that – in another few weeks she'd be cruising round the Greek islands, and she couldn't see that being very conducive to weight loss.

I'm a big, fat failure, she thought. I can't lose weight, I don't seem to be able to find a decent man, and I'm behind schedule with my sewing. Drastic action was called for. She would just not eat and she'd not arrange to meet any more of these 'hearts' for the time being. None of them so far had set her pulse racing, and most of them involved some form of food. So: no men, no food, and she'd work round the clock. At least she might get Amber's wedding dress tacked together and Mrs Byron-Sommers's monstrosity finished off.

She was pleased to see Shirley had returned from her grandmotherly duties.

'Don't look so downhearted!' she said as Tess plonked herself on the adjacent seat. 'I think you're looking great.'

'Thanks,' Tess said, giving Shirley a smile. 'But that Judy is such a taskmaster, and I don't know if I can lose as much weight as I want to in time for the wedding.'

'What does it matter if you don't? As long as you're well and happy with yourself when the big day comes.'

Tess grinned. 'You're a tonic, Shirley. I hope you're still OK for that meal on Friday week?'

'Looking forward to it.'

Stopping off at the shop on the way home, Tess found Orla on the laptop, making copious notes.

'It's gone quiet,' she informed Tess, taking a sip of her coffee. 'Just thought I'd check up on a few things.'

'Things?' Tess repeated, grinning. 'Could that be *men*? And what about Paul the plumber?'

Orla sighed. 'I never did get my bathroom, and I don't see him that often now anyway. But listen, there's a guy on here that I really like the sound of. He's got a *hotel*, Tess, with a cocktail bar and a spa! What's not to like? He's probably too good to be true, but he's surely worth a punt. Silver surfing might just be about to pay off.'

Tess decided to say nothing.

Tess did a minimum-calorie shop in Sainsbury's to get her through the week ahead. She'd arranged to have most of the week off from the shop. Now, staggering through her door with a mountain of fruit and vegetables, she decided to be vegetarian for a few days, and drink only water. She'd take long walks in all weathers and catch up on her work. As expected, Lisa had rung to ask if Tess could make 'a little dress for Ellie for the wedding', so that was an extra task.

She ate fruit for breakfast, soup for lunch, and some sort of vegetable casserole for dinner, accompanied by a glass of water; a diet that meant that she spent a considerable amount of time in the toilet. To take her mind off food, she worked hard. By Day Three she added some fish to her menu, and by Day Four she added some chicken and a glass of Merlot. By Day Five she added some potatoes and had two glasses of wine. By Day Six, Mrs Byron-Sommers's vast mauve outfit was completed, Amber's dress was ready for fitting and Ellie's dress was cut out. And, according to her bathroom scales, Tess had managed to lose six whole pounds.

Even Orla noticed that she looked slimmer when she arrived at the shop on Saturday morning. And Tess couldn't resist asking, 'How was the date? Wasn't he a hotelier or something?'

Orla rolled her eyes. 'Where do I begin?' Then she said, 'While I was waiting to meet him in reception I could just hear the receptionist murmur to a waiter who was passing by, "That's the latest one, over *there*! How many do you reckon that is altogether?" And the waiter, who was foreign, said, "I can only count up to ten in English," and they both fell about laughing. Then the guy appeared, and he was really good-looking, Tess, but I just *knew*! You can tell these Lotharios a mile off, can't you? And this guy – *Andy* was his name – would you believe it, he'd suggested I take an overnight bag, so I had a good idea what he had in mind. But I decided I'd risk one cocktail since I'd taken the trouble to drive all the way over there, and he was a real smoothie, you know, intent on telling me how hard he'd worked to make his way up in the world and to get this hotel, blah, blah, blah. And when that same waiter delivered the drinks I saw Andy give him a wink. What an idiot!'

Tess couldn't quite believe what she was hearing. 'So, what did you do?'

'Well, I drank his bloody cocktail and then I said, "I think I'll go now, Andy, but I expect you've got the next one in the queue lined up. Thanks for the drink." And I just got up and left.'

'What did *he* do?'

'Do? He didn't do anything, just sat there. Probably in shock. Let's face it, Tess, at our age we've all been round the block a few times and you can spot these guys a mile off.'

'Oh, indeed,' said Tess, sitting down quickly at the service desk.

'In the meantime,' Orla went on, 'how about you and I have a look around for *cruise wear*? We need to look the part, don't we? Don't tell me you're going to wear that boring old black one-piece swimsuit again? Why don't we look for one of those with the cut-out bits?'

'Because,' Tess replied, 'all the fat would bulge out through the cut-out bits. You've got to be really slim to wear that sort of stuff.'

'So you'll resurrect that boring old black one again. Well, I'm going to buy something bright, and I might just get a jumpsuit too. Jumpsuits are very *in* at the moment.'

'It's just such a palaver when you go to the loo,' Tess said, and then wondered if she sounded dull. Perhaps she could cope with a jumpsuit. And, for sure, she didn't want to look boring. Or *wholesome* – oh no! She'd buy that bright pink backless swimsuit she'd seen in her catalogue somewhere, and she might even look for a jumpsuit that didn't have a million buttons so she could go to the loo easily. And a long sundress with a great big split up the side, or the back maybe. She wouldn't tell Orla what she was planning to buy; she'd just wait to see Orla's face when she unpacked her suitcase on the boat. Because the new Tess Templar had no intention of being dowdy.

On Friday evening Shirley arrived, brandishing a bottle of Shiraz. 'I know we shouldn't,' she said.

'Ah, but I've cooked a very low-calorie meal, with masses of vegetables,' Tess said, 'which gives us plenty of allowance for wine.'

'A girl after my own heart!' said Shirley, looking around. 'Love your place! And your cat!'

Dylan had emerged from his favourite resting place on Tess's bed and come down the stairs to see what all the fuss was about. He made a beeline for Shirley, who stooped to stroke him.

'You're very honoured,' Tess informed her. 'Dylan is fussy. Some people he ignores completely.' She thought the cat was probably no bad judge of character, and wished she could take him along with her to suss out some of these tiresome 'hearts'.

'Have you always lived here?' Shirley asked as she sat down.

'Since my divorce more than ten years ago,' Tess replied. 'Before that we lived in Hawthorn Road. What about you?'

'I moved to a flat after Ken died, but I don't much like it. The flat's nice but there's a very noisy couple upstairs and a very nosy old bat who lives opposite.' Shirley looked wistful. 'And I miss having a little garden.'

'Perhaps you should look for something like this,' Tess suggested.

'Perhaps I should.' Shirley was silent for a moment. 'I don't mean to pry, but have you got anyone, you know... I mean, are you in a relationship?'

Tess shook her head. 'I was with a lovely guy for three years, but sadly he was killed in an accident. That was almost three years ago now but sometimes it's still quite raw. I really miss him.'

'Oh, I'm sorry, Tess. Do you feel lonely? Because I know I do sometimes.'

'I thought the lonely feeling would have worn off by now,' Tess admitted, 'and, although I'm much better than I was, I still feel sad and alone sometimes. He was such a nice guy, and so humorous. Whenever I hear or see something funny, I long to tell him so we could giggle together. I'm not explaining this very well but, you see, the contrast between him and Gerry – my ex-husband – was so pronounced! Gerry was hell-bent on expanding his business, making contacts, chatting up the right people. I hated it. Then David came along and he couldn't give a toss about *anything* like that. He had his own little business, he loved his cars, but he also loved living. And laughing.'

'It's so important to laugh, isn't it? Ken was one of the funniest men I've ever met. I don't know how a relationship survives when it's devoid of humour. But you can't live in the past, can you? Do you think you might be ready yet to meet someone else, Tess?'

Tess felt she could be honest with Shirley. 'Yes, I am, I think,' she said, and told Shirley a little about MMM and her disastrous dates. 'I miss the closeness and the companionship. I kid myself that all I want is an escort for my daughter's wedding in July, but it isn't just that. I *would* like to meet someone special.'

'I'm sure you will,' Shirley said.

'I'm not so sure. I've met a few guys, none of whom are really what I'm looking for. I keep hoping that the next one I meet might be different. My friend Orla, of course, just thinks it's all a big joke. Silver Singles or Single Surfers, she calls us. What about your love life?'

Shirley stroked Dylan, who'd leapt up onto the sofa beside her. 'Well, here's the thing,' she said. 'Would you believe I met this really nice guy while I was up in Manchester?'

'Manchester?' Tess echoed, wondering if she should consider extending her fifty-mile radius.

'Yes, I had to ferry my younger grandson to and from school because it's about seven miles away from where they live. Anyway, while I was waiting at the school gates, I met this guy. He just happened to be waiting for his granddaughter, who just happens to be in Todd's class, would you believe! He was attractive and very nice, and we got chatting. He's called Charlie and, while I was there, he took me out a couple of times for a meal.'

'Lucky you!' Tess made a mental note about school gates; Ellie would be starting school in September.

'You'd be surprised how many grandparents were there,' Shirley continued. 'So many mothers work these days.'

'And he's not married?'

'No, he lost his wife to cancer some years ago. And he's had bowel cancer himself, but he's fine now. As he said, we've either had it, got it, or someone close to you has. When I think of it, years ago we'd have broken the ice talking about pop music or something! Now it's operations!'

They both laughed as Tess refilled their glasses. 'Will you see him again?' she asked.

'Oh yes,' Shirley replied. 'He's coming down for a few days next week. And, before you ask, yes, he is staying with me. We've already had a couple of nights together and, at our ages, what's the point in making him wait?'

'That was my mother's mantra,' Tess laughed. '"Make him wait, he won't respect you otherwise!" None of us paid a lot of attention to that, did we?'

'No, we didn't. But you'll have plenty of opportunity to meet men soon, when you go on your cruise. You did say something about going on a cruise, didn't you?'

'Yes, in June. But it's organised by MMM, the dating site I'm with and, like I said, I haven't had much luck with the guys I've met so far.'

'Perhaps you should try your luck at the school gates,' Shirley joked.

'And extend my boundaries,' Tess said thoughtfully. So what if the right man happened to come from Liverpool or Leeds or

Leicester? Better, surely, to find the right man miles away than the wrong one on your doorstep, even if it limited the time you could spend together. Hopefully the 'hearts' on the cruise would hail from every corner of the country.

As they sat down to Tess's Mediterranean chicken, they spoke about their families. Shirley had one brother, Simon, who was an actor, currently filming in eastern Europe somewhere, but Tess had never heard of him. She had two sons, the one in Manchester and the one in Canada, whom she was hoping to visit in September, and was the main reason she wanted to get in shape. And there were five grandchildren. She was sixty-five, a retired nurse, and she did some volunteer driving to take people for hospital appointments and 'stuff like that'.

All in all it was a really enjoyable evening. Tess liked her new friend, who didn't depart until nearly eleven o'clock, promising to reciprocate in the next few weeks.

'After Manchester Man's visit,' Tess said. 'I shall look forward to a detailed account!'

CHAPTER TWELVE

WILLPOWER

Two months and at least ten pounds still to go! Tess hadn't yet bought her wedding outfit although she'd earmarked a couple on the Internet, along with another possible contender for the dubious privilege of accompanying her to the wedding. This one was called Walter Watson, and Walter ('call me Wally') liked being outdoors. He'd done the London marathon and he loved 'keeping in shape', so Tess could identify with that. He appeared clean-cut, bright-eyed and healthy, and probably just what she needed at the moment was someone to keep her on the straight and narrow.

So, another guy and another pub. The Travellers' Rest was a timber-framed, ye-olde-sawdust-on-the-floor type of establishment, and a favourite haunt of Thameside walkers. At the weekends, city types ventured out here to drink real ale at low prices and to give their four-wheel drives an airing. As a result, it was always crowded. It would certainly make a change from the Beeches, an experience Tess was trying hard to forget. Even Orla had seen through Andy's thinly veiled lust, so why hadn't she? Why did she always expect people to be straightforward and on the level? Orla was quite right when she said Tess had been round the block a few times, but perhaps not as many times as Orla. Even so, she should not have been so gullible.

Even on this still chilly day in May there were lots of people sitting outside, clad in shorts and T-shirts and the like. Tess, wearing a warm sweater and jeans, shivered as she got out of the car, and wished she'd brought a coat. She'd given Wally the registration number of the car and agreed to stay in it, or beside it, until he found her. She still wasn't keen on going into pubs on her own and looking around for someone she'd never met before, with the added horror of getting there first and not knowing whether to order a drink or to stand in a corner and hope she didn't appear too gormless. The car park was a much better bet.

She didn't have long to wait before a tall, muscular man dismounted from a racing-style bicycle and headed in her direction. He wore shorts, a fleece and a helmet. And he had a rucksack on his back. He looked like he was heading for the Tour de France.

He smiled as he approached her. 'Hi, Tess!' He held out his hand. 'Let me just park the bike over there and I'll be right with you.' He had nice blue eyes and had already acquired a tan. She admired the well-developed calf muscles, the broad shoulders, the complete lack of flab. There was a little bit of a resemblance to Gary Lineker here. She wondered if he'd ever played football.

As he walked back towards her he said, wiping his brow, 'It's such a nice day, so shall we sit outside?'

Tess did not wish to appear a wimp, so she said, 'Yes, lovely.'

He dumped his rucksack on the bench. 'What's your poison?'

'Just a lime and soda, please.' Tess was thinking of the weight she'd lost and the praise she'd got from Judy. And she liked the fact that he hadn't tried to persuade her to have something stronger.

When he reappeared with the lime soda and a half-pint of real ale for himself, he said, 'Who'd want to be inside a stuffy old pub on a glorious day like this?'

Well, I would, Tess thought. Again she wished she'd brought a jacket. The wind was cold and there was only intermittent sunshine but, nevertheless, most of the people sitting outside were in T-shirts or cropped tops and shorts. She was always amazed each year, when the calendar signalled the approaching summer, how many people immediately ditched their winter clothes and emerged in public half naked, regardless of the weather. The reverse process normally took place in September, often one of the warmest months, when the girls in particular, bored with their summer uniform, were back in duvet coats, leggings and boots. She'd have liked a duvet coat today.

They spoke about this and that for a few minutes before Wally asked, 'Do you do any running, Tess?' He regarded her seriously, plainly not referring to an occasional dash for a bus.

'No, can't say that I do.'

He sighed. 'That's a pity. It's nice to go running with someone.'

'Yes, I'm sure it must be.' Tess thought for a moment. 'I have to admit I'd like to tone up though, and lose some weight, so perhaps I should have a go?'

'Do you jog?'

'No, I don't do that either.' Tess was feeling as if she must be incredibly lazy. 'I try to walk most days…'

'You could start with jogging,' Wally went on, wiping beer foam from his mouth. 'Walk fifty steps, jog fifty steps, that sort of thing.'

'Mmm,' Tess said doubtfully.

'Would you like me to get you started?' he asked.

'Well, I—'

'Next week?' Wally interrupted. 'I'm not supposed to know where you live, so why don't we meet up at Mansell Park?'

Mansell Park was a ten-minute drive from Milbury and was one of those places Tess had avoided in the past; full of runners, joggers and cyclists, all with headbands, sweating and water-swigging. Not particularly her scene but, hey, all that had to change!

'OK,' she agreed. 'I'll be there.'

'I hope you've got some decent trainers,' he said, frowning as he looked down at her M&S loafers.

No, she didn't have trainers. Neither did she have a tracksuit or, heaven forbid, shorts. She thought momentarily of her fat, wrinkled thighs (now less fat but more wrinkled), and her batwing arms, and shuddered.

'You've got trainers, haven't you?' Wally asked.

'Oh yes,' she lied. 'Don't worry, I'll be wearing my trainers.'

He asked her a few questions about herself and then informed her that he was a widower, his wife having perished as the result of a massive stroke some years ago. And she was only fifty-seven. This had made him sit up and take stock of his own life. From that day on he vowed to give up smoking, drink very little, eat healthily and ramp up his exercise routine. He was sixty-seven but he didn't look it, did he? Tess wasn't sure how a man of sixty-seven should look, but he appeared pretty average to her. He went on to tell her he played football with a seniors' team, and he loved golf. Did Tess play golf? No? What a pity, oh well. He loved tennis too; did Tess play tennis? She told him that she'd played occasionally in school, but not since. She noticed he was frowning as he finished off his beer and wondered if he already considered her a lost cause. Was this relationship also destined for the scrapheap?

'So,' he said suddenly. 'If you're free on Wednesday I could meet you in Mansell Park, and we could make a start. Seven o'clock, say?'

'Seven o'clock? In the evening?' Tess asked.

He looked at her as if she were mad. 'In the *morning*, Tess.'

'Oh, the *morning*! Right then! How long will we be there?'

'An hour should do it,' he replied. 'It's so important to start the day with some exercise. You'll become addicted to it, just you wait and see!'

'I will?' Tess drained her glass, wishing she were drinking something stronger.

'You will,' he confirmed. 'I'll see you by the pond, seven o'clock sharp.'

'OK,' Tess said, standing up. 'See you then.' No mention of a lunch, or a dinner, or even a breakfast after getting up at the crack of dawn and an hour's exercise.

As he headed back towards his bike, Tess headed for the shops. She needed to buy a pair of trainers.

Trainers, Tess discovered, were expensive. You could buy a pair of white lace-up shoes that looked like trainers for a lot less money and, as Tess wasn't planning to make this a long-term project, she found a stylish-looking pair in the sale.

The following Wednesday she set her alarm for six o'clock and wondered if she was going crazy. Only the thought of herself, slimmed and toned for her cruise, forced her out of bed and into a T-shirt and jogging bottoms which she'd found in the charity shop. She added a sweater, which she'd wear knotted casually round her waist when the going got hot, and the new shoes. After a hasty cup of tea she drove to Mansell Park. It was a cool, cloudy morning but at least it wasn't raining; that would have been the ultimate nightmare and she'd probably have cried off, citing some mystery ailment.

She hadn't told Orla about Wally and the jogging because she knew it would be a source of great mirth for Orla, who would doubtless tell her what an idiot she was and that she'd probably give up after five minutes. In a few weeks' time she hoped to be able to impress Orla with her athletic prowess, her toned body, and perhaps even an athletic partner.

The athletic partner in question was waiting for her by the pond at seven o'clock on the dot, clad in a royal blue tracksuit and a pair of hefty, expensive-looking trainers.

'Good morning, Tess!' He gave her a hug, then asked, 'Haven't you brought any water? It's important to keep hydrated, you know.'

'Oh, I didn't think,' Tess muttered, realising she'd probably fallen flat at the first hurdle. 'But I have a bottle in the car. Shall I go back for it?'

He sighed. 'OK, but be quick.'

Why, she wondered, was there any great hurry? As she headed back to her car, she prayed that there was indeed a bottle of water in there. If there was, it was probably very ancient, but it would have to do. After much burrowing amongst a collection of shopping bags and tissues, she finally found the bottle of water and, as she walked back towards Wally, realised she hadn't any pockets in which to store it. Well, she'd just have to carry it in her hand.

'OK, let's go!' she said cheerfully.

'Fifty brisk steps,' he ordered, jogging alongside her.

She set off, counting to fifty, before he yelled, '*Now*, start jogging!'

Tess began to jog and got as far as forty before, breathless, she stopped.

'You are *so* out of condition!' said Wally, sounding exasperated. 'OK, so you'll have to go back to walking. *Brisk* walking, Tess!' He appeared to be a little short on humour so Tess stifled the urge to giggle. How ridiculous all this was!

She began to wonder if his late wife had suffered her fatal stroke while obeying his strident instructions. Perhaps he had her running marathons and perhaps she'd run one marathon too many... but then Tess remembered that he'd said it was her early death that had prompted him to do all this. Tess had had enough after forty minutes, having dropped her jogging efforts to a mere twenty steps for each fifty she'd walked, a fact that clearly disappointed Wally.

'We have a lot of work to do,' he said sadly, swigging from his water bottle. Having carried her water bottle in her hand for the entire ordeal, Tess thought she should take a sip too. She wasn't very thirsty but she was hot and sweaty, and the new white shoes had blistered her heels.

As if on cue, he looked down at her feet.

'You looked like you were limping back there,' he said, replacing the bottle into the royal blue depths of his trouser pocket.

'I think I've blistered my heel,' Tess admitted.

He carried on staring at the shoes. 'These don't look like proper trainers,' he remarked. 'Look how thin the soles are! These soles of yours are so thin that they can't possibly protect you when your foot hits the ground.' He placed one large foot alongside hers and pointed at the tyre-tread soles on his own enormous grey trainers.

'Well, I've had enough for today anyway,' Tess said, dreaming of a cup of tea and a bacon sandwich. And getting the shoes off.

'Right,' he said. 'Let's arrange for another go in a couple of days' time. Same time, same place, *different footwear*! OK? Now, I'd suggest you have a light breakfast or something, but I'm afraid I'm not going to be able to join you because I've got to be at the golf club for eight thirty.' He glanced at his watch. 'Big tournament, so I mustn't be late. In the meantime, why don't you buy some decent trainers and have a go by yourself tomorrow morning.'

As Tess limped back towards her car, he gave her a peck on the cheek and headed for the bicycle rack. Did this man have a car? Or a sense of humour? Tess was none too sure she wanted to bother finding out.

It was tempting to forget the whole thing, but Tess didn't feel she could give up so easily. She decided she would buy proper trainers and perhaps a little rucksack as well, in which to carry the bottle of water and the sweater. After all, she thought, it was almost like having a personal trainer, and for free! Let's face it, you wouldn't expect a personal trainer to be laughing at your uselessness or offering breakfast. And she'd have a little jog round Milbury in the morning, avoiding Penny Lane of course.

With sticking plasters on both heels, Tess ventured forth to seek appropriate footwear and found a seriously suitable pair on sale. And they were, she had to admit, very comfortable. And expensive, despite the discount. She'd do her Milbury jog very early in the morning in the hope that she wouldn't be seen by anyone she knew: Orla, for instance. Orla was already finding Tess's dates a subject of great mirth, and Tess could only guess at how she might react to hearing about the Andy incident. And now Wally, and the jogging. She'd probably split her sides.

At quarter to seven the next morning, she was up and half walking, half jogging with the new trainers on her feet and a rucksack on her back to hold the obligatory bottle of water. She walked briskly up the road and round towards the little shops on the High Street before she began jogging. She felt she'd improved slightly on the previous day's attempt, and she'd reached her twenty-ninth step when 'Pastry' Parker, taking a breath of fresh air outside his shop, called out, 'Good morning, Mrs Templar! Getting ready for summer, eh?'

Damn and blast! She'd forgotten that bakers would be up very early to knead the dough, or whatever it was they had to do. Orla bought her buns and stuff there, so Tess hoped fervently he wouldn't mention this early morning sighting.

'Good morning!' she replied, suddenly aware that she hadn't felt in the least tempted to buy one of his mouth-watering pastries.

Then she almost managed a forty-forty ratio of walking to jogging, before she collapsed onto a bench on the edge of the green. She was hot, sweaty and thirsty, so she was probably doing something right.

Tess felt quite perky on arriving at Mansell Park the following morning. Wally was already there, waiting by the pond, running on the spot. He pecked her on the cheek and, looking at her feet, said, 'Well, *those* are more sensible!' And off they set again, Tess feeling more confident and more suitably attired. She didn't do so well with Wally as she had on her own, probably due to the fact that she was less relaxed under his critical eye. But she wasn't going to give up, and managed almost an hour before he said, 'I can see a tiny bit of improvement. Fancy joining me for a cuppa?' There was a café on the edge of the park where they were serving breakfast to half a dozen workmen, condensation running down the windows, and a very appetising smell of bacon cooking. They sat down at a Formica-topped table by the window and Tess, who was ravenous, said, as the elderly waitress approached, 'Don't know about you, Wally, but I'm having a bacon butty. And a large mug of tea.'

Wally whistled. 'Not the healthiest of choices, Tess. I'll just have a black tea.'

'Two teas, one black, one bacon butty,' intoned the waitress, before she shuffled her way back to the kitchen.

'It's important to keep your fluid intake up,' Wally said, leaning forward, 'and your calorie intake down.'

'I'm sure you're right,' Tess said, rubbing a hole in the window steam so she could see out.

Wally lowered his voice. 'Not only that, they cook with *fat* here, Tess! None of your olive oils in this humble establishment. But if you need your arteries furring up, you've come to the right place.'

As she bit into the delicious butty, Tess said, 'Well, you've got me started on some exercise, Wally, but when it comes to my diet I do try to be careful but I like a treat occasionally. And that's exactly what I'm having now!'

'Each to his own,' Wally said piously.

'I take it we're not going to be wining and dining any time soon?' Tess asked, wiping the fat from her chin.

He looked confused. The idea had obviously never entered his head. 'I'm vegan,' he said after a moment, 'have been for a couple of years now. But perhaps I could cook you a vegan meal some time when I'm not too busy?'

Tess grinned. 'Like I said, we're probably not going to be wining and dining any time soon.'

They parted company amicably and politely. He wasn't *that* much like Gary Lineker anyway.

'Any time you fancy a jog, Tess,' Wally said, 'you just email me.'

Tess looked down at her feet, knowing she must justify having bought these trainers. But she'd be happier going it alone.

'I'll do that,' she said, as he gave her the obligatory peck on the cheek before jogging off in the opposite direction.

Plainly there was no spark there for either of them, and there was never going to be. But at least he'd set her off on the right track to rediscovering exercise.

Fired up with enthusiasm, Tess continued to rise early to jog her way round Milbury in the mornings, avoiding Penny Lane. Only Pastry was around at that time, and a few men on their way to work. Every bone in her body was aching when she arrived at Curvaceous on the following Saturday morning. Orla had got there first, opened up, and was now filling the kettle. Tess saw the box of cupcakes on the counter and groaned. She'd been to the baker's, after Tess had worked so hard to keep running past it.

'Rumour has it,' Orla said cheerfully, 'that there's been a sighting of some old bird staggering round Milbury at the crack of dawn. Can't imagine who that might be.'

'Fancy that,' Tess said drily. But it would be worth it. No pain, no gain, and all that. And she'd certainly got the pain.

'Isn't this taking things just a tad too far?' Orla persisted. 'It's only a bloody wedding! All over in a matter of hours, and everyone's going to be gawping at the bride, not her mother.'

Tess didn't bother replying. She knew perfectly well – and so did Orla – that women eyed each other up and down on such occasions. Particularly the mother of the bride, and particularly when her successor was Ursula. Ursula was quite fit to upstage the bride, never mind the bride's mother.

The following day Ellie, accompanied by Lisa, arrived at Temple Terrace for a dress fitting.

'There may be a tantrum when she discovers the dress is cream and not pink,' Lisa warned. 'She's mad about pink.'

'Ah, but I've made a pink sash, and she'll have pink roses in her hair,' Tess replied. She called out for Ellie, who'd disappeared into the back garden to find Dylan.

Ellie came running in, took one look at the dress and said, 'But it's not *pink*…' Her lower lip began to tremble.

'We have to do what Auntie Amber wants,' Lisa said, rolling her eyes at Tess, 'and Auntie Amber wants cream.'

'But it's got a lovely pink sash, and we're going to put pink roses in your hair and in your posy,' Tess put in quickly. 'You're going to look *so* pretty. Now, shall we slip this on and see how it looks?'

'It looks lovely,' Lisa said a few minutes later. 'You look beautiful, Ellie.'

Ellie didn't look altogether convinced, until Tess added the pink sash and told her to imagine the flowers. 'They'll be pink too and very sweet-smelling. I think you'll be as beautiful as the bride!'

'Can I have pink shoes, Mummy?' Ellie was now pirouetting in front of the mirror. 'With high heels?'

'You may be able to have pink shoes, but certainly not with high heels!' replied her mother.

'Why not?'

Lisa sighed. 'Because you're four years old! You're a little girl!'

'So I need high heels to make me bigger, don't I, Nana?'

'They still wouldn't make you as big as Mummy and me, so why don't we go for some lovely flat pumps like ballet dancers wear? I'm sure Auntie Amber would agree to them being pink.'

'Can I wear it now, to go home in?'

'No,' said Lisa, 'you can't. You can't wear it until the wedding.'

'And I still have to finish it off,' Tess added.

'I want to wear it *now*!'

'Well, you can't,' shouted Lisa. Then, as Ellie's lip started trembling again, she said to Tess, 'God, I wish I wasn't pregnant; I need a bloody gin and tonic!'

Tess realised then that this wedding was stressing them all out, one way or the other.

CHAPTER THIRTEEN

LAND OF LEGEND

Orla's enthusiasm for the cruise had waned a little ever since she met someone called Ricky, who owned and drove a large articulated truck all over the country. If he could handle one of those enormous monsters, Tess thought, he could probably handle Orla. This Ricky delivered anything and everything everywhere so found it difficult, he said, to form lasting relationships. Orla was keen to rectify this.

'He's so nice,' she told Tess, 'and he's offered me a lift anywhere I want to go. Sometimes he even goes across to Ireland, so wouldn't it be great to go over to see my brother? And, after we get back from the cruise, he's going to drop me off in Birmingham for a couple of days while he goes up north somewhere, and he'll pick me up again on the way back. Maeve lives in Birmingham now, so I could spend a couple of days with her.'

'Well, that's fine,' Tess said, 'but you never know who you might meet on this cruise.'

'But I don't really want to leave him,' Orla moaned.

'Surely he could come too, if he wanted to? You met him via MMM, didn't you?'

'Oh, he can't take much time off because he works for himself, and he has contracts all over the place to deliver this and that.'

Tess was getting worried that Orla might pull out. 'But since he's away so much of the time,' she said, 'you'd probably only be seeing him for a couple of days in the time we're away. Won't do him any harm and, if you'll forgive the cliché, absence makes the heart grow fonder and all that.'

Orla looked doubtful. 'I hope so.'

'And here's another cliché – there's plenty more fish in the sea, as you're forever telling me. It's Ricky who should be worried about you swanning off round the Greek islands with a boatful of old singletons all hoping to find a partner.'

'He's not the jealous type.'

'Because you haven't *made* him jealous yet. You're there, all ready and waiting, when he comes home.'

'I suppose you're right.'

'Of course I'm right, Orla! Don't let him take you for granted.'

'Hmm, OK. So, to change the subject, do you think I should take my bikini?'

Tess stopped in the middle of hand-stitching a hem and stared at Orla in horror. 'Orla, you're sixty-three!'

'I *know* how old I am!' Orla snapped.

'And you're overweight!'

'Well, thank you very much for pointing *that* out!'

'It's the truth!' Tess said. 'You gave up on Slim Chance because Paul or someone said they liked larger ladies. That doesn't mean they'd want to see you prancing around in a bikini! Come on, Orla, very few women our age can get away with wearing a bikini. You have to be slim and toned, or Helen Mirren.'

'What about shorts then?'

'Well, I'm not wearing them because my thighs still leave a lot to be desired. But you wear shorts if you want to, so long as they're not *short* shorts.'

'Have you finished lecturing me?'

'I'm not lecturing you! I just want you to look nice. And you *did* ask!'

Tess worked well into the night during the week prior to their departure. She had several large outfits to finish off, and she had Amber's wedding dress to tack together, ready for a final fitting. And then there was Ellie's dress. Ellie had finally accepted the idea that the dress had to be cream, because Amber didn't like pink. Somehow or the other Tess had to get that little dress finished too before she went away. Then, hopefully, she'd only have to finish off Amber's dress when she got back.

Amber came for her fitting two days before Tess went away.

'You look tired, Mum.'

'I *am* tired. But I just need to get on top of everything before I leave. Then I shall rest and relax for a whole week.'

'Sounds good. Just be careful not to put the weight back on with all that wine, all that baklava.'

The more Tess thought about it, the more she prayed for a restful time. She sincerely hoped they weren't going to be organised into groups to play stupid games or, heaven forbid, bingo. She'd heard about these singles' holidays before and had sworn to give them a wide berth. She could only hope that MMM, with its mature clientele, would be a little more sophisticated.

Orla offered to drive to Gatwick, and they'd share the cost of the car park. The flight departed at 2 p.m. and they'd been advised to arrive around midday. Orla, with her Mini, was a fast driver but, as usual, the M25 was manic and the M23 not much better.

'Where the hell are they all *going*?' Orla ranted at no one in particular, as she braked yet again, staring in fury at the sea of red lights ahead.

'Probably Greece.'

'It's not as if it's the bloody rush hour!' Orla went on.

'No, but it is Friday and lots of people are on the move. It's holiday time, in case you've forgotten.'

By the time they got to the car park and then the terminal, they were both severely stressed. Diet or no diet, Tess decided, I'm going to be having a stiff drink if we get to the departures lounge on time. When they finally got through security there were only minutes to spare and, by the time they'd bought some bottled water and newspapers, the flight was on final call. Tess's stiff drink had to wait.

She and Orla had aisle seats across from each other. The ancient couple seated between Tess and the window on her side of the aisle – who were obviously *not* MMM hopefuls – appeared to have brought their lunch with them, as they happily opened up Tupperware boxes of pies, pastries and a very yellow cake, plus cling-film-wrapped packages, scattering crumbs everywhere.

'We had a flask of tea,' the old man told Tess, 'but they wouldn't let us take it through. We don't like the stuff they give you on these flights.'

Tess, who'd had nothing to eat since a couple of slices of toast at breakfast, was beginning to wish she'd got some Tupperware boxes too. While she waited for her meal she treated herself to a gin and tonic, as did Orla, who'd wasted no time getting into conversation with the man seated next to her.

'He's a "heart"!' Orla muttered to Tess, leaning across the aisle. 'He's going on the cruise and he's not *bad*.'

'Are you telling me you fancy him?' Tess murmured back.

'No, I'm thinking he'd be good for you. He's a craftsman, a furniture maker.'

'What do I want with a furniture maker? I've got plenty of furniture.'

'No, no, Tess! What I mean is that he's *creative*! And you're creative!'

Tess tried to get a look at him. Was he shaven or bald? Whatever he was, his head was gleaming in the afternoon sunshine that was streaming in through the window.

'I'll reserve judgement,' Tess said.

Athens was two hours ahead of British Summer Time, meaning that it was nearly nine o'clock and dark by the time they reached the hotel MMM had booked them into for one night. There was a bar and a pool, and the twin-bed room was basic but clean. In the bathroom was that inevitable notice asking you not to flush any paper down the loo, but to deposit it in the bin supplied below, indicated by an arrow.

'Do you know, I came to Greece when I was nineteen and this loo paper business was the same then. Wouldn't you have thought they'd have got their sewage systems sorted out by now?' Orla grumbled.

'You would,' Tess agreed, kicking off her sandals as she opened her suitcase.

'So let's go down to the bar for a nightcap. Time we had an ouzo. What say you?'

'I say that's a very fine idea, Orla,' Tess replied.

The bar was dimly lit and very busy. They took their ouzos out onto the small terrace by the pool in the hope of finding some cooler air, and had hardly had a sip when the furniture maker and his friend, a nervous-looking little guy, appeared.

'Orla!' he exclaimed.

'Alan!' Orla waved her arm towards Tess. 'This is my friend, Tess.'

'Pleased to meet you, Tess,' he said. 'And this is a mate of mine, Barry.'

Alan of the gleaming head was of medium height and stocky build. He had blue eyes and several chins, but wasn't bad-looking. He wore a blue shirt which, Tess noted, exactly matched his eyes. The shirt was unbuttoned almost to the waist where, on display amid his luxuriant grey chest hair, was nestled an assortment of silver chains and medallions. He also had several large rings adorning his large hands, and an earring in one ear. Poor old Barry was thin and grey-haired with a buttoned-up shirt and no ornamentation whatsoever.

'I was telling Tess you're a craftsman and make furniture,' Orla said to Alan. 'Tess is a dressmaker so you probably have lots in common.'

Tess and Alan surveyed each other in bewilderment.

'What I mean is,' Orla went on, 'you both have to take bits of stuff and put them together to make something recognisable. And beautiful, of course.'

'Well, that's one way of looking at it,' Alan said, grinning at Tess.

'I can always lend you some scissors,' Tess joked.

'And you can borrow any of my saws any time, provided you don't wreck them hacking through all those silks and satins.'

Tess laughed. 'I'll bear it in mind.' At least he has a sense of humour, she thought. Pity about all the silverware.

'So,' said Orla, 'we're all going to be cruising tomorrow. But we thought we could squeeze in a quick visit to the Parthenon in the morning before we leave.'

Barry nodded but said nothing.

'Are you two friends?' Tess asked.

'Yeah, we've known each other for years,' Alan replied. 'We've just paired up 'cos Barry here wants to see all these old ruins and things. And I'm just after a bit of sun, on that cruise boat, what's it called?'

'The *White Rose*,' Barry confirmed.

'Funny old name for a ship,' Alan said.

'Like "The White Rose of Athens", I expect,' Tess said. 'Nana Mouskouri sang it years ago. Lovely song.'

'Talking of Greek warblers,' said Orla, 'does anyone remember Demis Roussos?'

Alan groaned. 'That big bloke in a frock?'

'It was a kaftan,' Orla corrected. 'And he was lovely.'

'If you fancy that type you might as well hang around Athens,' Alan joked, 'and save yourself the price of the cruise.'

'Good idea!' said Orla, 'but I have to keep an eye on Tess here. She's bound to go off the rails if I'm not around to keep her in check.'

'Are you planning to go off the rails, Tess?' Alan asked, grinning. 'Let me know if you do!'

Tess laughed. 'I shall try to stay on track!'

Barry smiled, nodded and said very little. They downed another ouzo before Tess yawned and said, 'Well, I'm turning in. It's been a long day and I'm knackered.'

'We must be getting old,' Alan moaned. 'A few years back we'd all have been looking for discos and nightclubs!'

'Not tonight,' Orla confirmed. 'Hey look, Barry's asleep!'

Barry's head had dropped forward and he was emitting soft snores. Alan shook him gently, causing poor Barry to jump and to start apologising in what was definitely a Scouse accent. It was the most he'd said all evening.

When they got back to their room, Orla asked, 'What did you think of Alan?'

'He's all right,' Tess replied. 'And he's got a good sense of humour. But just imagine being crushed up against all that silverware on his manly chest!'

'Yeah, it must cost an awful lot of money to look that cheap!' Orla retorted.

'And what about Barry?' Tess asked.

Orla pulled a face. 'Can't imagine what he's doing here.'

'He's probably just very shy,' Tess said. 'And, let's face it, he didn't get a chance to say much with Alan doing all the talking. Anyway, we can share a taxi to go to the Parthenon with them in the morning, and then we can probably lose them on board the boat.'

Tess slept deeply but not for long. Wide awake at 6 a.m., she then gave up on the idea of further sleep, got up and quietly opened the French doors, discovering a tiny balcony filled to capacity with two plastic garden chairs. They were several floors above a long, narrow street full of parked cars and shuttered houses. Water bottle in hand, Tess sat down on a chair and stared across at one of the shuttered windows opposite. It was already very warm. Tonight they'd be on the *White Rose*, somewhere out at sea, and heading for their first port of call, Mykonos. She decided it didn't matter if she didn't fancy anyone on board because she'd enjoy briefly exploring those beautiful islands and, in between, she'd relax and work on her tan. She wondered briefly if she and David would have been sailing on the *White Rose*. This was not how she'd imagined arriving in Greece. But she must put the past behind her and, even if she *never* found her soulmate, at least she could arrive at Amber's wedding with a healthy golden glow. But keeping slim was definitely going to be the biggest challenge during the coming week.

'What are you doing out there?' a sleepy-voiced Orla asked.

'Daydreaming.'

'It's only half past six, not properly daytime yet.'

'I know, but I couldn't sleep.'

Orla eased herself out of bed and tottered towards the open windows. 'Is there a stunning view of the Acropolis?'

'No such luck,' Tess replied. 'Only a stunning view of loads of parked cars and a heap of washing strung out on the balcony opposite.'

'They certainly haven't gone overboard – if you'll forgive the pun – to find us a luxury hotel. But I suppose we've got what we paid for, because I asked for a budget hotel in Athens. Alan was saying that, apparently, there *was* the option of flying out this morning and going straight to Piraeus. But then we wouldn't have seen anything of Athens.'

'Let's make the most of it then. What time's breakfast?'

'The blurb here says from 7 a.m., so that just gives us time to get beautiful!'

Breakfast consisted of the usual continental line-up of cereals, fruits, yoghurts and rolls. Orla reckoned the rolls had been dug up with other archaeological treasures from ancient Greece, and so Tess decided to stick with yoghurt, honey and some melon, hoping that wasn't asking for tummy trouble later in the day.

As they were drinking their second cups of coffee, Alan and Barry walked into the restaurant. Both were clad in T-shirts and shorts; Alan had replaced the medallions with a heavy silver chain choker, while Barry was unadorned and looked decidedly sleepy. In contrast to Alan's flip-flops, Barry wore socks and trainers on the end of his stick-thin legs, and carried a little rucksack.

'Thought we'd better get up early,' Alan said cheerfully, 'before it gets too hot. And we're going to have to be back here by lunchtime to get our stuff and head for the boat.'

'We thought the same,' said Orla. 'How about we share a taxi to the Parthenon?'

'Good idea.' Alan turned to Barry. 'That OK with you?'

'Yeah, but I have a load of pills to take first. They're in the room.'

No one dared ask what sort of pills they were or what problems he might have. They just nodded.

Bathed in golden sunshine, the ancient columns of the Parthenon stood proudly on the rocky outcrop that overlooked the city. It was the scene of countless postcards and travel programmes, but it still gave Tess goosebumps when she first saw it, and thought of all the centuries it had survived and the generations of people who'd strolled through these ancient columns.

'Nice to find something older than us!' Orla joked.

'It was completed in 438 BC and dedicated to the goddess Athena,' said Barry, 'which is where Athens gets its name from.'

The other three all turned round to look at him in amazement. Not only did he not have a guidebook, but it was the most any of them had heard him speak.

'You're very knowledgeable, Barry,' Tess said admiringly.

'I just like history,' said Barry.

'Blimey!' said Alan.

'It's the most important surviving building of classical Greece,' Barry continued, unfazed. 'In fact, it's one of the greatest classical monuments in the world.'

They digested this for a few moments before Tess asked, 'What exactly is the Acropolis?'

'An acropolis,' Barry explained, 'was a settlement in ancient Greece, or a citadel, built in an elevated position for reasons of defence. This one contains the remains of several ancient buildings, the Parthenon being the most famous.'

'I'm glad you came along!' Alan joked.

'I'm very glad you did,' Tess said. 'It's so nice to be with someone who knows their stuff. I shall be sticking close to you, Barry, when we visit some of these ancient ruins in the coming week.'

'It's just that I like history,' Barry said, blushing furiously. He made a few comments about Doric columns and then lapsed back into silence, as they stood taking photographs and marvelling at the magnificent view over the city.

What a nice man, Tess thought. He only seemed to emerge from his shell when surrounded by the ancient history that he loved so much. She wondered why on earth he'd come on a singles' cruise; was he *really* looking for a girlfriend? He was naturally so nervous and quiet that it must have been a real effort for him to join a group like this. She'd love to find out, and she decided that she would. He might not be a likely candidate for her longed-for soulmate, but he was certainly interesting.

There was a crowd of people waiting for taxis. Orla and Alan had got into the queue and were wildly gesticulating for Tess to do the same. Tess looked round to see where Barry had got to and finally spotted him, some fifty yards back, beckoning. He'd grabbed a taxi before it got to the rank.

'Come on!' Tess yelled at the other two. There was a lot of derogatory shouting from the patiently waiting queue.

'We're none too popular,' Orla remarked breathlessly, as they rushed back to Barry and his taxi.

'You've got to be ahead of the game,' Barry said quietly.

This little man was full of surprises.

CHAPTER FOURTEEN

THE WHITE ROSE

The *White Rose* was large, sleek and very white.

'Oh, it's beautiful!' Tess exclaimed as they got out of the taxi. What a wonderful setting for romance, she thought. All at once she could imagine a tanned, debonair, handsome man in a white dinner jacket leaning casually against the rail, handing her a glass of champagne, soft music in the background perhaps. She cast a glance at Alan and Barry. Perhaps not.

Their cabin was on the third deck, on the outside, with a small balcony. Orla said she'd decided they should pay extra to get some private outside space and views. They were relieved not to be any higher, as Tess knew that, the higher they were, the more likely they were to feel the motion of the ship and the possible seasickness that accompanied it.

As they arrived in their cabin, Orla was already raving about the fantastic-looking steward who'd welcomed them on board, all thoughts of Ricky disappearing into the azure and turquoise waters as the liner slowly made its way out of Piraeus.

Their cabin was immaculate: twin beds with snowy white bed linen, two blue chairs on either side of a white coffee table, blue and white cushions. Blue and white everything. They'd each been given a little booklet to show the location of the lifejackets and the ditching drill, as well as directions to the restaurants, pool and gym. A gym! Tess had occasionally toyed with the idea of going to a gym, but that was as far as it got. This would be her opportunity to work off the inevitable pounds gained in the wonderful restaurants: Greek, Italian, seafood, 'Vitality' (what was *that*?), speciality steaks, a snack bar and the romantic – and expensive-sounding – White Rose Room. Would she ever get there?

There was a gentle tap on the door. Tess paused her unpacking and opened it. There stood a handsome steward, dark eyes flashing, white teeth gleaming, clutching a large basket of fruit.

'I am Spyros,' he said with a charming accent, 'and I am here to look after you.'

Orla emitted a gentle groan. 'Yes, please!'

'And I have brought you fruit.'

'Thank you, Spyros,' Tess said, casting a reproving glance at her friend. 'I am Tess, and this is Orla.'

He gave a little bow. 'I am honoured to be of service.' He placed the basket of fruit on the coffee table. 'There is the button.' He pointed at the bedside console. 'You just press, and I can get you anything. I hope you will enjoy this voyage.' With that he retreated back into the corridor.

Orla sighed. 'If only I was forty years younger!'

'You're not here to ogle crew members who could be your grandsons!' Tess said, laughing. 'You're here to meet guys your own age.'

'We'd better start looking then.' Orla hung up the last of her outfits. 'And I'm starving!'

'Let's find the snack bar for now, and we'll sound out the bars and restaurants later,' Tess said.

The snack bar had no end of tempting titbits and, while Orla loaded up her plate with pies and pastries, Tess settled for tzatziki – a yoghurt, cucumber and mint salad that surely shouldn't be fattening – along with some dolmathes, the stuffed vine leaves. But she couldn't resist a glass of retsina to go with it. After a coffee, they set off on an exploration trip, beginning with the pool area which was up on the sixth deck. The pool was large and inviting and already crowded, with all the sunbeds occupied. Just beyond was the sauna, a beauty salon and several shops selling colourful beachwear. There was also the gym.

'There's hardly time to do everything!' Tess exclaimed. 'We're only on board for a week and we have to explore these islands as well.' Perhaps she might have to give the gym a miss.

They went on to find the restaurants on the upper decks, and had a peep through the shutters at the White Rose Room on the very top level.

'This,' Orla remarked, 'is presumably where you come when you find the man of your dreams – and preferably one with deep pockets, because this looks mighty expensive.'

The tables for two were already set up with pristine white tablecloths, sparkling crystal and gleaming silverware.

'In that case,' sighed Tess, 'we're very unlikely to be customers.'

'They clearly expect some people to make it,' Orla said, standing back from the windows.

'Since it's probably *not* going to be us,' Tess said, 'shall we have a look at the other eating places?'

'What about sitting at the captain's table?' Orla asked. 'Where does *he* sit? And where do we find him?'

'I should think that, if he does these oldies' cruises every other week, he'll have the good sense to keep well out of the way. Probably has to barricade himself into his cabin to keep the mob at bay.'

'He might be an oldie himself,' Orla said wistfully. 'And on the lookout. You just never know.'

'Pigs might fly,' said Tess.

They found a couple of steamer chairs positioned a little way along from the fourth-deck restaurant, and plonked themselves down to look out at the passing coastline and the incredible blue of the Aegean. Tess thought about David and how he'd have loved to be here. And how she'd have loved him to be here.

Orla adjusted her sunglasses. 'I think a few drinks at the bar tonight, followed by some Greek nosh and then, maybe, a nightclub.'

At seven o'clock they headed towards the Athenian bar, Tess in a full-length green sundress with a split up the side and Orla in a knee-length floral number with a plunging neckline. Both had blow-dried their hair and applied their make-up with great care, and both had varnished their fingernails and toenails. Alan, who was chatting to a tall blonde, gave them a welcoming wave and carried on talking. Tess looked around and reckoned, as she'd expected, there were two women to every one man. And there was no sign of Barry.

'I suppose we'll just have to weave our way around,' Orla said, looking doubtful.

Tess, for a brief moment, wanted to escape back to their cabin, read a book, watch a film, order room service and wait for tomorrow. Anything was better than trying to make conversation with all these complete strangers.

As if reading her mind, Orla said, 'We haven't paid all this money to hide ourselves away, and we look just as good as anyone here. Come *on*!'

Orla was right. They had to make some effort. Tess looked around but no one caught her eye, except for a very handsome Asian man in a white jacket, who was chatting to two tiny grey-haired women, both of whom appeared to be hanging on to his every word. She got to the bar, ordered a gin and tonic, and a tall bespectacled man standing alongside said, 'No point in asking, I suppose, if you come here often?' He was wearing a natty yellow bow tie over his buttoned-up black shirt.

'No point whatsoever!' Tess laughed, sipping her drink.

'Well, I *have* been here before,' the man continued, 'last year, when we went to Lesvos and Kos. I'm Ed, by the way.'

'I'm Tess. And why then, Ed, would you come here two years running?' Was he desperately looking for a lover? she wondered.

'Please don't take this the wrong way, but I like to people-watch, mainly as research for a book I'm compiling: a photographic record of the social habits and love life of the over-sixties.'

Tess gulped. 'Oh,' she said. 'Well, you've probably come to the right place.'

'It's largely untapped territory, you see,' he continued.

'I would imagine the social life of the over-sixties is very similar to that of the under-sixties, isn't it?' Tess asked. 'Surely people don't change that much?'

'Ah,' said Ed, 'but their circumstances change. They're more likely to be widowed or divorced, kids flown the nest and that sort of thing. All of which can equal loneliness. And, of course, health problems increase with age. Not too many over-sixties go to parties and discos, so where do they find a partner?' He looked at her questioningly.

'I should think it's a safe bet to say they come somewhere like this,' Tess said.

'That's because you joined MMM, I assume? Bear in mind that not all over-sixties are very computer-savvy, are they? And not all over-sixties have enough spare cash to indulge themselves in something like this. We're the lucky ones.'

'I guess you're right,' Tess said, wondering for a moment what she would have done if she didn't use a computer or had to live entirely on her pension. After a minute she said, 'I'd probably have taken up ballroom dancing.' Why hadn't she thought of that before?

'That's very good,' said Ed approvingly. 'Very good. You'd get exercise, a bit of fun, and a partner for an hour or two at least.'

'But in case you hadn't noticed,' Tess went on, glancing around, 'there are at least two women here for every one man, so how do you solve that one? It's the women who have the problem, not the men.'

'It's the women I'm interested in,' Ed began but, before he got any further, Orla appeared.

'This,' said Tess, 'is my friend, Orla. I just know she'll be happy to help provide you with some relevant information. Orla, this is Ed.'

Orla gave one of her famous snorts, cleared her throat and said, 'And what do you need to know, Ed?' just as Tess made her escape.

She scanned the bar, hoping to see the good-looking Asian man – and there he was, looking just like Art Malik, now deep in conversation with a tall, willowy blonde. Tess's heart sank. Never mind, there were more fish in the sea, as Orla never tired of reminding her. And so there probably were – all around them in the depths below – but precious few in here.

Tess wasn't keen on small talk; she could never think of anything interesting to say to people she didn't know, and was seriously considering going out on deck when Orla reappeared at her side.

'Thanks *very much* for that introduction,' she said sarcastically. 'What a pontificating old bore! Anyway, I've given him something to think about. And I've just left him with an eighty-year-old who's busy telling him she's having the best sex of her life.'

'God bless her,' said Tess.

'Let's get out of here and go to eat,' said Orla.

They opted for the Greek taverna where, predictably, Orla went into raptures about the waiters. 'Aren't they just *gorgeous?*'

'Gorgeous or not, you can't have them,' Tess said. 'You'll just have to settle for an Alan, or a Barry, or an Ed!'

'In that case, let's turn our attention to the food,' Orla said.

They settled for some *kolokithakia gemista*, which consisted of plump courgettes stuffed with minced lamb and herbs, served with an egg and lemon sauce. Tess had vowed to avoid desserts but, seeing Orla about to order baklava, she decided she'd have it too. Just this once. And then she panicked at the sight of all the delicious-looking layers of filo pastry, but she ate it anyway. All this was washed down with a large carafe of red wine. Tomorrow, Tess vowed, she'd *run* round Mykonos!

Orla hiccupped. 'Fancy some disco dancing?'

'I fancy my bed,' Tess said.

'Me too,' admitted Orla.

They were both sound asleep by eleven o'clock.

CHAPTER FIFTEEN

MYKONOS

Tess woke up just after six o'clock, rubbed her eyes, yawned, stretched, and made her way out onto the balcony. And there, bathed in the early morning sunshine, was the island of Mykonos, with its blindingly white buildings along the waterfront and up the hill. And windmills!

Tess had always been intrigued by the rather squat white windmills that featured in so many photographs of the islands. And this island was theirs for the day. She was here to enjoy the sun, the scenery and the culture, so what did it matter if she found a soulmate or not? After all, there were still several 'hearts' yet to meet after she got home… not that she'd be holding her breath.

They must have cruised around a hundred miles overnight and then anchored offshore until dawn.

'Oh, wow!' Orla had suddenly emerged from the cabin. 'That looks so beautiful!'

'It is, isn't it?' Tess said dreamily.

'Talking of beauty,' Orla went on, 'shall we ring for that gorgeous Spyros to bring us some breakfast? After I've beautified myself a little, of course.'

'Why not?'

Twenty minutes later Spyros was duly summoned, and appeared with a jug of freshly squeezed orange juice and a big smile. 'Good morning, ladies!'

'Good morning, Spyros!' Orla beamed. 'I think we could manage a light breakfast before honouring Mykonos with our presence. Just fruit, rolls and coffee – what do you think, Tess?'

Tess nodded and Spyros flashed them another of his smiles before disappearing.

'How old do you reckon he is?' Orla asked.

'Far too young for us!' Tess laughed. 'But since you ask, probably mid-twenties.'

Shortly afterwards the object of their admiration reappeared with a laden tray. As he turned to leave, Orla asked, 'What should we be seeing in Mykonos, Spyros?'

'Very beautiful place,' replied Spyros. 'You like beach? Beautiful beaches. You like nice food and wine? Many good tavernas. Many hotels, many rich peoples, many old buildings. You will like.'

'I'm sure we will, Spyros, thank you,' said Tess, dishing herself up a generous portion of yoghurt and honey. The rolls were obviously freshly made and smelled delicious. She'd ration herself to one and one only, and then walk as much as possible in an attempt to keep her weight from rocketing.

'That Spyros sends my hormones haywire,' Orla muttered.

'What about Ricky?' Tess asked. 'Five minutes ago you didn't want to be leaving him!'

'Just because you've got a luscious pair of Manolo Blahniks, doesn't mean you can't admire a gorgeous pair of Jimmy Choos,'

Orla informed her. As Tess attempted to work out the logic of this, Orla added, 'Anyway, Ricky's already emailed and says he's missing me, so it'll make him appreciate me all the more.'

'Didn't I tell you just that?' Tess asked.

'You did. And I hope you're right. He's in Grimsby at the moment. Do you suppose they've got attractive women in Grimsby?'

'Why wouldn't they have?'

'Just so long as he doesn't meet any. Now, what are you planning to wear today?'

At ten o'clock Tess, wearing a yellow sundress, and Orla, in a sleeveless top and shorts, waited to disembark, with strict instructions to be back on board by 6 p.m. In front of them was Mykonos Town. They'd been told it was customary in Greece to give the principal town the same name as that of the island. But to confuse matters, it was known as Chora by the locals.

Tess thought the town was enchanting, with its narrow cobbled streets, the white buildings with their colourful shutters and doors, and the shops selling all manner of souvenirs, icons, pottery and clothing.

'They must be rubbing their hands with glee when they see us coming,' Orla reckoned. 'And I bet they double their prices whenever they see a cruise liner on the horizon.' She stopped to examine some postcards. 'I wonder if I should send one of these to Ricky?'

'There's a very good chance Ricky'll see you before he sees the postcard,' Tess said. 'If it's anything like Italy, I think they get sent by carrier pigeon.'

It was already very hot and there was the whole island to see, which Tess had to admit was not walkable. Spyros had advised them to take a taxi. 'Very cheap,' he'd said. Tess somehow doubted that anything would be very cheap round here, but there seemed little alternative if they were to do any exploring. There had been a fleet of taxis waiting when they got off the boat and Tess wondered if they'd all be gone by now, as they retraced their steps. They were in luck. One taxi still remained. The driver introduced himself as Grigoris. He looked about sixty, tall, craggy, wearing jeans with a snazzy red shirt unbuttoned just enough to display a forest of grey hair on his chest, adorned with just the one silver chain.

'I take you nice places,' said Grigoris. 'We have very good day. I very cheap.' He wasn't very cheap but, after some mental calculations, Tess and Orla decided he was probably worth it if they wanted to see anything of the island.

'Very comfortable,' Grigoris continued, ushering them towards his Mercedes. 'Also air-conditioning and music. You like music?' With that he switched on the CD player and some very loud bouzouki music blared out.

After persuading him to turn it down a decibel or two, they set off round the island. Orla wanted to know if he had anything by Demis Roussos. Yes, he did, and he had Nana Mouskouri too, because foreign visitors had never heard of anybody else in Greece. Except maybe Melina Mercouri.

'You like?' he asked, waving his arm out of the window as they passed some luxury hotels and beautiful sandy beaches. 'Many tourists here,' continued Grigoris, lighting a cigarette and blowing the smoke out of the open window. 'Very cosmopolitan. Some men, you know, they come here to find… um, other men. You know?'

'I didn't know,' said Orla. 'Just our luck!'

'Ah,' said Grigoris, 'but most Greek men here prefer the ladies. *English* ladies.'

'That lets us out,' Tess sighed.

They went to Ornos, described as a typical Greek island village: cobbled, whitewashed, with geraniums everywhere and lots of little old ladies dressed in black. Exactly as the postcards decreed it should be.

'You go now to taverna for lunch,' Grigoris ordered, one hand resting lightly on the steering wheel, the other waving at everyone he passed. 'I take you to nice place.'

'Probably belongs to his brother or his cousin,' Orla muttered, but they were both becoming decidedly peckish and needed a break from Grigoris's endless chatter. He deposited them at an ancient building with a garden alongside, filled with vines, geraniums, and rustic tables and chairs. A very attractive Greek woman came to take their order and recommended something unpronounceable, which turned out to be a filo pastry concoction with spinach. They both declined the tray of sweet pastries proffered afterwards, and Tess worried again about her weight. Since it didn't look as if they'd be doing much walking today, perhaps she could run round the deck later, when it was cooler?

They found Grigoris outside, deep in conversation with a man who looked just like him.

'My brother,' he explained as he led the way back to the car.

'Does he live here?' Tess asked.

'Of course,' replied Grigoris. 'The taverna belong to him.'

Orla nudged Tess. 'I *told* you so.'

As they set off again Grigoris informed them that Mykonos had, over the centuries, been under the control of the Romans, the

Catalans, the Venetians and the Ottomans before becoming part of Greece. Then his mobile rang and he chatted animatedly to the caller with one hand holding the phone to his ear, the other just touching the wheel as he drove with his elbow out of the window.

'He wouldn't get away with all that at home,' Tess said, praying they wouldn't meet anything on the sharp bends, which he navigated with a couple of fingers.

'I don't suppose they have many more accidents than we do,' Orla said dismissively.

Tess tried to concentrate on the landscape. She was fascinated by the windmills. They were such a defining feature of the countryside and, according to Grigoris, were built by the Venetians but repurposed over the years, and many had now been converted into homes. They stopped briefly at Lena's House, a nineteenth-century traditional Mykonian residence which had belonged to a wealthy shipping family. Some of the original furniture was still preserved in what was now a museum. And there seemed to be a terrific number of churches. When Tess remarked on this Grigoris told them that, for years, if an islander wished to build a house, he was required to build a church on his land first. Then, near Kastro they stopped outside the Panagia Paraportiani, the Church of Our Lady which, they were informed, was one of the most famous architectural structures in Greece.

'I'm beginning to suffer from an overdose of culture, so how about taking us to a nice quiet beach for an hour or two?' Orla suggested.

The ever-obliging Grigoris knew just the place and, after about fifteen minutes, they drew up near a small deserted cove. 'I return after one hour,' he said, 'to take you back to ship.'

'Why on earth didn't I bring my swimsuit?' Tess moaned, looking at the inviting turquoise water as they strolled barefoot on the sand.

'Well, I'm going in there in my bra and pants,' Orla said. 'There's no one around and, even if there was, would it matter?'

'I don't suppose it would,' Tess said, watching Orla stepping out of her shorts and removing her top. The allure of the sparkling sea was too much, and she pulled her sundress off over her head and ran, laughing, into the water. It was like stepping into a warm bath, and they had to wade out some way before it was deep enough to swim.

'Oh, this feels wonderful!' Tess exclaimed, as she plunged into the cooler, deeper water and commenced a careful breaststroke. As she swam, she thought of long-ago summers when she and her sister had braved the icy waters of the sea at North Berwick. All gritted teeth and gooseflesh. But this was something else! She thought about her sister then. Was Barbara coming to the wedding? Omar had died some years previously but she had decided to remain in Nice, where the climate suited her better because the British weather did nothing to alleviate her arthritis. She rarely came back, even after their parents had died, but she did email Tess occasionally. Her only son had emigrated to Australia and he most definitely was not coming to the wedding. But Barbara? Who knew? She'd been sent an invitation, of course, but was still yet to give a firm response. Well, in spite of all the hoo-ha at the time of her elopement, she'd had a long and happy marriage with a successful, wealthy man, even if the source of his income remained in some doubt. But as ever, Barbara was a law to herself.

As Tess pondered over her sister, she heard Orla shout, 'I'm going back to dry off.'

Reluctantly, after about ten minutes, they both made their way back to the beach.

'Wish we'd thought to bring towels,' Tess said.

'We'll just sunbathe until we're dry,' Orla said. 'It shouldn't take long in this heat.' Then, glancing at Tess, she said, 'Just as well Grigoris isn't around, because your knickers have gone all transparent!'

Two hours later, they were back on board the *White Rose*, having thanked Grigoris profusely and sworn that they would, of course, hire him again next time they came to Mykonos.

'As it's taken me sixty-two years to get here for the first time,' Tess mused, 'I don't think he needs to count the days until our return.'

It was as they were heading back towards their cabin that Tess caught sight of someone vaguely familiar, running along the deck towards the swimming pool. She stopped dead.

'What's up?' Orla asked.

'That guy,' Tess said, pointing to where she'd seen him running. 'I'm sure he's the one who had me jogging all over the place. Wally, he was called.'

'It could be him, I suppose,' said Orla. 'But then again, there must be dozens of guys running around who all look much the same.'

'I expect you're right. I can't imagine him going on a cruise anyway, particularly as he's vegan.'

'I seem to remember from the brochure that one of the restaurants – "Vitality", I think it was called, specialises in vegetarian and vegan food, so he wouldn't starve,' Orla said.

Tess then forgot about him as she showered and got dressed for the 'Greek evening' during which, according to the brochure, there would be typical Greek food, wine, music and dance, plus a chance to meet guests from all the other groups on board.

'I've not seen *that* before,' Orla remarked, as Tess appeared in a silky black and white patterned jumpsuit. 'When did you get *that*?'

Tess resisted saying, 'What, this old thing?' and said instead, 'I bought it for the cruise. You're the one who was going on about jumpsuits being the *in* thing. So I decided to get with it.'

'Well, it's very nice,' said Orla.

It must be, Tess thought happily, because Orla does not dish out compliments lightly.

The event was to take place al fresco, with the main deck transformed into an enormous dining room, tables and chairs positioned round an area where three bouzouki players were strumming as they arrived. It was already dark, and hundreds of tiny lights were strung overhead. On one side was a long bar, and on the other a long table on which the buffet was laid out. There were already crowds of people milling around, and the first person they met was Alan, tonight attired in a white shirt, unbuttoned most of the way to best display his collection of medallions on a bright pink, sunburned chest.

He raised his glass. 'Hi, girls! You look like you've caught some sun!'

'Not as much as you!' Tess exclaimed. 'Where did you get yours?'

'Right here, by the pool,' Alan replied.

'Didn't you want to explore the island?' Orla asked.

'Didn't see the point,' he said. 'I can see it from here. I've taken a few photos, so that'll do me.'

'It's such an interesting island,' Tess told him. 'You should have gone ashore. Where's Barry?'

'Not feeling so good. He's staying in his cabin.'

Tess felt sorry for Barry, who seemed so sadly out of place amidst all this colour and laughter. He would have liked some of the places they'd seen today, though, and would no doubt have been a mine of information. Perhaps he was simply shy. She wished she'd taken the trouble to knock on his door this morning and persuade him to join them.

There was no sign of the jogger that might have been Wally, but Tess noticed the man with the Art Malik looks again. Tonight he was wearing a black shirt with white trousers, and standing near the bar talking to a small fat man with a shock of white hair. She wished she had the confidence to go up and introduce herself, as Orla would surely have done, but could only hope that their paths would cross at some point. Was he from MMM or some other group? While Orla chatted to Alan, Tess found herself in conversation with a jovial gang of four women from Sheffield, all members of MMM, and all on the hunt for a man.

'We thought it would be a laugh,' said Peggy, who appeared to be their spokeswoman. 'And, who knows, one of us might just snare someone!' Much guffawing ensued. Peggy was a large lady with dyed auburn hair and an enormous bosom precariously contained in a low-cut strappy top.

'Trouble is,' put in one of her companions, with pink hair and protruding teeth, 'there's twice as many women as men here.'

'So we'll only get half a bloke each!' Peggy added, and they all collapsed in further giggles.

'At least we'll get tans,' another one with bright green eyelids said, 'and the wine's not bad.'

The wine was cheap and there was plenty of it. As Tess edged her way towards the bar, she collided with the good-looking Asian man, who was now on his own and drinking what looked like an orange juice. He was even more attractive up close. They both apologised at the same time.

'My fault entirely,' he said, smiling. 'May I get you a drink?'

'Oh, thank you, yes, that would be lovely. I'd like a wine – red wine, please.'

'No problem.' He pushed his way towards the counter.

Tess could not believe her luck. She checked that her bra straps weren't showing and fluffed up her hair with her fingers. As he waited at the bar, where the two bartenders were working flat out, she composed several sentences in the hope she'd be interesting enough when the conversation began.

When he came back and handed Tess the wine, he asked, 'And what do I call you?'

'I'm Tess,' she said, accepting the glass. 'And you are…?'

'Sanjeev,' he replied. 'Nice to meet you, Tess. And what do you think of the *White Rose*?'

'She's a beautiful ship,' Tess said.

He nodded in agreement. 'I was pleasantly surprised. I've never fancied cruising before.'

'I planned to come on a cruise once but it never happened,' Tess said. It wouldn't be a very good start to the conversation if she admitted that her previous cruising plans had involved a past lover, and that now she was only there in the hope of meeting someone like him.

'And where do you come from, Tess?'

'Originally from a little place near Edinburgh, but for the last forty-odd years I've been living in Surrey, not far from Kingston upon Thames. A small town called Milbury. How about you?'

'I live in London, for my sins. Fulham, to be exact.'

'Do you work there?'

'Yes, at the Royal Marsden.'

'Oh, so you're a doctor?' He looked like a doctor, she decided.

'Yes,' he said. 'An oncologist, actually. I specialise in bone cancer.'

'How interesting!' Tess was impressed. 'What a very worthwhile profession!'

Sanjeev smiled. 'It is, and I consider myself very fortunate to be doing this work. Do you work, Tess?'

'I'm a dressmaker,' Tess replied. 'I run a little boutique with a friend of mine, who's here somewhere.' She cast her eyes around but could see no sign of Orla.

'Ah,' he said, 'so you have clever fingers.'

'It's the only thing I'm much good at,' she admitted sadly.

'Nonsense! I'm sure there are many other things which you haven't even tried yet.'

What a charmer he is, thought Tess. He had beautiful eyes, the brown very dark and like velvet, the white bright and shining. And framed with the most gorgeous long black lashes. And he had a natural charm, not just chat-up lines. Here at last was someone clever, handsome and charming. Trouble is, she thought, there's an awful lot of women on this boat who are probably all thinking exactly the same thing. Not least Peggy and her gang. She'd be killed in the crush.

At that moment the tall, willowy blonde whom Tess had seen him talking to the previous night appeared from nowhere. 'Sanjeev!' she exclaimed. 'I've been looking for you!' She laid a proprietorial hand on his arm. 'Remember I was telling you about my friend, Professor Woodrow? Well, he's on this cruise with his delightful wife, and very interested in meeting you.' She didn't even glance at Tess.

'Well…' He hesitated. 'Do you mind, Tess? Lavinia knows how much I'd like to meet this gentleman. Perhaps we'll run into each other again? I do hope so. Will you excuse me?'

'Yes, of course,' Tess said, turning away and silently cursing Lavinia, who was purposefully leading him away, her hand on his elbow. To make matters worse, Lavinia only looked to be in her mid-forties and was beautiful in a cool, Scandinavian sort of way. Perhaps he liked a contrast to his own dark good looks? And that Lavinia had seemed as if she were out for the kill. Was *she* an MMM member or part of another group? Tess wondered. Never mind. She sipped her glass of wine and supposed she should look for Orla.

She found Orla deep in conversation with the tall bespectacled Ed of the previous day. Tonight he was wearing a snazzy multicoloured blazer with a white T-shirt and trousers.

'Oh, there you are!' said Orla. 'Look who's turned up again!'

Tess was surprised at Orla's change of attitude; perhaps he wasn't such a pontificating old bore after all.

'Did you know Ed is a photographer?' Orla asked.

'Yes, he mentioned it yesterday,' Tess replied.

'Ah, but did you know he's having an exhibition in the art gallery on deck four after we leave Crete, to display all the great photos he's taking?'

'Places or people?' Tess asked him.

'Both,' Ed confirmed. 'But I'm looking for unique shots. Offbeat moments, unusual angles, that sort of thing. I'll bring my camera along when people start to loosen up, have a few drinks, throw a few plates, start to dance. Everyone's far too inhibited at the moment.'

'Sounds intriguing,' said Tess, resolving not to have too much wine.

'It's the story of a voyage,' he continued. 'People coming on board, uptight, nervous, feeling their way – right up to the time when they finally disembark, friendly, relaxed, maybe even partnered.'

'Chance would be a fine thing!' chortled Orla. 'And did you know, Tess, that we're supposed to wear an MMM badge so that we can all recognise each other? Apparently there's a group of doctors and bigwigs from some chemical company or other on board and, believe it or not, a group of over-eighties on an archaeological beginners' course. Everyone has different badges.'

'You are kidding!'

'No, I'm not. Here's yours.' Orla handed her a tiny gold badge in the shape of a heart. 'Pin that on somewhere.'

Tess was still trying to get her head round the archaeology course for the over-eighties. Antiques chasing antiques! Then she tried to remember if Sanjeev had been wearing a gold heart, but she couldn't recall that he'd been wearing any kind of badge. Perhaps he was from the doctors' group, or whatever they were. Perhaps Lavinia was his wife or partner? Heaven forbid! She decided she would waste no further time dwelling on his eligibility.

She turned her attention to the buffet. 'I'm hungry.'

'Me too,' Orla said. 'Fancy eating with us, Ed?'

'Yeah, thanks.' He gazed at the buffet. 'Don't suppose there's a cat in hell's chance of getting steak and chips?'

'Doubt it,' Tess said. 'This is, after all, a Greek-themed evening, on a Greek ship, in Greece.'

Ed sighed. 'Minced lamb and aubergines have a limited appeal night after night. Then again, the Greeks aren't known for their culinary expertise, are they? I've been told the Italian restaurant on deck five is very good, so I might try that tomorrow.'

They found a table and then headed for the buffet. Tess chose the *kotopoulo lemonato* – chicken cooked in a lemon and basil sauce – along with *horiatiki*, a tomato and feta salad. Ed had organised a large bottle of red wine from the bar, the bouzoukis were in full swing, and everyone was eating, drinking and relaxing. There was no further sign of Sanjeev or Lavinia. It was becoming more and more crowded, and the atmosphere was jovial and friendly. Ed had his camera at the ready but nothing had caught his eye yet. He seemed nice. He was from Newcastle, and was divorced with four adult offspring. He owned a photographic shop, he said, selling all manner of cameras and equipment, because photography was his thing.

Tess abstained from even looking at the desserts, but Orla found some orange cake and Ed tackled some *loukoumades*, yeast and honey buns. In the meantime, the wine flowed and people began to get up to dance. The bouzoukis predictably struck up the theme from *Zorba the Greek* and about twenty people rushed from their seats, linked arms and attempted to dance Greek style, most tripping over their own feet.

'Come on, you two!' Ed was already standing up. Laughing, Tess and Orla joined him and, insisting on being in the middle, he proceeded to do the steps faultlessly while they stumbled around trying to emulate him. He seemed to have a natural aptitude for the rhythm and the footwork.

'You've done this before!' Tess said.

'No, I haven't. I'm just lucky I've got good coordination. I'm waiting for my invitation to *Strictly Come Dancing*!'

By this time, almost everyone was on the floor doing their own version of the dance. When the music paused, one of the managers took to the floor to implore people not to throw their plates. 'I know that is what we are known to do,' he said, 'but not here, please!' Everyone cheered.

The three wandered back to their table and Tess, laughing, said, 'Now I'm convinced I've got two left feet!'

'Well,' said Ed, 'I've only got that one.'

'What do you mean?' Orla asked.

'Just the left foot,' he replied, grinning. 'Because I haven't got a right one.'

'You are kidding!' said Tess.

'Nope,' Ed replied, stretching out his leg and lifting up the fabric of his trousers. Tess and Orla both stared in disbelief at his prosthetic leg.

'My God!' Orla exclaimed. 'It *is* artificial! How on earth did that happen?'

'Motorbike accident when I was seventeen. I've been living with Jake for a very long time.'

'Jake?' Tess queried.

'Yes, that's what I call him. Do you remember the song that went "I'm Jake the peg, with my extra leg"? It just seemed like a good name.'

'But how on earth can you dance so well?' Tess was full of admiration for anyone with the gift of good coordination and the ability to remember a set of steps with two feet, never mind just one.

'You have to adapt,' he said. 'Just look at all those one-legged runners in the Paralympics. They'd outrun most people any day of the week.'

Tess sighed. 'A snail could outrun me!'

There followed a cabaret, during which some professional Greek dancers took to the floor, arms resting lightly on each other's shoulders, their dancing and the music becoming faster and faster, everyone clapping in time. Then there was a girl with a haunting voice who sang several folk songs, as well as more popular ditties such as 'Never on Sunday'.

At this point Ed had found some brandy, and was waving the bottle in the air saying, 'Some decent booze at last!' Tess thought the very least they could do was have a few little nightcaps and was surprised, when she consulted her watch, to discover it was nearly one o'clock. By now she was feeling decidedly tipsy and leaned back to close her eyes for a moment, which was not a good idea as everything started spinning around. When she opened them, she noticed Ed had just put his camera down on the table.

'I hope you haven't taken my photo!'

Ed grinned. 'As if!'

The music had slowed, and there were only a few couples left swaying together on the dance floor, groups of women looking on wistfully. And no sign of that lovely doctor or anyone Tess recognised, other than Orla and Ed, who had joined the others on the floor. Ed had been the perfect companion, dancing with them both in turn throughout the evening. In between numbers he'd headed off with his camera at the ready, hoping to catch people unawares.

Tess had had enough. It was time for bed – if only she could stay on her feet and find her way to their cabin. Why, oh why, had she been persuaded to drink those brandies?

Thankfully Orla returned and said quietly to Tess, 'I'm ready for bed, how about you?'

Bidding Ed goodnight, they linked arms and set off unsteadily towards their cabin.

CHAPTER SIXTEEN

SANTORINI

Tess woke just after nine o'clock with a massive headache. Where the hell had she packed the Alka-Seltzers? She rose slowly and, trying not to wake up the still sleeping Orla, rummaged in her suitcase until she finally located them. She poured herself a glass of water and dissolved a couple of tablets before venturing slowly out onto the balcony. All that was visible was sea. If they were moving at all it was very slowly, but they should be docking in Santorini later in the morning. The sun was already very warm but there was a soft breeze.

Then some movement caught her eye. She looked down to the promenade deck and saw a vaguely familiar figure, in shorts only, jogging round and clutching a water bottle. It *was* – it *had* to be! Tess was almost certain it was Wally, although she'd seen no sign of him yesterday evening. Being Wally, of course, if he wasn't running he'd probably be in the gym or eating vegan food. He would not be suffering from a hangover, that was for sure. Still, it had been a fun evening.

But alcohol equals calories, and Tess knew from her bloated waistband that she'd already gained a few pounds. With only a month to go until the wedding, she still had half a stone, and hopefully a little more, to lose before the end of July; and she certainly didn't want to go back home with a single extra pound. Somehow or other she had to work it off and watch her alcohol intake.

As she went back inside, she heard some grunting from Orla.

'What the hell sort of brandy was that?' she groaned, easing herself up and clutching her head.

'The usual kind,' Tess replied. 'We just drank far too much of it.'

'Where are the Alka-Seltzers?'

Tess poured Orla a glass of water, and handed it to her along with a couple of tablets.

'It wouldn't have been so bad if we'd had a romantic evening with a couple of fabulous blokes,' Orla muttered as she watched the bubbles fizzing up through the water. 'Instead of boring old Ed.'

'Well, he was very gallant taking us up to dance like that,' Tess said. 'He's a nice guy and, my word, can he dance!'

'Amazing, that,' Orla mumbled, gulping her drink. 'Couldn't you manage to fancy him a bit?'

'No,' Tess replied. 'Could you?'

'Nope. What are we doing today?'

'Well, I think we should be arriving in Santorini about now. According to the booklet there's a very good winery tour.'

Orla grimaced. 'No way! I'm not touching a drop of *anything* today!'

'I'll believe that when I see it,' said Tess. 'Shall I ask Spyros to get us some coffee?'

'I can't let him see me like this,' Orla said, heading for the bathroom. 'You deal with it.'

'I'll take that as a yes,' Tess said, pressing the button.

*

An hour later they docked in Santorini, where there were buses to take them anywhere they wanted to go on the island and a shuttle service going to and from the boat every hour. Feeling marginally better after their coffees, Tess and Orla decided they could cope with sitting on a bus, but not much else. They nodded at everyone they recognised as they boarded, and Tess was relieved to see Barry had finally emerged from his cabin.

'Have you been feeling rough?' Tess asked him, looking into his thin, pale face.

'Oh, just a bit, but I'm feeling OK now, thanks,' he replied.

Tess felt sorry for him. The sea had been smooth ever since they'd set off from Piraeus, so it couldn't have been seasickness, surely? She still didn't feel she should pursue the subject though.

'I'm afraid I didn't see much of Mykonos,' he said sadly. 'But I know a little bit about Santorini. Do you see how rugged the landscape is? That's because this island was devastated by a volcanic eruption around 1600 BC. And the main towns are Fira and Oia, which are perched on the cliff edges, or so I've read.'

He was right. Both towns appeared to be clinging to the cliffs overlooking the incredibly blue sea. Again, the streets were narrow and crowded with tourists, with the usual quota of gift shops and restaurants. And again Tess was enchanted by the whitewashed houses with their blue shutters and doors, the pots of geraniums and the spectacular sea views. She would always remember this trip in shades of blue and white: the blue of the sea, the white of the buildings, the white and blue of the boat, the white and blue decor of their cabin, and even the Greek flag! Plus, of course, the relentless heat of the sun, which gave these islands their sunbaked, bronzed background scenery.

There was time to have some lunch before they had to think about exploring further, and then finding the bus to take them back to the boat. Having only had coffee and fruit for breakfast, and now feeling almost normal again after the excesses of the previous evening, Tess said, 'I'm beginning to feel hungry.'

'Hmm,' said Orla. 'I suppose I could manage something.'

They'd been browsing in a ceramics shop and Tess had bought a plate with which to decorate her kitchen wall, adding to the collection already there. As they came out onto the street, Tess spotted Barry gazing into the window of the shop opposite.

'I think we should ask him to join us for lunch,' she said. 'Poor wee soul.'

Orla shrugged. 'He looks like he could do with a decent meal.'

He jumped as Tess tapped him on the shoulder.

'Didn't mean to scare you, Barry, but would you like to join us for something to eat?'

Barry looked confused for a moment. 'That's kind of you,' he said, 'but I don't eat very much.'

'You need to eat something,' Tess said to him. 'Come on, we'll find a morsel to tempt you.'

It was cool and quite dark inside their chosen taverna, where the menu was chalked up on an enormous board attached to the wall, featuring some interesting spellings such as 'God's Roe Paste' and 'Lamb and Fate Kebabs'.

'I'm hoping not to meet my fate just yet,' said Orla, 'but assuming it's feta, that'll do me.'

Tess settled for courgettes stuffed with egg and lemon sauce, while Barry looked bewildered. Eventually he was persuaded to try some stuffed vine leaves and, while he waited, he fiddled about with a bread roll but ate very little of it.

'Do you have some tummy trouble then, Barry?' Orla asked, picking up the carafe of red wine which was already positioned on the table, and pouring out three glasses.

'I seem to remember, about five hours ago you said were never going to drink again,' Tess murmured, consulting her watch.

Orla ignored her.

'Yes, I have some tummy trouble,' Barry admitted. 'Bit of a nuisance really.'

He ate only about half of the vine leaves and drank a few sips of wine, but said no more on the subject. Seeing that he was unlikely to be forthcoming about his lack of appetite, Tess changed the subject.

'Have you known Alan long?' she asked.

'We were in the same sports club together,' Barry replied. 'We both played football and we got friendly, mainly because we both supported Liverpool. The football team. I come from Liverpool originally, you see.'

'Are you married, Barry?' Orla asked.

'My wife died eight years ago,' Barry replied. 'And I still miss her. Her name was Heather.' He turned to Tess. 'She was Scottish, like you.'

'And are you hoping to meet someone else?' Tess asked.

'Not now.' He looked sad for a moment. 'Alan is, though. I came along to keep him company really, and I've always wanted to see the Greek islands. It's on my bucket list.'

'Well, hope you're not planning on kicking the bucket any time soon,' Orla said cheerfully.

'It wasn't in my plan,' Barry said quietly, pushing the vine leaves round his plate.

Tess was intrigued but decided to pursue the subject no further. She watched as he filled up his glass with water, withdrew a small box from his pocket, emptied several pills into the palm of his hand, and then proceeded to swallow them one by one. Tess didn't want to stare but, out of the corner of her eye, she reckoned he must have taken at least five. She shook her head at Orla, who, she could see, was about to ask him something.

There was a short silence before Tess said, 'Shall we get the bill?'

They'd done very little walking, but she'd seen an attractive church at the top of the hill which she'd planned to visit before they left. But Tess's dream of walking quickly faded as she realised Barry was having difficulty keeping up. He was obviously unwell, and she planned to quiz Alan about him whenever she had an opportunity.

The church was, of course, white, with a rounded red-tiled roof topped with a gold cross. Inside Tess was relieved to find it cool and dark, with an abundance of gold detail everywhere.

'Not a lot different to the Catholic Church,' Orla observed, as she studied the paintings of saints and the icons, all embellished with gold.

'It's similar. In fact, the Greek Orthodox Church is one of the oldest institutions in the world, founded by St Andrew, the apostle.' Barry had come into his own again. 'But, Orla, it's governed by bishops, not the Pope, and was in communion with Constantinople, as opposed to Rome.'

'Gosh, Barry!' Orla looked impressed. 'Is there anything you *don't* know?'

'And don't forget,' Barry added, 'that the New Testament was written in Greek.'

'Are you interested in religion then, Barry?' Tess asked, as they walked slowly back down the hill.

Barry shrugged. 'Not especially. I just like history. I read a lot, you see.'

'If you feel up to it,' Tess said, 'you must try to come sightseeing with us in Rhodes and Crete. You have so much knowledge up your sleeve, and we'd love to have you with us!'

Barry went noticeably pink but didn't reply.

They found the shuttle bus in the town centre and, as they boarded, he said, 'Thanks for letting me join you, girls.' He sat down across the aisle from them.

As the bus filled up and it trundled its way back to the harbour, Orla murmured, 'That guy is not at all well.'

Tess nodded. 'He swallowed five pills in the taverna.'

'Six,' Orla corrected. 'I counted. He took six.'

'But obviously he doesn't want to talk about it, so don't go quizzing him, Orla.'

'Changing the subject,' Orla said, 'there's still time to do that winery tour.'

'No,' said Tess. 'Much as I love wine, I don't feel like tasting any more at the moment. But you go if you want to.'

Orla considered for a moment. 'Would you mind? I'll stay on the bus and go back to the town.'

'Of course I don't mind you going but I've had enough for today, particularly after last night.'

As she spoke, Tess realised how much she'd relish some time on her own, to sit quietly and gaze at the scenery. Daydreaming time. When you live on your own, she thought, you get used to having time to daydream, reminiscing about the past and wondering about the future.

Having waved goodbye to the other two, Tess headed back to her cabin on the boat, got into her new pink swimsuit, and stretched out on the sun lounger on the balcony. She thought about poor Barry for a few minutes. Then she thought about Amber and the dress she was making for her, and wondered if she'd manage not to cry at the wedding; better remember to get some waterproof mascara. She also thought about how hopeless it was to try to meet someone within a specified time limit. Of course she wasn't going to meet the love of her life in the next month! What had she been thinking of? These things only happened when you least expected them to, when you weren't even *looking* for love, and sometimes when you didn't even *want* to meet someone. It was the main reason marriages broke up, including hers.

Nevertheless, she'd plod on with the MMM dates, if only so she could claim her £150 back and forget the whole thing. And anyway, what was wrong with going to a wedding on your own? As long as she felt good and looked good, what did it matter?

Feeling completely relaxed, Tess drifted off to sleep.

She woke up to the sound of Orla letting the door slam as she came back into the cabin.

'Oh, there you are!' she exclaimed, as she spotted Tess on the balcony. 'You missed a good tour. Lovely wines.' She hiccupped. 'I haven't seen that swimsuit before, have I?'

Tess yawned and glanced at her watch. She'd been asleep for nearly two hours.

'No, you haven't,' she said. 'I wasn't sure whether to wear this or the emerald green. Black swimsuits are so passé, are they not?'

'Hmm. I think I need to lie down,' Orla said, stripping off. 'Otherwise I won't make it through the evening.'

'And I need some exercise,' Tess said as she headed towards the bathroom. 'I think I'll go for a little jog round a bit of the promenade deck.' She'd brought some shorts along, purely for the exercising that she wasn't doing. As she slipped them on, she was glad to see that her legs were tanning nicely, which hid some of the cellulite. Anyway, what did it matter? Was *anyone* looking? Did anyone *care*? And, as she was now resigned to *not* meeting a prospective suitor on this cruise, she might as well concentrate on the facilities on offer. In her T-shirt, shorts and flip-flops, she made her way to the promenade deck. When she got there she realised it would be foolish to try to run in flip-flops. It seemed like a good way to break her neck. Just as she was pondering the matter, a voice behind her said, 'It's Tess of Milbury marathon fame, or do my eyes deceive me?'

She swung round and came face to face with Wally.

'I *thought* it was you I saw running around,' she said, noting his well-developed hairless chest and impressive biceps, none of which she'd been aware of when he was fully clothed.

True to form, he cast a disapproving look at her feet. 'Where are the trainers?' he asked.

'In my cupboard at home,' Tess replied. 'I wasn't planning on any marathons.'

'Tut, tut!' He shook his head in exasperation. 'After all I taught you! Well, take those ridiculous things off, because you can't run in them.'

'Who said anything about running?' Tess asked, knowing she sounded a little petulant.

'I just did. You're going to need to work all these Greek calories off, aren't you? Isn't it you who's going to a wedding or something?'

Damn the man! She'd only planned a gentle jog and some brisk walking, and she recalled him being a hard taskmaster.

'Don't you worry about me,' she said.

'I only worry you'll break your neck. Take those damned things off!'

Tess did as she was told.

'Leave them behind that lifeboat stowage thing over there,' he ordered, 'and you can collect them when you get back.'

'Do you mean we're going to run *all* the way round?' Tess reckoned it would be a long run because it was a big ship. 'And I hope there's no sharp bits on these decks.'

'These decks are immaculate. I know because I run round twice a day. Now, flex your insteps and your toes, and off we go!'

Tess realised how out of condition she was after she'd been jogging for only a couple of minutes. That was the trouble with any form of exercise, she thought – you have to keep at it, otherwise you stiffen up.

Wally had to slow down to let her catch up. 'You haven't been running regularly, have you?'

'No,' she gasped, 'I haven't. Now don't start bloody lecturing me!'

'Wouldn't dream of it,' he said.

Tess had had no idea just how large this liner was. She trotted, she walked, she gasped, and she stopped twice to get her breath back. 'I've got a stitch in my side,' she moaned.

'Nonsense!' said Wally. 'It's because you're not holding yourself properly. You need to work on your core. You need to go to the gym.'

'I am *not* going to the gym,' Tess said through gritted teeth. 'Particularly if you're there brandishing a whip.'

They continued trotting, passing groups of people, seeing Santorini for a mere couple of minutes, then sea, sea and more sea. Perspiration was streaming from her hairline into her eyes, dripping between her breasts and trickling down her back. She didn't think she could walk another step, far less jog or run. Wally ran on for several yards before he realised she was no longer with him. He stopped and looked back at Tess, who was clutching the rail and trying to get her breath.

'You giving up already?' he asked, grinning.

'This,' Tess gasped, 'is one enormous ship, and I have just run right the way round it for the first and last time. I am not going one step further. My sandals are just over there.'

'Nonsense! You should be doing this every day. Although it would be more comfortable when it cools down a little. Fancy a drink?'

Tess hobbled over to where she'd hidden her flip-flops and slid her feet into them. 'I'm a mess,' she moaned. 'I can't go anywhere like this.'

'Of course you can! Everyone's hot and sweaty at this time of day. C'mon, I know where there's a nice little open-air bar, just round the corner.'

'I'm not sure I can walk another step!'

'Just think of a lovely ice-cold beer,' he coaxed.

She tottered along and sat down with relief under a yellow sunshade at a small white table, while Wally went to the counter. They were the only customers. When he returned with two beers he sat down opposite her, clinked glasses and asked, 'Are you here on your own?'

'No,' Tess replied, taking a gulp and then holding the cold glass against her hot face. 'I'm with my friend, Orla. How about you?'

'I'm with my mate, Greg. We're in the same sports club at home.'

'So where's Greg?'

'Weightlifting at the moment.'

'Don't either of you ever *stop*?'

Wally laughed. 'Occasionally. We're taking part in a darts match this evening in the Seagull bar. Fancy coming along?'

'Not really,' Tess said, 'but nice of you to ask.' She had visions of a group of men swilling beer and aiming at a darts board, probably followed by a vegan meal.

'So what do you do in the evenings then?' he asked.

'We eat, drink, talk, listen to music, dance occasionally,' Tess replied.

'All the more reason why you should do some exercise to keep in shape.'

Tess drained her glass. 'I'll keep it in mind. Thanks for the beer. Right now I'm off for a shower.'

No doubt about it, Wally had set her off on the right track, but now she was doing things her way. And it seemed to be working out pretty well so far.

'Ah well,' Wally said, 'see you around.'

CHAPTER SEVENTEEN

RHODES

Orla was still asleep and snoring when Tess limped into the cabin. She stared in horror at her sticky, sweaty reflection in the bathroom mirror. She desperately needed a shower. And after that she'd have a luxurious soak in a scented bath to ease her aches and pains.

As she stood under the gushing hot water, Tess decided she would have a run round the promenade deck *every* evening, but at her own pace. Wally was right – she did need to burn the calories off – but she'd wait until it was cooler and, in the absence of trainers, would continue to do so barefoot.

After she'd showered, she ran a bath and squeezed in the sachet of White Rose Beauty Bath, which had been displayed on the shelf, then lay back in the scented bubbles and relaxed. She'd almost fallen asleep when Orla staggered in, bleary-eyed.

'I wondered what all the splashing was about,' she said. 'Sorry to disturb you, but I need a pee.'

'Be my guest,' Tess said, waving an arm in the air. 'What's the plan for tonight?'

'I thought,' said Orla, flushing the toilet, 'we might try the Italian. And would you mind if Ed came with us?'

'Of course not,' Tess replied. 'But I seem to remember you considered him to be boring.'

'He's not so bad when you get to know him,' Orla said.

Tess wondered for a moment if that lovely doctor might frequent the Italian restaurant. She hadn't seen him around anywhere else. No, probably best to forget him; leave him to Lavinia. 'Do you fancy him then? Ed, I mean?'

'No, of course I don't *fancy* him,' Orla said, 'but he's a nice guy. And, let's face it, there aren't many fanciable guys around, apart from all the lovely Greek waiters and bartenders.'

'Well, you don't want to be done for cradle-snatching, do you?' Tess asked, as she got out of the bath and draped herself in one of the large fluffy white towels.

Orla snorted. 'I'm almost ready to risk it. Stay out here, do a Shirley Valentine!'

'Have you forgotten the sainted Ricky so soon?'

'It would do him good to have a bit of competition,' Orla replied. 'Have him come out here looking for me. In the meantime there's Ed.' She yawned. 'Right, my turn for the shower.'

An hour later, bathed and beautified, Tess and Orla made their way up to the top deck bar, where Ed was sitting in a solitary state at a white wrought-iron table, his camera on his knee, with a bottle of Prosecco in an ice bucket and three glasses. He was looking quite jaunty in a short-sleeved purple shirt and cream jeans.

'My word, you two look very stylish!' Ed exclaimed, standing up.

Tess had chosen a white shirt with dark blue straight ankle-length trousers, and Orla was wearing a turquoise shift.

'You don't look so bad yourself,' Orla remarked.

'Then shall we three beauties have some fizz? Sorry it's not Bollinger or anything, but this is a really nice Prosecco.' With that Ed filled up the three glasses. Then, picking up his own, he said, 'Chin-chin!'

'Salute!' said Tess, doing the same.

Orla took a gulp. 'Ooh, that's nice!'

There were bowls of various coloured olives on the table, along with a little dish in which to deposit the stones. They discussed the day's events and sightseeing. Ed had hired a moped and got round a large chunk of the island where, at one point, he'd come across the group of over-eighties avidly making notes at some archaeological dig, while being lectured to by an attractive young Greek lady. 'All I could hear,' Ed said, 'was her telling them that, when they got home, they should campaign to have the Elgin Marbles returned to Greece.'

The bar was rapidly filling up with passengers, their skins varying in colour from bright pink to scarlet to bronze. Tess was glad she'd plastered herself with factor thirty while they were sightseeing, and she was acquiring a good tan.

Ed was refilling the glasses yet again, and thought they should have another bottle. And some Aperol, perhaps? Tess knew that, although Aperol was very low in alcohol, when mixed with Prosecco it was only too easy to gulp it down like lemonade. She really had to pace herself, particularly after overdoing it last night.

'Mmm, nice!' Orla said, glugging it down.

'Go easy!' said Tess. 'You've been drinking wine all afternoon!'

'Only for research,' Orla said, grinning. 'You have to show some appreciation when they tell you about the various types of grape and then take the trouble to explain how each wine matures. It would be rude not to have a few slurps.'

'And then you spat it out, of course?' Ed asked, raising an eyebrow.

'Are you *kidding*?'

'Time to eat,' said Tess.

The Trattoria Aegeana had candles and tablecloths, plus baskets with rolls and breadsticks on each table, along with dainty dishes of olive oil and balsamic vinegar for dipping. It also had Graziano, who waxed lyrical about every dish on the menu. 'Everything come from Italy,' he informed them proudly and then, curling his lip, added, 'No kebabs, no feta, no terrible Greek wine!'

Tess chose Neapolitan veal cutlets with mascarpone, and the other two opted for artichoke and olive spaghetti, accompanied by a very good Chianti. It was delicious. Then Tess averted her eyes while Orla tackled her *zabaglione* and Ed devoured a generous slice of Sicilian cheesecake. But she couldn't resist the amaretti biscuit that came with her espresso.

'Fancy the cabaret?' Ed asked, wiping his mouth with the large napkin.

'Oh, most definitely,' said Orla. 'Do you think it'll be any good?'

'Well,' said Ed, 'there's only one way to find out.' He tapped his camera. 'Should get a few shots.'

It was as the three were leaving the restaurant that Tess saw Sanjeev heading towards them with two other men. But no Lavinia. When he saw her, Sanjeev excused himself from his companions and walked straight up to her. He touched her arm.

'Tess!' he said. 'I was hoping to see you and to apologise for deserting you so abruptly the other evening.'

'Oh, no problem!' Tess said. Oh Lord, he really was a good-looking man. And he'd remembered her name!

'These gentlemen are colleagues.' He indicated the two men who were standing waiting. 'We're just about to have dinner, but hopefully you and I can catch up soon.'

'I hope so too,' Tess said. 'We're going to the cabaret now.'

'Not sure I'll make that tonight, but I'll be sure to look out for you.' He squeezed her hand, gave her a dazzling smile and a little wave, and then he was gone.

'Who was *that*?' Orla, who'd been standing back with Ed, asked.

'His name is Sanjeev,' Tess replied. 'And he's a doctor. An oncologist. I met him briefly a couple of nights ago at the bar.'

'Wow!' said Orla. 'Great-looking, great profession, great escort to Amber's wedding – problem solved!'

'Don't be daft!' Tess hoped she wasn't blushing. 'I hardly know him.'

'Well, hang in there, Tess!'

Ed had stopped further along the corridor to chat to Peggy, the leader of the Sheffield four. Tonight Peggy was wearing a backless top, displaying a large blue dragon tattooed across her shoulder blades. She and the girls were going to the cabaret too; they were all in the loo at the moment, doing up their hair 'and all that'. Peggy's hair was starched into spikes and Tess wondered if she'd ever before seen such long false eyelashes; she looked as if she had a spider dangling from each eyelid.

In fact, the cabaret was better than expected. As they sipped Mediterranean Martinis – which consisted of raki, sweet vermouth and drops of orange bitters, she was informed – Tess was mesmerised by a group of Greek males, just like Il Divo at home, singing in perfect harmony. Their rendition of 'Nessun Dorma' brought a tear to her eye. They were followed by some acrobatic Ukrainian dancers, and then an ageing English pop singer named Riff Pritchard, who warbled his way through 'The Young Ones' and 'True Love Ways'. During the entertainment, Tess noticed Ed's arm snaking its way round the back of Orla's chair. Did he fancy her? Did she fancy *him*? Tess was intrigued. She had given up on the cocktails and was now sipping a low-calorie ginger ale, but these two were still knocking them back and God only knew what that might lead to. Tess didn't plan to wait around to find out. It was already late and tomorrow they would be in Rhodes, probably the most interesting of the Dodecanese islands.

The entertainment over, Orla and Ed got up to dance and Tess slid quietly away.

When she woke next morning, Tess was aware that she was on her own in the cabin. So, where was Orla? She lay still for a few minutes and pondered the likeliest situation: Orla and Ed! It had to be! Then Tess began to worry. What if Orla wasn't with Ed? What if she'd been accosted on her way back to the cabin? Surely that wouldn't happen on a boat full of mostly middle-class middle-aged people. Should she worry? No, she shouldn't. Orla wasn't exactly in her first flush of youth, and had hopefully retained a few grains of common sense. She was a mother, a grandmother, a businesswoman, a respected member of the community, and she was free to do exactly as she pleased. And she usually did just that.

Tess washed, dressed, and was just about to buzz for Spyros to ask for some coffee and rolls when the door opened and in walked Orla, still in last night's clothes, make-up smudged and hair uncombed.

'Morning!' Orla said cheerfully. 'You ordered any coffee yet?'

Tess looked at her in bewilderment. 'Where the hell have you been?'

'I'll give you three guesses but I'll bet you'll think the worst. I fell asleep on his bed, because I was knackered, but we didn't *do* anything,' said Orla, heading for the bathroom. 'Can't have Spyros seeing me like this.'

'So you've been with Ed? Presumably he's got his own cabin?'

'Yes, of course he's got his own cabin.' Orla applied liberal amounts of make-up remover in front of the mirror.

'I didn't think you fancied him,' Tess said.

'I don't. I told you, nothing happened, but I thought there was no harm in a kiss and a cuddle, if only I could have kept awake. He was still fast asleep and snoring on top of the bed when I left. But hey, he's a nice guy.' Orla continued wiping off her make-up. 'No problemo, Tess! You weren't worried, were you?'

Tess sighed. 'I should know better than to worry about you. But Ed's quite a character.'

'Yes,' said Orla, 'he is. But my heart belongs to Ricky, and anyway Ed lives up in Newcastle.'

'I suppose,' Tess said, suppressing a giggle, 'you could always get Ricky to drop you off there on his travels?'

'Ha ha, very amusing. So, are we savouring the delights of Rhodes today?'

'Doesn't Ed want you all to himself?'

'Don't be daft! We're not *teenagers*. We'll go as a threesome, unless you want to ask Barry?'

'Yes, I would like to ask Barry,' Tess replied. 'He's such a nice wee soul and so informative.'

Orla yawned. 'We thought a day on the beach might be nice. Apparently there are some great beaches on Rhodes.'

'There's also an awful lot of interesting history in Rhodes, you know. So I'd like to see some of that first. That's where Barry comes in.'

'We might even be able to persuade Alan to get off his arse and come with us too,' Orla suggested. Tess thought this was extremely unlikely. But she did wonder if the lovely doctor might be making some excursions too. She still couldn't work out if he was an MMM member or not, although it seemed more likely he was part of the medical group, or whatever they were. Surely, by the law of averages, they'd run into each other again before they got back to Piraeus?

She decided to wear her wraparound cotton skirt, because she could always let her legs emerge to sunbathe, and a camisole top. She'd got to get the tan going as well as the exercise. She noticed there was more material to wrap around than usual, which was good. She was surely losing weight. Greatly cheered, she agreed with Orla when she suggested they meet up with Ed in the breakfast bar. And there was Ed, reading a three-day-old *Daily Mail* that he said he'd found abandoned by the pool when they left Santorini.

'Hi!' He gave Orla a wink. 'Ready for breakfast?'

There was an extensive selection of cereals, fruits, cold meats, cheese, bread and pastries on offer. As Tess made her choice she spotted Alan, his pink chest bedecked with chains, sitting with

Peggy and her gang. As she left the buffet he looked up, waved and said, 'Hiya! Coming to join us?'

'Thanks,' Tess said, 'but I'm with Orla. Just wondered though if I could have the number of your cabin, Alan, so I can ask Barry if he wants to join us to have a look round the island? That's if he feels up to it.'

Alan gave her the number and directions to deck seven.

'He'd like that,' he said. 'And I think he's feeling OK today.'

Tess would have liked to ask him about Barry's health, but it didn't seem like an opportune moment with four pairs of female eyes scrutinising her. When they'd finished their breakfast, she set off to find Barry, wondering if he'd eaten anything yet. She eventually located the cabin, and he opened the door clutching a banana.

'Just wondered if you'd like to come to explore Rhodes with us, Barry?' Tess said. 'If you've had breakfast?'

'That's very kind,' Barry replied, chucking the banana skin into the waste bin, 'and yes, I have had breakfast.' He was wearing navy knee-length shorts and a plain grey T-shirt. 'I'll just find my sandals.'

Tess noticed a tiny breakfast tray with half a glass of orange juice and half a roll still remaining. And, while Barry was searching around for his sandals, she noticed the pill dispenser on his bedside table. It was one of the type that had separate compartments for pills to take morning, noon and night, all counted out and, as far as Tess could see, for the week. There were numerous pills of every colour and shape in each compartment. Then, when he finally found his sandals, he produced the little pill box and, with his back to her, filled it up with what was presumably his lunchtime quota and slipped it into the pocket of his shorts. Donning some sunglasses, he said, 'Ready?'

They joined Orla and Ed in the coffee shop, where Tess introduced Barry to Ed. 'Barry's great on history,' she informed Ed. 'And Rhodes has plenty of that, I'm told.'

'Not too many old ruins, I hope,' said Orla, draining her coffee. 'I fancy the beach a bit later on.'

They set off together, heading to the city of Rhodes where, in the Old Town, Barry led them into the medieval Street of the Knights which, he explained, referred to the Knights of St John during the Crusades. Then he directed them towards a castle-like building which he told them was the Palace of the Grand Master, once captured by the Ottomans and later held by the Italians, and which was now a history museum. Barry said he'd explore the museum later, or tomorrow, since they were here for two days. When it came to history, all of them were interested in where the famous Colossus of Rhodes had once been. This was the enormous statue of the sun god Helios, one of the Seven Wonders of the Ancient World, Barry explained, as he shepherded them to the area where it had reputedly stood at the harbour.

'It was said to be thirty-three metres high,' he informed them, 'and made of bronze but reinforced with iron.'

They all stared in awe, trying to imagine how it might once have looked.

'Didn't I read that it straddled the entrance to the harbour?' Ed asked.

'Technically impossible,' retorted Barry. 'Then it was toppled by an earthquake somewhere around 225 BC. And later, when

Arabian forces raided Rhodes, they broke up the statue and sold the bronze for scrap.'

'I must buy a guidebook,' Ed said. 'I'd like to read about all this.'

'And you can't come to Rhodes without seeing the acropolis and the Temple of Apollo,' Barry continued, studying his map.

'Why don't we take a taxi?' Ed suggested. 'We can have a look at your temple and then the driver can take us on to the beach.'

They all agreed this was a good idea. The Temple of Apollo was situated on the western edge of the city and on the top of a hill. The taxi driver agreed to wait while they walked round the columns and ruins of the ancient temple. By this time they'd all had enough history, and Barry looked even more exhausted than usual.

'Come to the beach with us,' Tess implored. 'You can look at your museum later. We need to find some lunch and relax in the sun.'

The beach, obviously popular, had a busy restaurant, with sunbeds and sunshades for hire.

'I'm ravenous,' said Ed.

'Me too,' said Orla.

'Are *you* hungry?' Tess asked Barry quietly.

He smiled ruefully. 'Not very. I could probably manage a sandwich and I could murder a beer.'

Barry asked for a cheese and tomato sandwich while the others had kebabs and Greek salads.

'Hope we've all got our swimming cossies,' said Ed as he tackled his kebab, juice running down his chin.

'I'm wearing my *bikini* under this,' said Orla, casting a glance at Tess, who rolled her eyes.

'I've got my costume with me,' she said, patting her tote bag, which contained her other brand-new one-piece, the emerald green. 'What about you, Barry?'

'Yeah, I'm wearing trunks underneath,' he said. He nibbled half his sandwich and drank about half of his beer, saving the other half, Tess guessed correctly, with which to swallow his pills. Again Barry brought out his little box and proceeded to swallow them one by one. Ed stared but said nothing.

They paid for sunbeds and sunshades to get as close to the water's edge as possible, bearing in mind that Ed, if removing the prosthetic, would have to either hop or crawl into the water. Orla was wearing her pale blue bikini which, in Tess's opinion, should have been passed on to the charity shop years ago. Her boobs and her belly bulged precariously over the cotton fabric, which was stretched to breaking point. Tess wore the emerald green and, for the first time in years, felt she looked good.

'I haven't seen *that* one before either,' Orla remarked. 'Glad you finally ditched that old black number. Now I fancy a dip.'

'I can only hop so far,' said Ed, surveying the sea. 'I'll need a bit of support.' He glanced at Orla.

Meanwhile, Barry had removed his shirt to display his neat, hairless chest. Tess was horrified to see the zigzag of scars across his front. While she was trying to decide whether to ask him any questions or not, Orla said, 'Jaysus, Barry! You've been through the wars!'

Barry smiled. 'We all have to fight our demons,' he said, as he lay down on his sunbed. Orla caught Tess's eye and shrugged. Barry was not about to give out any information.

What disturbed Tess was that some of these scars were clearly recent. Her knowledge of anatomy was not good and she couldn't decide whether these cuts had been made to access his stomach, his intestines or what. No more was said because Ed had stripped off to reveal his prosthetic leg, causing much interest all around. The leg had been amputated just below the knee. 'I suppose I should have brought my crutch,' he said, waving the leg in the air, 'but I'd have had to leave it on the beach and, to be honest, I just didn't think about it.' As always, Ed's humour saved the day. 'OK,' he said. 'Maybe I've lost a bit of myself, but most people lose bits and pieces in a lifetime. What about you two girls?'

'Only my tonsils,' said Orla. 'Where I come from in Limerick, the first time you had a sore throat they yanked out your tonsils.'

Tess thought for a moment. 'The first ever thing that was removed from me,' she said, 'was Matt, my son, who flatly refused to come into the world in the normal way. So I had to have a caesarean, otherwise he'd probably be in there yet. However, since then I've had a hysterectomy and a chunk out of my left breast.'

'Sure nobody's perfect!' said Orla.

Barry appeared to have relaxed a little. But he didn't add much to the general chat. When Orla helped Ed hop into the water, Barry turned to Tess and asked, 'You OK now?'

'So far so good,' Tess replied. 'I hope I stay clear, but with this bloody disease you never quite know. What about you?'

Barry sighed. 'Not so good. They can't do much more; it's gone all over the place.'

Tess tried not to show her horror. 'Oh, Barry!' she said, and leaned across to squeeze his hand. 'I'm so sorry.'

'I'm OK,' he said with a grin. 'The pills do their job.'

'It's a bugger, isn't it?' Tess said sadly.

'Couldn't have put it better myself!'

Tess looked across at the sparkling sea, where Ed had made it into the water and was splashing Orla. She continued to watch as he dived into the waves and swam strongly out to sea, Orla laughing and following in his wake.

'It's why I wanted to make this trip,' Barry went on. 'I've always wanted to see the Dodecanese. I'm not here to meet anyone, but when Alan said he was coming on this cruise, it just seemed like a golden opportunity. Alan's very kind, you know.'

'I'm sure he is,' Tess said, thinking guiltily of how she'd giggled at his chains and his medallions.

'He's been great,' Barry went on. 'Even got up in the middle of the night a couple of times to get me stuff. I really hope he meets someone nice on this trip.'

Tess wondered for a moment how he was getting on with Peggy and her dragon-tattooed shoulder blades. There I go again, she thought, all too keen to judge books by their covers. She glanced at Barry, who was now lying on his side and appeared to be asleep. Talking to him, and being impressed by Ed's positivity, helped to put everything into perspective. What did it matter if she went to Amber's wedding on her own or not? What was important was the here and now, to have all her limbs, good health, good family and good friends. She was a lucky woman and to wish for more was pure greed.

Tess had dozed off and only woke when Orla returned, followed by Ed on all fours. 'Still got a knee, so might as well use it!' he said cheerfully. 'It's got me quite an audience though!' Several children had followed him, saucer-eyed, from the water.

'It was either that or a three-legged race,' Orla said, laughing, as Ed brushed the sand from his knees.

Barry appeared to still be asleep, so Tess decided to have a short swim on her own. The heat was fierce, even beneath the sunshade, and she felt uncomfortably hot and sticky and desperate to plunge into the cool of the water. She paddled close to shore, surrounded mainly by locals smiling and splashing. The Greeks were a friendly bunch. The *White Rose* was not sailing on to Crete until the following afternoon, and Tess looked forward to an evening here in Rhodes instead of on board. You couldn't fault the boat – it was beautiful and offered every facility – but it wasn't the real Greece. When she went back to join the others, they were discussing exactly that.

'I just fancy sitting outside somewhere,' Orla was saying, 'in one of the squares with all the bars and tavernas, just to eat, drink and watch the world go by. It must be magic by night.'

'I couldn't agree more,' said Tess.

'That's exactly what we'll do then,' said Ed.

'Shall we ask Barry if he'd like to join us?' Tess suggested. She looked across at Barry. 'We should wake him up – he shouldn't be sleeping in the sun like that.' She shook him gently, and he slowly came round, sat up and looked a little bewildered. 'Are you OK, Barry?'

'Yes. I'm fine,' he said, 'but drenched with sweat. I think I'll have a quick dip.'

As he headed towards the water, Orla said, 'He's such a nice inoffensive guy, but what about all those awful scars?'

'Yes, he is nice,' Tess agreed. She decided to say nothing of the conversation she'd had with him earlier. If he wanted them all to know about his problem then he'd tell them himself.

As he emerged from the sea, Barry looked happier than Tess had ever seen him before.

'That beats Scarborough any day of the week,' he said as he towelled himself dry. 'You need to be pretty hardy to brave the North Sea without a wetsuit.'

'That's for sure,' Tess agreed, thinking of North Berwick.

As they gathered up their belongings, Ed turned to his audience of local children, who had reappeared as he began to put on his prosthetic leg. The biggest boy spoke some English. 'You swim OK?' he asked.

'Oh yes,' said Ed, 'of course I can.'

'And he can dance,' Orla added.

'And do lots of things, including chasing away little boys!' Ed got to his feet and pretended to run after them, which caused many screams of laughter as they all ran off.

As they headed back towards the boat, Tess noticed for the first time that Ed was limping slightly.

Back in their cabin, Tess and Orla compared tans. They both had freckly skin, but nevertheless had acquired a good colour. Orla patted her tummy. 'There's one place *you* won't get bronzed,' she said to Tess. 'You and your one-pieces. Mind you, that green number's quite nice – so much better than that dreary black thing you used to wear.'

Tess pirouetted in front of the mirror. 'I've no intention of baring my middle,' she said, pleased with her silhouette and with Orla's comments.

'But I have to say you look nice and slim,' Orla added.

This was again music to Tess's ears, since Orla was not forthcoming with her compliments.

'I'm going for my run now,' Tess said, 'since I want to stay that way.'

'At least until after the wedding,' Orla said, grinning.

'Oh, definitely until after the wedding!' Tess agreed.

She ran round the promenade deck for about twenty minutes but there was no sign of Wally, only some regular runners and walkers that she'd already begun to recognise, as they acknowledged each other with a cheery wave. As she ran she realised that this wasn't just for the wedding, but for herself, because she enjoyed feeling slimmer and fitter. And she intended to do her best to keep it up.

Barry opted out of the evening, admitting he was exhausted after his day on the island and he wanted to conserve his energy for visiting the museum the following morning.

It was dark when the three of them returned to Rhodes and located a square they'd earmarked earlier with its bars and tavernas, lamps glowing at regular intervals, and candles lit on all the tables. It was already packed with tourists talking, laughing and sipping their aperitifs, and somewhere in the background was the sound of the inevitable bouzoukis.

Later, while they were eating, a group of singers, strumming guitars, strolled from table to table. Tess enjoyed people watching, but didn't at first recognise anyone else from the *White Rose*. Then, a couple of tables away, she spotted a vaguely familiar-looking cool blonde. Lavinia? She was almost certain it was Lavinia, but she wasn't with Sanjeev tonight. She was with two prosperous-looking elderly men. So, where was Sanjeev? And did this mean that Lavinia and Sanjeev weren't *an item*, as Orla would say? Not that it would do Tess much good, considering how rarely their paths crossed. Anyway, she'd already decided that she didn't need a man. She relaxed, enjoyed her wine, ate her red mullet grilled in vine leaves, listened to the music and chatter all around, and decided that life was pretty good.

The following morning, Tess and Orla decided to explore the local shops in Rhodes. Tess needed to buy a little souvenir for Ellie, and perhaps a piece of pottery or something for Amber. Then again, what would Amber do with a piece of pottery in that monastic, minimalist flat she shared with Peter? Better to buy some miniature bottles of local liqueurs for both Amber and Matt, and hope they'd survive the flight home in her suitcase. She found another plate that would look terrific on her kitchen wall and had it bubble-wrapped in the hope that it, too, would survive the flight.

As they pushed their way through the throngs of tourists, Tess wondered what it would be like here in the winter after all the visitors had gone home. It would belong to the locals again, who probably sighed with relief to be on their own once more. She decided she wouldn't mind coming here in the winter and being able to explore everything in peace. And surely the weather would be better than in the UK.

The *White Rose* was sailing at 5 p.m. Tess decided she'd get back to do her run at that time so she could watch the island slipping away as the boat set sail for Crete, their last port of call, where it was scheduled to dock the following morning. She wanted to be up early to see the approach into Heraklion and, more importantly, the former leper colony of Spinalonga as they sailed past. She'd also arranged to meet up with Barry at 9 a.m. to visit the famous Archaeological Museum in Heraklion. It was the best time to visit, Barry assured her, before the crowds got there. She wasn't a history buff like him, but nevertheless she'd read about it in the guidebook and thought it would be well worth a visit. She couldn't understand the Alans and Peggys of this world who never set foot off the boat, but lounged all day by the pool instead.

After her run, Ed suggested a sauna, a massage and an early supper in the Ocean bar. Tess didn't feel much like any of it, and fancied a few precious minutes to herself. So she wandered back to the cabin, where she sat on the balcony and watched the moon weaving silvery patterns on the sea.

CHAPTER EIGHTEEN

CRETE

The *White Rose* sailed past Spinalonga at 7 a.m., and Tess was on deck to gaze at the island where once lepers were banished from their homes and families, never to return. It must have been a desperately sad place, and yet she'd read that the lepers built themselves a community and got on with it. She'd have loved to visit the island, but this cruise was proving to be a mere taster for places she'd like to see in much more detail. She vowed to return. She couldn't work out either why they'd had the best part of two days in Rhodes, but were only scheduled to have one in Crete, which was the largest island and where she'd have liked to spend more time. Ed reckoned that the captain probably hailed from Rhodes and he fancied the extra day with his family. Whatever the reason, if they wanted to see anything of this island, there was no time to waste.

As Spinalonga was left behind, Tess gazed at the White Mountains in the distance and the sprawl of Heraklion ahead, then returned to the cabin for an early breakfast before meeting up with Barry for her daily dose of culture. Orla, in the meantime, was going to have her hair done and would meet Tess for lunch, and to explore the shops.

'I'm having withdrawal symptoms in the absence of any retail therapy,' she moaned.

Tess set off and found Barry looking quite jaunty in a smart red shirt and white shorts. He too had acquired a tan, and was bright-eyed in anticipation of a few hours in his magic world of history.

Sailing into Heraklion, the first thing they saw was the impressive Koules Venetian fortress on the harbour walls, but their initial impression of the city itself was disappointing: dusty, noisy, chaotic, with cars, scooters, trucks, angry drivers and masses of concrete. Of course, it was the rush hour, Tess thought, looking around, but she doubted somehow that she was going to like this place very much. However, the museum did not disappoint. It housed a wealth of Minoan artefacts; the Minoans, Barry informed her, were the first advanced society on European soil some four thousand years ago. There were also classic Hellenic and Roman sculptures, frescoes, jewellery and pottery.

Barry was in heaven. And he'd been absolutely right: by the time they'd got round the greater part of the museum, the hordes of visitors were arriving in force.

As they emerged blinking into the sunshine of the square, Barry announced he was getting a bus to the Palace of Knossos, a Bronze Age settlement about half an hour's drive away. Tess felt some concern at him setting off on his own. 'Will you be all right?' she asked, hoping not to sound too anxious.

'I'm fine,' he said, 'I'll be sitting on a bus most of the time, and I have my phone with me.'

Tess was already regretting that she couldn't go with him, but she'd arranged to meet Orla outside the museum. After all, you could see the shops any old time, but she was gaining a taste for history now. She'd also like to see so much more of this beautiful island, as opposed to just its capital. There simply wasn't time to do everything, and she resolved to come back one day in the not-too-distant future.

She and Barry parted company, and Tess waited for Orla, who was late as usual. When she arrived, Tess said, 'After lunch and the shops I'd like to do some kind of short tour, to see something of the island.'

'OK,' said Orla, 'we'll have a gander round a few shops before lunch, and then we'll do something else this afternoon.'

They gazed at outfits they couldn't afford in the windows of the designer outlets on Daedalon Street and then, purely by chance, found the Zeus international restaurant, flying the flags of every nation and displaying an impressive selection of menus outside.

Tess laughed. 'I've read that Zeus was born in a mountain cave in Crete, but there was no record of him being in catering!'

'Good old Zeus!' said Orla, studying the menus intently. 'And look! We don't have to have anything with lamb or aubergines or bloody vine leaves! Hey, steak and chips, lasagne, curry – have we died and gone to heaven?'

'Don't get too excited,' Tess warned. 'We haven't tasted any of it yet. But I'm willing to give it a go.'

The proprietors had done their best to create a rustic atmosphere, though it was somewhat marred by the roar of traffic outside. But the staff were pleasant, there was wine already on the tables, and a nice garlicky smell permeated the air. Orla settled for the steak and chips which, she later admitted, provided a dental challenge. Tess had a lasagne and salad, which would not have been approved of by any passing Italian, but it was edible. Unfortunately the Greek wine, so generously provided, would be unlikely to have been approved of by anyone. Nevertheless, they needed something to wash it all down.

'There are days,' sighed Orla, 'when I dream of Boulters and our lovely lunches.'

'I'm inclined to agree with you,' said Tess. 'Do you want a second glass of this stuff?'

'Oh, go on then. I suppose it's better than nothing.'

What are we like? Tess wondered to herself as she refilled their glasses. At least it was free.

There wasn't enough time to do a tour of any length, so they opted for the yellow hop-on, hop-off double-decker open-top tour bus, which transported them to the traditional parts of the city. It also took them to the fortress and out as far as Knossos, both of which Tess wanted to explore, but time was limited. She wondered how Barry was faring, but of course there was no sign of him during their brief stop at Knossos. She would be coming again, but it was extremely unlikely that poor Barry would. She'd love to see the mountains with their caves, and the cliffs on the south coast, all of which she'd read about in the brochure. Even without disembarking at any of the tourist spots, they only just made it back to the boat on time.

An hour later, as the liner slowly sailed out of Heraklion, Tess did her final lap of the promenade deck. Tomorrow they would be back in Piraeus and the cruise would be over. As she headed towards the cabin, she espied Alan coming towards her.

'Hi!' he shouted. 'Had a good day?'

'Yes, we did,' Tess replied. 'But did Barry get back OK?'

Alan nodded. 'He did, but the poor guy's completely knackered. Don't think he's feeling too good either.'

'Oh, poor Barry.' He'd obviously overdone it, she thought. 'He did tell me about his problems.'

Alan nodded. 'I was worried about bringing him along, you know. He was given a matter of months a year ago, and he's still with us. But you just never know when…' His voice tailed off.

'I think it's great that he came along, Alan. I know it must be a worry for you, but he's so happy when he's pottering round museums and things.'

Alan grinned. 'Yeah, makes it all worthwhile. He's a really nice bloke and life's dealt him some rotten blows. But I have to admit I'll be glad to get him home. And thanks for inviting him to join yourself and Orla.'

'It really was a pleasure,' Tess said sincerely.

'Well, just on my way to meet up with Peggy,' he said. 'See you around!' And, with a wave, he was off.

As she emerged from the shower soon after, Tess decided tonight was the night to wear the white shift dress she'd brought with her and, at one point, had wondered if she'd ever get into again. She'd bought the dress years ago in Pisa, on a Tuscan holiday with David, back when she'd been reasonably slim.

'That dress is absolutely *you*!' he'd said. 'But you'd better not put any weight on!'

Admittedly it had been a neat fit even then, and she'd never been slim enough to wear it since. She'd even hesitated to bring the dress with her, wondering if she could wear something so closely connected with David without feeling sad. But she was now recovering from that sadness, and he'd surely have approved of both her weight loss and tan, although he'd always insisted he loved her just the way she was. The dress was beautifully cut and a classic shape, but needed the tan to set it off. Tonight's the night, Tess decided.

'Wow!' said Orla as she came out of the shower. 'Don't you look fantastic! What a pity there isn't a half-decent bloke around here to appreciate you! There is that dishy doctor, of course, if you can ever manage to run into him again.'

Tess had been thinking along the same lines, particularly as it was their last night on board. Since she'd hardly set eyes on him all week, it seemed unlikely she'd run into him now. And it was a pity, because the dress fitted better than it ever had. Never mind – she was looking good for *herself*.

Tonight Ed's camera shots were on display in the art gallery. She and Orla headed up there; Orla in a very attractive red dress, Tess feeling better than she had in years. The art gallery had some colourful paintings by Greek artists, which lined the walls. Some of them Tess liked very much, and might have been tempted to buy had they not been flying home with one suitcase per person.

Ed's photos were displayed in a long line down the centre of the gallery, where Ed himself was holding court clad in a pink shirt and blue jeans. He was a talented photographer and had taken some wonderful unposed informal shots of passengers at hilarious moments; and of Greek scenes, old men and local children. There was one of Peggy tripping on the dance floor, several of people pulling faces as they talked, and one, Tess realised with horror, of herself fast asleep on the chair after too many drinks on that first night.

Orla roared with laughter. 'I've seen that old bat somewhere before!'

'I've seen this old bat around too,' said Tess with glee, pointing at a particularly unflattering shot of Orla pulling a funny face.

'Bloody hell!' exclaimed Orla. 'Whenever did he take that? I'll throttle him!'

Then, as Tess turned round, she looked straight into the dark brown eyes of the dishy doctor. God was in his heaven after all!

'Tess!' he said. 'Don't you look lovely!'

Tess was dumbstruck for a brief moment before she was able to say anything. Then she said, 'Thank you, Sanjeev!' She wanted to add that he didn't look too bad himself in his dark blue shirt and white jeans.

'I'm finally free,' Sanjeev said, 'as the lectures are over, and so are the organised meals and sightseeing. It's been interesting, but a little restrictive.' He smiled.

'I hadn't realised you were on some sort of course,' Tess said.

'Well, it wasn't exactly a course, more a series of lectures. Beautiful surroundings, of course, but quite intense. It has certainly improved my knowledge, as some of the professors who were giving the lectures are the best in the world. It was expensive, but worth it. Anyway, enough about me! Have you enjoyed the voyage?'

'I have,' Tess replied. 'So many stunning places, but not enough time in any of them.'

'I couldn't agree more. This was one reason why I've never fancied cruising. I like to get to know a place, to get the feel of it, meet the locals, that sort of thing, and not to be forever moving on. Now, would you like to have a drink?'

'Yes, please,' Tess replied, hoping she didn't sound too eager.

'Have you been up to the Seagull's Nest, next to the White Rose restaurant?'

'No,' Tess replied. 'I haven't yet reached such dizzying heights.'

'Time you did then! Shall we go?'

'Let me just have a quick word with my friend, otherwise she'll wonder where I've got to.'

Tess found Orla standing next to Ed, who was surrounded by admirers asking about cameras and shutter speeds and a barrage of technical questions.

She nudged Orla. 'I'm going with the lovely doctor up to the posh bar next to the White Rose restaurant.'

'Good for you! At last! Enjoy,' Orla said. 'Wish I was coming with you, but Ed's in his element here rabbiting on about his bloody photos. To be honest I don't understand the questions they're asking, far less the answers. See you later – maybe?'

'Some excellent shots,' Sanjeev remarked when she re-joined him. Tess prayed he hadn't come across her less than flattering photo. She relaxed a little as they left the gallery.

The Seagull's Nest was a calm oasis in mainly green and white – as opposed to the blue and white that appeared everywhere else. There were seagulls painted on the walls, and a great deal of foliage.

'What would you like to drink?' Sanjeev asked. 'A cocktail, perhaps?'

Tess had sudden unwelcome memories of Sarasota Sunsets.

'I'm told the Aegean Sunset is very good,' he added.

Another damned sunset! Did she dare? Well, she thought, Sanjeev is not the type of man to be putting me to bed and, even if he were, at least she wasn't wearing her big knickers.

'I'll have an Aegean Sunset then, please.'

Tess sat down on a green chair at a white table and looked around. Everyone was well groomed, talking quietly, and there wasn't a tattoo or a medallion in sight.

'Here we are!' He placed two tall glasses on the table. Tess's was a foamy concoction, topped with pineapple and a sprig of greenery which looked like mint, but wasn't. Sanjeev's looked different.

'Cheers!' They toasted each other and Tess asked, 'What's your cocktail called, Sanjeev?'

'Ah,' he replied, 'this is called a Dis-Crete Devil! Clever play on words! Actually it's a *mocktail*, no alcohol. I don't drink, you see.'

'Oh,' said Tess, not quite sure what to say.

'Not particularly for religious reasons,' he added, as if sensing her discomfort. 'I just don't much like alcohol.'

With this in mind, Tess decided she'd better not gulp down her delicious drink, which she guessed was rum-based. She didn't want him to think that she was too fond of her booze; that wouldn't do at all. She'd concentrate on being ladylike and take delicate sips.

'So, are you with a group, Tess?' he asked.

'Um, yes,' she admitted, feeling slightly awkward. He was plainly awaiting some detail. 'We're called MMM, a social group.'

'What does that stand for?' he asked. 'MMM?'

Tess hadn't time to dream up an acceptable answer. 'Well, it's actually Meetings for the More Mature,' she said.

He didn't flinch. 'And are you all ladies?'

'No, there are a few men as well.' But not nearly enough, she thought.

'So, I take it you're not married or anything?'

'Good heavens, no!' Tess replied. 'I was once, though. A long time ago. We divorced, and since then I've had a lovely partner, but sadly he died. What about you?'

'Yes, I too was married years ago, but my wife died also. Cancer, would you believe? And I could do nothing to help her. Nothing. It had spread too much and she had concealed her symptoms.' He looked sadly into space. 'It's made me all the more determined to do everything I can to help eliminate this disease.'

'I'm so sorry about your wife. Did you have children?'

'Oh yes, I have two sons. One is also a doctor, but he's a GP, and the other's a lawyer. I'm very proud of them both.'

'I'm sure you must be. I have two children also; Matt's a computer whizz-kid, works for Apple. Goodness knows where he gets his talent from – certainly not from me. And my daughter, Amber, is a make-up artist. She works on films and TV.'

'We are very fortunate to have such clever offspring,' Sanjeev said, smiling. 'Are you enjoying your cocktail?'

'It's delicious,' Tess said, remembering to take only a delicate sip because the glass was nearly empty, and wondering if he'd offer her another one. Then, out of the corner of her eye, she noticed Lavinia sitting at a nearby table with three men. She couldn't resist asking, 'Isn't that your friend over there?'

He turned round. 'Friend? They're all members of our group, but none of them is a special friend.'

'The lady… she's very pretty.'

'What, you mean Lavinia?' He frowned. 'She's one of the organisers. Very bossy!'

'Oh!' said Tess, trying not to appear too delighted. She took a final sip, feeling much more relaxed now, much less inhibited. She had to be careful though.

'Did I see you running round the deck the other evening?' he asked.

'That was me,' Tess admitted. 'I've been trying to get into shape.'

'You're a very nice shape,' Sanjeev said, smiling.

'Thank you. But I wasn't, you see. I was really fat, and I've been dieting and exercising for months.'

'Would it ruin your diet to have another cocktail?' Sanjeev asked, looking at her empty glass. She noticed his mocktail was still half full. Well, bugger it.

'No, not at all,' she replied. 'I still have a few weeks to go.'

'Until what?' he asked, picking up her glass.

'Until Amber's wedding. That's my daughter, the make-up artist.'

'You must tell me all about it. But would you like to try a different cocktail this time?'

'No, no, an Aegean Sunset would be perfect.' She resolved to drink this one very, *very* slowly. It had quite a kick, and that was on top of the awful wine she'd imbibed at lunch. Lousy it may have been, but she'd still downed two glasses. What would he think of her?

When he returned with the second Aegean Sunset, he asked, 'This wedding, will it be a very grand affair?'

'Not *grand*,' she replied. 'Just big. And probably full of my ex-husband's business associates.' Tess took a gulp. 'And his wife.'

'He's remarried?'

'Yes, to Ars… er, Ursula. She's very glamorous.'

'Ah,' he said, 'but you're very glamorous too.'

'Well,' she said, 'I'm doing my best.' What a lovely man he was! She took a large gulp. 'I joined MMM originally in the hope of finding a nice escort for Amber's wedding.' Best to be honest; she was a bad liar anyway. 'But it's not worked out. And do you know what? I really don't care.' She wondered why on earth she'd told him all that; he must think she was pathetic. Nevertheless, she felt she should qualify her last statement. 'In this day and age women can choose *not* to have partners, and I'm certainly not going to bother.' Not entirely true, of course.

'Good for you!' He sounded genuine.

Anyway, she was unlikely to ever see him again, so what did it matter?

Then he said, 'I think perhaps we should eat.'

'Yes, we should,' she agreed.

'Shall we try the White Rose restaurant next door? It's supposed to be special and this is our last evening. This time tomorrow night we'll be reduced to airline food, most likely.'

Wait until I tell Orla, she thought. *The White Rose restaurant!*

'No hurry!' he added. 'Finish your drink.'

She was aware that the second Aegean Sunset was diminishing somewhat rapidly, while he was still finishing off his original Crete-whatever-it-was-called. One thing was for certain. She would not be having wine with dinner. Of course he wasn't aware of the two glasses of that lousy plonk at lunchtime, but he *must* have noticed how quickly she'd glugged the cocktails.

When they stood up, she felt as if she was gliding. It was a good feeling. The White Rose restaurant was all white. White painted floorboards, white tablecloths, white chairs, stunning arrangements of white roses on every table for two. And here was Tess Templar in her white dress! Just as well she had no plans to down any red wine this evening; it could have been disastrous. One slip of her hand…!

'Would you like to see the wine list?' Sanjeev asked, as the white-clad waiter hovered over the table.

'Oh, no thank you,' she replied, hoping she sounded suitably virtuous. 'Just water, please. And not fizzy.'

'Make that for us both,' said Sanjeev. The waiter looked sulky as he handed her the menu.

'I'm vegetarian,' Sanjeev said, 'but I'm told they have some excellent dishes here. Are you veggie by any chance?'

There was no point in pretending she was. 'No,' Tess replied. 'I do like meat occasionally, although I must admit I don't eat nearly so much of it as I did years ago.' And that was the truth. Furthermore, she decided it would probably not be a good idea to tuck into a rare steak right under this ethical man's nose. She settled for smoked salmon as a starter, and sea bass for a main. And she'd kill for some lovely chilled Chablis to go with it… But no, no, *no!*

While they ate, he spoke about his sons, their wives, the grandchildren. One of his sons was having problems in his marriage, he said, sighing. They'd chosen their own wives, of course, whereas he'd had his wife chosen for him.

Tess nearly dropped her fork. 'You had an *arranged* marriage?'

'Oh yes,' he said, 'my generation frequently did. My family knew her family, you see, and I'd always known Nadira and that we'd be married one day.'

Tess was fascinated. 'And you didn't *mind?*'

'Why would I mind?' He looked genuinely astonished. 'She was right for me.'

'But were you in love with her?'

'Love?' He shrugged. 'Love comes in time, along with respect and shared interests. The thing is, Tess, it *worked*.'

Tess had a feeling she'd been put in her place. 'And mine didn't,' she said.

'Many marriages don't work these days,' he went on, 'and yet the couples concerned professed great love for each other when first they met. Isn't that so?'

Tess nodded. It was a no-brainer; he was absolutely right. Time to change the subject. She told him she'd had breast cancer.

'I'm sorry to hear it,' he said. 'But the prognosis is generally very good these days if it's caught in time. Did you have chemotherapy and radiotherapy?'

'Yes, both. It wasn't pleasant but hopefully it's done the job. I hated losing my hair.'

'Of course you did – most women do.' He surveyed her newly styled locks. 'It always grows back though, and yours looks very thick and healthy.'

'It is,' Tess agreed. 'It's actually thicker and in better condition than it was before.'

She told him about Barry and how brave he was, and then wondered if she should be talking about cancer at all. After all, this man was on a holiday of sorts and probably glad to get away from the subject, if only for an evening.

'I'm sorry,' Tess said, 'I'm sure everyone you meet socially tells you about their problems. It can't be much of a break for you.'

He laughed. 'I'm used to it. And to be honest, I don't have a lot of time for a social life. My family tell me I'm far too absorbed in my work, and they're probably right. It's just the way I am. Now, to change the subject – are we going to have a dessert?'

The last night! Throw caution to the wind! 'Yes, please.'

She chose the *ravani*, diamond-shaped orange cakes served with cream, while Sanjeev settled for baklava. Then tiny coffees, strong and dark. And it was while she was sipping her coffee and wondering how the evening would progress from here that her phone rang. She was very tempted to ignore it, but then worried there might be a problem at home. It wasn't; it was Orla.

'Tess,' she said, 'really sorry to bugger up your evening, but I've just seen Alan and he's desperately worried about Barry, who's not at all well. Alan wondered about calling out the ship's doctor, but I told him that you were with a cancer specialist and that perhaps he might do the honours? Could you ask him to have a look at Barry? I know it's a big favour…'

'Leave it with me,' Tess said. 'I'll call you back.'

She turned back to Sanjeev. 'I'm really sorry,' she said. 'It's Barry, the guy I was telling you about. I hate to ask you, but he's very poorly and we wondered if you could possibly have a look at him?'

'Of course I can,' he replied. 'I don't have any strong drugs with me because of customs regulations, but hopefully there may be some on board.'

He signalled for the waiter and paid the bill, refusing her offer to pay her share. 'I wouldn't hear of it!' he said. 'I asked you to dinner and I am paying.'

Tess thanked him profusely as they headed back down to the lower decks, towards Barry's cabin. As they walked, he handed her a business card. 'That's me,' he said, pointing to the mobile number. 'Have you got a card, or can you let me have your number and I'll list it on my phone? I'd like to see you again when we get home.'

Tess's spirits soared. 'Oh yes,' she said, rooting around in her shoulder bag. 'I've got some somewhere.' She was sure she'd had a batch of Curvaceous cards, but could only find one, dog-eared and grubby. 'I'm sorry it's so tacky,' she said.

'Thank you,' he said, pocketing it just as they reached the cabin and a very anxious Alan opened the door. There were introductions all round and then Sanjeev went to the bed, where Barry was lying on his back, waxen-faced and moaning softly.

'Oh my God,' said Tess.

'He's scaring me to death,' said Alan.

Sanjeev spoke quietly to Barry, felt his pulse, and studied the vast array of pills by the bedside.

'I will need to see the ship's doctor,' Sanjeev said.

Alan found the telephone list, called the relevant number and then passed the phone to Sanjeev. Much to everyone's relief the ship's doctor said he'd come straight away. The doctor was young, probably in his mid-thirties, and was wearing an open-neck white shirt which was tucked half in and half out of his jeans. 'Poor guy was probably getting ready for bed,' Alan murmured.

The two medics conferred together for a few moments before a syringe was produced, the contents of which were injected into Barry's skinny arm. Almost immediately Barry appeared to respond, some colour returning to his face and his breathing becoming more peaceful. After a moment, Sanjeev wandered over to where Tess was standing just inside the door.

He spoke quietly. 'Don't wait, Tess. I might be here for another hour or so to see how he reacts to this.' He leaned forward and kissed her gently on the cheek. 'Thank you for your company this evening. I'll be in touch.'

'Thank *you*, Sanjeev.' Tess spoke with feeling. It was nearly eleven o'clock and he was right; there was no point in hanging around because there was little she could do except get in the way. As she walked back towards her cabin, she felt very sad. She only hoped Sanjeev could do something to alleviate Barry's suffering. As far as her so-called 'romance' was concerned, that seemed to be fated. Perhaps Sanjeev *would* get in touch when they got home.

When she got back to the cabin there was no sign of Orla. Well, it was the final evening and, in spite of Orla's denials, Tess was sure that she and Ed were getting on very well indeed. It would be interesting to see how *that* one panned out when they got home, and whether Ricky was still in the picture. Holiday romances – who knew?

Tess went out onto the balcony to sit and watch the moon and the stars and their reflections on the water, as the liner slowly made its way back to Piraeus. Tomorrow night at this time they'd be at Gatwick again, and then all this would rapidly become just a memory. It was always nice to get home, of course, but always a little sad that holidays, and the individuals you met, could never be recaptured. She could hear some distant conversations, and some faint bouzouki music. She wondered if she should ring up either

Sanjeev or Alan to find out how Barry was, but decided against it in case it woke him up.

Tess sat gazing at the water for nearly an hour before she decided to go to bed.

CHAPTER NINETEEN

HOME AGAIN

Orla had obviously had a very late night and was still sound asleep the following morning. She woke just as Tess was beginning to pack.

'Oh, Lord!' she moaned, glancing at Tess's suitcase. 'That's what I should be doing, after I've had my shower though. Anyway, how did it go last night?'

'Well, Sanjeev had to contact the ship's doctor to get the appropriate drugs, but they seemed to have got Barry settled when I left. I don't really want to ring anyone yet in case they're all still asleep.'

Orla sighed. 'Oh dear, poor Barry. And it couldn't have done your romance a lot of good either.'

Tess gave a rueful grin. 'Somehow or the other we always seem to get interrupted. But we had a lovely evening and – wait for it – we ate in the salubrious White Rose restaurant!'

'I'm glad one of us made it up there,' Orla said. 'But tell me, are you going to be seeing the dishy doctor again at home?'

'We've exchanged phone numbers,' Tess said.

'Well, that's a start I suppose. Do you think he might be "the one"?'

'I'm not sure,' Tess replied truthfully. 'He's a lovely guy, he's handsome, he's clever…'

'I can sense a "but" coming,' said Orla.

'But I just don't know. We've led such different lives.' She told Orla about the arranged marriage, losing his wife, dedicating himself to medicine.

Orla pulled a face. 'But surely none of that would matter a toss if you'd fallen for him hook, line and sinker? Doesn't love conquer all?'

'Oh, come *on*, Orla! I've only just met him, and it's far too early to talk about love. I'm nearly sixty-three, for God's sake! And I haven't asked him, but I'm pretty certain he's only in his fifties.'

'So what? You wouldn't want to wind up with some old codger, would you?'

Tess laughed. 'I don't know if I want to wind up with anyone, and I'm not at all sure I'll be lucky enough to find someone like David again.'

'Of course you will! And in the meantime, wouldn't he be just the cat's whiskers to take to the wedding?'

'Changing the subject,' Tess said, carefully packing one of the plates she'd bought between some layers of clothing, 'do you have Alan's mobile number?' She glanced at her watch. 'I could probably risk ringing him now.'

At that very moment Tess's phone rang.

'I hope I haven't woken you,' Sanjeev said.

'Oh, I've been up for ages,' Tess replied. 'But tell me, how's Barry?'

'We got him to sleep,' Sanjeev went on. 'I've just been round to have a look at him and he seems a lot better. Hopefully he's strong enough to get on the flight home this evening. None of us want him to end up in hospital out here. We'll pump him up with medication before we leave the ship, and I'll be with him on the flight. Thank you again for your company last night; I really enjoyed our evening and I'll contact you when we get back.'

'Thank you, Sanjeev, for all you've done and are doing. This, for you, is what we call a busman's holiday!'

When she related the conversation to Orla, Orla said, 'He's almost a bloody saint!'

'Did I tell you he was vegetarian?' Tess was folding up the white dress very carefully.

'Extremely healthy. Nothing wrong with that, if you can forgo juicy steaks and roast dinners on Sundays.'

'And he doesn't drink.'

'You're joking!'

'Of course I'm not. What's wrong with that? That's healthy too, you know.'

Orla snorted. 'I'm not so sure now that he's right for you. You could get a bit fed up looking at someone sipping lemonade for the rest of your days. In the meantime, shall we call for that sexy Spyros to bring us breakfast for the very last time?'

The bus awaiting them at Piraeus took them straight to the airport. Ed was flying to Newcastle a couple of hours after their Gatwick flight, and there was much hugging and kissing as he bade farewell to Tess and Orla in the departures lounge.

'Do you think you'll see him again?' Tess asked as they headed towards the gate.

'Probably not,' Orla said. 'Newcastle's so far away.'

'Rubbish!' Tess said. 'What if he lived in Australia or somewhere?'

'That's true. But my heart belongs to Ricky. I *think*.'

There was a long queue at the gate, headed by Barry, who was being transported in a wheelchair, with Alan and Sanjeev in attendance. They boarded ahead of everyone else, along with some families with young children.

The flight was uneventful, the aisles congested with a succession of trolleys selling perfumes, aftershave, gadgets, spirits and cigarettes; everything except decent food.

'I remember the days when you got a three-course meal on a tray,' Orla moaned. 'And free booze.'

And then Tess saw Wally coming down the aisle, obviously heading for the toilet. He grinned when he saw Tess.

'I spotted you doing your run a couple of times,' he said. 'I'm very proud of you. I can see quite a difference. Hope the wedding goes well!' And then he was gone.

Sanjeev also managed to navigate his way down the aisle from the front of the cabin to where Tess and Orla were sitting at the back. 'Just to let you know, Barry's OK,' he said, 'but he really shouldn't have come on this trip. He's going into a hospice when he gets back.'

Tess felt her eyes brim with tears.

'Don't be upset,' Sanjeev said. 'He's quite happy. He only missed out on Mykonos, otherwise he's seen most of what he wanted to see.'

At Gatwick, as they waited at the carousel for their luggage, Tess and Orla said their goodbyes to Alan and Barry.

'Thank God we've got him home,' Alan said, medallions jingling. 'I had a few bad moments back there.'

Barry himself looked quite cheerful. 'I'm fine, I'm fine,' he assured them. 'Don't worry! But thanks, everyone, for your help. I hope I haven't been too much of a pain in the arse.'

Tess hugged him. 'All the best, Barry, and thanks for sharing your knowledge about all those relics and things!'

Sanjeev had already got his suitcase and waved as he headed towards the exit.

Orla's case was one of the last to appear. 'Let's go home,' she said.

Back to reality! At least Dylan was pleased to see her; he kept edging his way into her suitcase as she tried to unpack. Amber had phoned, Matt had phoned. Did she have a wonderful time?

When Tess first got home all she could think of was falling into bed. Now, wide awake at 6 a.m., she needed to check her emails, check her post, unpack, do some grocery shopping, and get to Curvaceous for two o'clock, to meet up with Orla and take over from poor Lauren, who'd been slaving away for eight whole days.

It wasn't cold but it was overcast and grey and, as Tess battled her way round the aisles in Tesco, she was already dreaming of the blue skies and sunshine of the Greek islands. She might not have met the man of her dreams – or had she? – but never mind, she'd enjoyed it all and she'd taken in some culture. She'd also stepped on the scales after she'd showered, and was delighted to see that she'd only gained one pound, probably due to her deck jogging and filling up with fruit, to counteract the alcohol. She weighed twelve stone exactly, and was determined to lose a few more pounds in the three weeks before the wedding. And she'd acquired a good tan. Would

Sanjeev get in touch? And Barry... what about Barry? Would Orla and Ed meet up again? Would Alan and Peggy make a go of it? Or were they all destined to be just holiday romances?

At two o'clock on the dot Tess was back at the boutique, unsure of exactly what she might find. She found Lauren, reading a Jilly Cooper and drinking a coffee. 'It's been manic,' she told Tess. 'I've sold almost everything in the shop. You're going to be doing a lot of sewing, Tess!'

No doubt about it, Lauren had done a good job. Even Orla was impressed when she arrived a few minutes later, although she was hell-bent on not admitting it until Lauren had disappeared.

'Well, she has to be good at *something*,' she said, dismissing her daughter-in-law with a wave of her hand.

That afternoon, Mrs Byron-Sommers appeared to collect her outfit. To Tess's relief Reg had obviously decided it was worthy of payment, and Mrs Byron-Sommers handed over a cheque for the whole amount, with much sighing and grunting. The woman did not believe in card payments or any form of technology and, as she'd once informed Tess, at great length, she'd never give house-room to a computer.

She grudgingly admitted that the dress and jacket were exactly what she'd asked for and that she *supposed* she'd wear them some time. And she'd quite like to have another look at the midnight blue silk. She then waddled out of the shop, clutching the carrier bag, and collapsed onto her motorised scooter before rattling her way over the cobbles in Penny Lane and back to the High Street.

'If that woman lost about ten stone, she wouldn't need that thing,' Orla remarked, peering out of the window. 'Talking of which, are you going back to Slim Chance? How is it these days?'

'Slim Chance has done a great job,' Tess replied, feeling proud of her hard work.

At her Slim Chance session later in the week, Tess discovered she'd lost a further three pounds due, in no small way, to the fact that she'd starved herself for the past four days since her return. Only four more pounds and she'd have lost an amazing two and a half stone – *thirty-five pounds!*

Now it was time to go in search of The Outfit. Tess tramped round Milbury's one and only department store, with no success. She looked online and then wondered how many dresses she'd have to return if they didn't come up to her exacting standards. Even if she had time to make something for herself, she realised that she'd love – just for once – to be blown away by a ready-made dress. Naturally she had a critical eye for style, colour and finish. She'd been known, much to the embarrassment of whoever was accompanying her, to turn ready-made items inside out to examine the seams and the lining, causing much exaggerated sighing from salesladies. A shopping trip to town was necessary.

She called Amber, who said she was free on Friday so why didn't her mother come up to town, and they'd 'do' Oxford Street and have a nice lunch somewhere as well? It sounded good to Tess so, on the Friday, she got the train to Waterloo and then the Tube to meet up with Amber at Oxford Circus.

'Hey, Mum, you're looking good! You're in great shape and I love the tan!'

Tess felt ridiculously pleased. Now she knew it had been worth all the exercise: getting up early every morning to jog around Milbury, running laps on the boat and, not least, queuing up to be weighed every week at Slim Chance. Amber was another one who did not dole out such compliments lightly.

Two and a half hours later, having tramped their way down half of Oxford Street, Tess was exhausted. She'd tried on a dozen possible outfits, none of which had particularly excited her.

'Let's have lunch,' Amber said. 'I know a great little place near Selfridges, and we can go in there afterwards.'

The restaurant served every kind of salad imaginable, along with a bewildering selection of low-calorie dressings.

'You see, Mum, I have your best interests at heart!' Amber laughed as her mother oohed and aahed over the menu.

They got through a bottle of Sauvignon Blanc as well, which Tess reckoned was perfectly OK because of the amount of foot-slogging they were doing; pounding the pavements, trailing round enormous fashion floors and trying to find escalators.

'I don't think Dad and the Arse are hitting it off too well at the moment,' Amber said chattily, popping some shrimps into her mouth.

'Really?' Tess laid down her fork.

'Yes, really. I saw Dad last Wednesday and he made several caustic remarks about Arsula, about how much money she was spending and how many business trips she was making – that sort of thing.'

'Well, that's a turn-up for the books,' Tess said. 'Divine retribution.'

'He asked about you as well,' Amber continued. 'Thought you'd lost weight, and were you OK? Funnily enough, he also asked if you were "seeing anyone", which I thought was a bit strange. So I said, "Mum? You must be joking!"'

'Well, thanks a bunch!' Tess snapped.

'But, Mum, you're not seeing anyone, are you?'

'That's not the point. I just don't see why it should be such a ridiculous idea,' Tess said, feeling slightly sensitive, knowing that her efforts at romance had mostly fallen on stony ground – not that she'd admit any of this to Amber.

'It's not so much that it's a ridiculous idea,' Amber went on, 'it's just so *unlikely*! I mean, you have your friends and your dressmaking and your shop…'

'That doesn't mean that I'm immune to the opposite sex,' Tess replied. 'It just means I'm busy.'

'Exactly! So I said to Dad, "That'll be the day when Mum gets round to finding herself a boyfriend," and we both laughed.'

Tess gritted her teeth. What was so damned funny about her not having a man friend? Did they pity her because she was on her own? And what was wrong with that anyway, in this age of female equality and independence? Nevertheless, this conversation had made her think it was now imperative that she find an attractive escort for the wedding. *Dare* she ask Sanjeev, if he ever phoned? Would he think it peculiar to be asked to a wedding amongst a family he didn't know?

Eager to change the subject, Tess asked, 'Can we have a dessert, do you think?'

'Yes, they have some really yummy yoghurt-based ones here which aren't a bit fattening. It'll give us the strength to plod our way round Selfridges.'

*

Tess had never had much luck in Selfridges before but, hallelujah, there it was! It was displayed on a pedestal and she spotted it as soon as she stepped off the escalator. The dress was emerald green and stunning. It had elbow-length sleeves, a V-neckline, and was semi-fitted and very elegant. It was, of course, expensive.

'It's *you*, Mum!' Amber enthused. 'It's stunning!'

'I don't suppose they have it in a size sixteen,' Tess sighed. 'If they do, I'll know it's meant for me!' She badly wanted it, although she didn't want to spend such an obscene amount of money.

'Go on! It's for my special day,' Amber pleaded. 'And you are the mother of the bride! So, ask if they have a sixteen.'

They didn't. But they did have a fourteen, said the saleslady, and she was sure a size fourteen would fit.

Tess felt deflated. It wasn't meant to be. She'd been a size sixteen, occasionally an eighteen and – lately – a *twenty*! She'd been so hor-rified she'd cut all the labels out. Now, even with her weight loss, a fourteen was too much to hope for.

'Go on, try it, Mum!'

What if it got stuck when she was trying to get it over her head? Or what if the zip broke? She'd die from embarrassment. But…

'OK, I'll try it,' she said finally, knowing that otherwise she'd think about it for weeks afterwards and wish she'd at least tried it on. And Amber would nag.

As they headed towards the changing room, Amber said, 'You know how these sizes vary, Mum. It's high time they were standardised.'

But the dress *didn't* get stuck as she slipped it over her head and the zip *didn't* break. Amber said it was too loose and she should try the twelve.

'No, this is fine,' protested Tess.

'These are generously cut,' said the saleslady. 'I think you should try the twelve.'

'Go on, Mum!'

Unbelievably, the fit of the size twelve was perfect. Tess was not given to conceit but she knew this dress looked terrific on her. It was pre-destined, surely! A twelve! She wouldn't be cutting the label out of this one.

'Mum, you look fabulous! Particularly with that tan!'

'Yes, it is lovely. But what colour accessories could I team it with?'

'For God's sake, Mum, cream or black or almost anything would go with it. Experiment when you get home.'

So Tess bought the dress.

Exhausted, Tess sank into her favourite chair with a big mug of tea. Normally she'd be imbibing a large glass of wine at this time in the evening, but the few glasses at lunchtime were now making her feel sleepy. She was thrilled about the dress, although less so by the hole it had made in her savings – but never mind. And, as Amber had pointed out, she could wear it anywhere, any time, and it would look perfect. A wardrobe investment, in fact. She left the dress hanging on the outside of the wardrobe door so she could admire it. She couldn't, of course, afford to put on a single ounce, which would surely spur her on to lose a few more pounds. Sound advice from Judy.

*

The following Monday, Orla climbed up into the passenger seat of the enormous juggernaut and set off for Birmingham with Ricky. Ricky appeared to be sixtyish, broad and brawny, with his remaining hair tied neatly in a ponytail. And Orla looked like the cat who'd got the cream.

By herself in the shop for a couple of days, Tess considered her own situation. Would Sanjeev phone? Probably not; just a holiday romance. Not even a proper holiday romance! There was, of course, still a chance, however small, to meet someone else in the next couple of weeks.

When Orla returned three days later, she was full of her trip to Birmingham with Ricky to see Maeve, and Maeve's amazing house. Maeve had married an architect and their home, which he'd designed, would make anything from *Grand Designs* look positively suburban.

'I kept walking into glass,' Orla said. 'Glass walls, glass everything. No blinds, no curtains, just press a button and the glass becomes opaque. Well, I hope it did anyway, otherwise half of Birmingham would have seen me undressing.'

'Doesn't sound very cosy,' Tess remarked, as she fitted a summery floral dress on Dolly the dummy. 'Did you enjoy it all?'

'And they eat organic,' Orla went on. 'Everything's organic. Maeve goes round peering at labels to see if they've listed any preservatives or artificial colouring, and all that.'

'You still haven't told me if you enjoyed yourself or not?'

'Well, I did, in a way. But I tell you what, I was ever so glad to see Ricky on the way back. We stopped off for fish and chips and, boy, did I wolf it down! And bright green mushy peas! Maeve would have had a fit! It was heaven! Anyway, what's happening with you? Any word from that Sanjeev?'

'Nothing. I'm meeting another "heart" tomorrow though. Desperate times call for desperate measures.'

CHAPTER TWENTY

RURAL RETREAT

Dougie Morrison was Scottish, lived near Maidenhead, and sold camping equipment for a living. He liked nice food, red wine, dogs, movies, travel and women with a good sense of humour. He also looked, from his photo, a teeny-weeny bit like Paul Newman. He was going to be in Surbiton for a camping exhibition but should be able to get away just after 5 p.m., so why didn't they meet somewhere for a drink and, perhaps, a bite to eat? Unless, he added, we really *don't* like the sight of each other, but somehow I don't think that's going to happen, ha ha.

Tess rather liked the sight and sound of him. More so than any of the other men she'd met – with the exception of Sanjeev.

He'd be happy to pick her up from home, he said, but realised he wasn't supposed to know where she lived, so why not meet in the Fox and Grapes, near Weybridge, at 6 p.m. – rush hour permitting. He would be driving a dark blue Jaguar and he'd be standing beside it, looking out for her, until she arrived.

Tess thought he seemed endearingly normal. It was a warm, sunny July evening and she decided to wear a summer dress that she hadn't been able to get into the previous year. Now it was, if anything, too large.

The traffic was predictably heavy, but she managed to find the pub without too much trouble, thanks to the satnav Amber had given her last Christmas. She was ten minutes late but there he was, leaning against his Jaguar, talking on his phone. When he saw her he put the phone in his pocket and came forward, hand outstretched. He was tall with greying hair which had, Tess reckoned, once been auburn, and very blue eyes. And Tess was a sucker for blue eyes. There was a *definite* resemblance to Paul Newman. He was wearing an open-neck short-sleeved shirt, dark trousers and a big smile.

'Sorry I'm late!' Tess said, shaking his hand.

Dougie grinned. 'I've only just got here myself. Hellish traffic. But good to meet you, Tess. Hey, that's a great tan! Can't believe you got it round here. Now, I could murder a pint! What about you?'

'A lager and lime would be lovely,' Tess said, trying to decipher from his accent which part of Scotland he hailed from. 'Shall we sit outside?'

'Good idea,' he said. 'Grab a table and I'll get the drinks.'

When he emerged carrying the two glasses he said, 'You really should see inside this place; they stock just about every wine on the planet, I should think! Good place to come if you don't have to drive. That's if you like wine, of course.'

'I love wine!' Tess replied with feeling. 'Now, tell me where you're from as I can't quite place the accent.'

'Born in Aberdeen, but we moved to just north of Perth when I was about seven. And, let me guess, you're from somewhere near Edinburgh?'

'Yes, a little place called Strathcoy. But I've spent all my adult life down here.'

'Me too. Did you say you were divorced, Tess?'

'I am, yes, and I assume you are too?'

He laughed. 'I don't think I'm very good at marriage.'

'I don't think I am either, but it would be good to have some nice company for occasional outings, holidays and all that.'

'Agreed. Where do you like to go on holiday, Tess?'

'I've just got back from a cruise round the Greek islands, which I loved. I love France and Italy too. I'm not keen on popular resorts heaving with Brits.'

Dougie laughed. 'I take it I won't be seeing you in Benidorm then?'

'Very unlikely!'

'Talking of holidays,' he said, 'have you ever been camping?'

'No, I haven't,' Tess replied. 'I know, of course, that you sell camping equipment but, to be honest, I've never fancied crawling in and out of a tent, probably in the rain, trying to keep dry. Or trying to light a Primus stove, or any of that stuff. I like my creature comforts too much.'

'I couldn't agree with you more,' he said. 'I like my comforts too. But camping's not like that any more, Tess.'

'I'll take your word for it,' Tess said, smiling.

'You must try it some time. Now, do you fancy something to eat?'

'Yes, but something light. I'm trying to diet.'

He regarded her appraisingly. '*You* don't need to be on a diet, surely?'

She was liking him more and more.

'Let's see what's on the menu, shall we?' he went on. 'There's bound to be a salad of some kind.'

There was. And, as they ate, they agreed to meet again the following week, somewhere near Farnborough where he was doing a sales pitch.

'This one is so nice,' Tess informed Orla. 'And he has the most amazing blue eyes!'

'Well, you're surely due someone half decent from MMM,' Orla retorted. 'But can you see this camping guy escorting you up the aisle and sitting beside you at the top table, or whatever?'

'Definitely,' Tess said. 'Anyway, next week we're wining and dining at a place he knows between Farnborough and Camberley, so that'll give me more time to decide.'

'No word from Sanjeev yet then?'

'No, not yet.'

'Aw, never mind. Like I said, you need more than one string to your bow. How's Amber's wedding dress coming along?'

'More or less finished. Just one final fitting. And now that I've got my lovely dress, everything's falling into place. Apart from the *man*! It would be such a relief not to have to meet any more of these "hearts".'

'Yes, but for sure you won't get your money back until you meet up with the lot, so you'll just have to keep going a bit longer.'

Tess groaned. 'Honestly, Orla, I'm losing the will to love.'

Tess and Dougie met the following Monday at the Bladon Bells, a not-very-picturesque pub near Camberley. It was rush hour again by the time Dougie had sold his camping stuff and got there. But it was another warm evening and his eyes appeared to be bluer than ever. Tess enjoyed his company, his humour and his enthusiasm for everything – and, as a bonus, he was also extremely fanciable. She'd get to know him a little better and then she'd bring up the subject of the wedding and the ex-husband and all that. With a bit of luck he *might* even say, 'Why don't I escort you to the wedding?' Or he might not. She'd have to work on it.

Instead he said, 'How do you fancy a night's camping in a luxury tent this week, Tess? I promise you it's quite opulent.'

The suggestion took Tess completely by surprise. As she struggled for a reply he said, 'No funny stuff! Separate bedrooms, if you wish. Beautiful countryside. I'll cook the steaks, and I'll bring gallons of wine!'

Put like that, it didn't sound such a bad idea.

'Well, yes, why not? Only thing is, I work on Saturdays, and I guess you were thinking of the weekend?'

He grinned. 'On the contrary. They're forecasting rain this weekend anyway, but the outlook for the next few days is good. Would it be too soon for a couple of days away? Say, tomorrow and Wednesday or Wednesday and Thursday? Unless you're working?'

Tess thought for a moment. Orla owed her a couple of days so, yes, she could do a short break, no problem. Tuesday and Wednesday would be fine. Was she crazy? What the hell! And she might even be able to squeeze in a visit to Slim Chance tomorrow morning before she left.

'That might be fun, Dougie!'

'You're never too old for a new experience,' he informed her, his blue eyes twinkling. 'And I promise you'll enjoy it.'

'I'm sure I will,' Tess murmured as she tackled her seafood salad.

'You're kidding!' Orla stared at Tess aghast. '*You? Camping?* Do me a favour!'

'You don't understand, Orla. This is not like Girl Guides or anything. These modern tents are something else! Glamping, they call it.'

'Call it what you like – he only wants to have you away, and on the cheap at that!'

'You have a one-track mind, Orla. This guy is really nice. And he's *Scottish*!'

'That doesn't make him into any kind of saint. I've met Irishmen who seemed to me like God's own gift to a maiden's prayer but, believe me, they were *not.*'

'And he's got the most amazing blue eyes. Like Paul Newman. Gorgeous!'

'Look, Tess, if you want to have it off under canvas with your blue-eyed idol then go ahead, for goodness' sake! You're sixty-two – you can do what you like. You're hardly going to end up pregnant, and I'll do the Wednesday for you, so no problemo!'

'Thanks, Orla. Thing is, Lisa's due to give birth any day now, so I feel a bit guilty if I go away for long."

'Well, she doesn't need you hovering over her, does she?'

'No, of course not. But I know Matt wants me to be around, probably to look after Ellie if she goes into labour."

'Well, you're not leaving the country, are you? You'll have your phone with you so what's the problem?

She'd been instructed to get the train to Maidenhead, where Dougie would meet her at the station and then whisk her off to the beautiful location he had in mind. She'd only need T-shirts, shorts or jeans, and perhaps some sort of waterproof because you could never tell with the British weather, even though it was the middle of summer. So she packed her nightie again, but not the big knickers this time; she'd learnt a salutary lesson there. Besides, she didn't need them now, being a size *twelve*!

Tess, with her overnight bag, arrived at Maidenhead station before Dougie did. For a few panic-filled moments she wondered if she'd been stood up, but then thought he surely wouldn't have asked her to come all this way if he had no intention of appearing himself. What would be the point? Then, just as she was considering whether or not to phone him, he appeared in his Jaguar towing a trailer laden with equipment, which Tess presumed would be transformed into their love nest. *Love?* She was getting carried away with her romantic notions. Whatever was she thinking of?

He was full of apologies: an urgent phone call just as he was leaving. She wondered where he lived, imagining him in a minimalist modern bachelor pad, possibly overlooking the Thames. She hoped she'd be invited to see it sooner or later.

'So sorry, Tess, were you getting worried? Did you think I'd stood you up?'

'No, of course not!' Tess lied, watching him sling her bag into the boot. 'Mind you, although I'd bought a return ticket I wasn't planning on using it straight away!'

She got into the passenger seat. Another nice car. Not quite so flashy as Benedict's Aston Martin, but very smooth nonetheless.

'Where are we going?' she asked.

'Towards the Cotswolds,' he replied. 'Near Woodstock, Chipping Norton – that area. Do you know it?'

'My ex and I took that road to Stratford many years ago.' As they roared up the M40 Tess recalled that particular trip, with Amber being car-sick, and having to stop every five minutes.

'A bit touristy this time of year,' Dougie said, 'but I know a nice spot off the beaten track.'

As expected, Woodstock was buzzing with tourists.

'Have you ever been to Blenheim Palace?' he asked. He looked at his watch. 'We can't stay long because I want to get the tent up before six or seven o'clock.'

Tess hadn't been to the palace, so they decided to have a quick tour. It was expensive but there was a lot to see, if you had the time. She only knew it was a World Heritage Site, that it was the home of the Duke and Duchess of Marlborough, and that Sir Winston Churchill had been born here. It was also the background for countless movies, Dougie informed her.

'And did you know,' he said, 'that it's the only stately home in Britain which belongs neither to the church nor to the royal family that bears the title of "palace"?'

For a moment, Tess was reminded of Barry and his treasure trove of knowledge.

There were some stunning collections of porcelain and furniture, and Tess was particularly interested in the Long Gallery where, apparently, Sir Winston loved to relax, and where every one of the ten thousand books had to be cleaned individually by hand. For a small fortune they could partake of an afternoon tea in the champagne bar but, as there was a tent to erect, this wasn't a great idea, Dougie said.

'We'll have our humble plonk later on,' he promised as they emerged into the glorious gardens. Tess would have liked to see lots more, and hoped that they might have time on the return journey.

They set off through the historic village with its buildings of mellow golden stone, and hadn't gone more than a couple of miles when Dougie turned off down a single-track lane, brushed on either side by nettles and cow parsley, the trailer bumping along noisily behind them. Tess hoped they wouldn't meet anything, as he drove fast and there were no passing places.

'Where on earth are we going?' she asked, holding tightly on to the armrests.

He laughed. 'Nearly there! I found this place years ago when I first started selling camping stuff. You'll love it!'

Tess hoped she would, if they arrived in one piece. And then, suddenly, they were in a meadow which sloped away to a panorama of miles of green, rolling countryside, with golden villages nestled in the folds. He switched off the engine. There were cows grazing in the next field, and Tess could hear them crunching the grass, along with the sound of a tractor in the distance.

'Oh, it's absolutely idyllic!' she exclaimed, as she got out of the car to admire the view.

'Parson's Meadow, it's called,' Dougie said. 'It belonged to the vicarage back in the eighteenth century, and these names stick. This land belongs to a mate of mind, Ollie Regan, up at Cresswell Farm on the main road. He said I can pitch my tent here any time, provided I don't spread the word, otherwise he'll be inundated with tourists and tents. I used to bring the kids here years ago, and they loved it.'

Tess loved it too. What a glorious spot! She watched Dougie lugging out the contents of the trailer. She wondered if she should offer to do something.

'Can I help?' she asked, knowing she hadn't the first clue how to assemble anything.

'Just sit and enjoy the view,' he replied, producing a folding canvas chair. 'It'll take me a little time to assemble this thing, but I'm used to doing it on my own. Don't forget, it's my job.'

Tess sat down, glad that he'd refused her offer of assistance. Apart from a glance now and again to see how he was progressing, she concentrated on the view and taking a few photographs. She'd often dreamed of a vista like this when looking out from her sitting room window in Temple Terrace, but then wondered if she could live happily in such isolation.

'Nearly finished!' His voice broke into her daydreams. She turned round, amazed to see the tall canvas structure, the size of a caravan, in position.

'Wow! It's huge!' she exclaimed, walking through the entrance without having to bend. Inside were two separate rooms with plastic windows.

Dougie flung a couple of large bags into each room. 'Inflatable beds,' he informed her. He then set up another folding chair and table outside, along with a portable barbecue, a big container of water, a large canvas box and a cool box. Inside the canvas box were cutlery, napkins, condiments and wine glasses. The cool box contained the promised steaks, salad and white wine. The red wine, he explained, was in a box in the rear seat of the car. What foresight! What a guy!

Dougie squinted at his watch. 'Time to open some wine, I think. It's well past six o'clock.'

They settled on the Shiraz. He even produced some anchovy-stuffed olives. How could he have known this was one of her favourite appetisers?

They chatted about their families. She told him about Amber and her fiancé, about Matt and his family, and about Gerry and Ursula. He didn't refer to his ex-wife much but spoke at length about his two daughters, both having done well for themselves. One had snared a city broker and produced twin sons; the other was still single and a qualified nurse at Charing Cross Hospital. He was inordinately proud of them both.

Their glasses were refilled. Tess told him about Orla and Curvaceous and her dressmaking. And the larger ladies, which he found hilarious. She certainly wasn't going to mention the disastrous set of 'hearts' she'd met thus far. Rejects, all of them. Then she wondered if he'd transported any other ladies to these pastoral delights. But it was too early to discuss such things; perhaps they'd compare notes later.

In the meantime the charcoal was heating up nicely, and he'd seasoned the steaks in readiness. Tess had done very little apart from setting the table and removing the lid from the Tupperware salad bowl. She felt relaxed and happy as he refilled their glasses yet again.

She permitted herself a little daydream where Dougie was accompanying her into the church, he in a smart morning suit, she in the green dress, and walking down the aisle afterwards, behind the bridal couple and Gerry and the Arse. She felt sure her worries were almost over. She might have lost her £150, but it would be well worth it.

The steaks, his rare and hers medium rare, were cooked to perfection. The salad was crisp, the dressing delicious, the view incredible, and his eyes bluer by the minute. He even produced his tablet and asked her what music she liked. She liked anything by Andrew Lloyd Webber, she said, or ABBA, or opera. Not too heavy, though. Verdi, Puccini, Bizet, that sort of thing. He had them all and played some of each. He opened another bottle of wine and edged his chair a little closer. She could see what he was trying to do, but she had no objections.

It didn't get dark until fairly late, and there was still a vestige of daylight as they danced together, barefoot on the grass, to 'The Music of the Night'. It was the perfect end to a great day. She'd sworn never to get into an alcoholic haze again and now, here she was! Well, why not? And he was looking more like Paul Newman by the sip.

'Do we need to inflate both beds, Tess?' he murmured into her ear.

'No, I don't think so, Dougie,' she whispered back.

At the touch of a button the bed in the larger of the two rooms ballooned into life, and it was a double. Surprise, surprise! He'd really thought of everything – even a couple of sheets and pillows. He unzipped a sleeping bag to make a cover. 'We should be warm enough with that,' he said, 'if we cuddle up close.' He nibbled her ear. 'You have such *pretty* ears, Tess.'

There was no denying it. She wanted him, and desperately. And there was little doubt, as she pressed against him, that he wanted her too. As they tore off each other's clothes, she thought for a brief moment about how surplus to requirements the nightie in her overnight bag always seemed to be.

Dougie's lovemaking did not disappoint. It was the best she'd experienced in years. In fact, apart from a hazy recollection of Andy, it was the *only* lovemaking she'd experienced in years. She had no objections to be woken again, in the early morning, for more of the same.

When Tess awoke at about eight, her lover was still fast asleep. She lay still for a while, studying him, before easing herself carefully up off the mattress and wandering out into the morning sunshine. She needed to pee, so she headed for some nearby bushes, hoping the farmer wasn't strolling around somewhere. She wondered if she could get the little stove to work so she could make a cup of tea – he had, of course, brought teabags and a couple of mugs.

While she waited for him to wake up, she fished in her bag for some wet wipes, and gave herself a perfunctory wash. After she'd donned her T-shirt and jeans she glanced again at Dougie, to see that his eyes were open but he still hadn't moved.

'Good morning!' Tess said brightly, half hoping he'd command her back to bed again.

He didn't answer for a moment, then muttered, 'I feel really weird.'

'What?' Tess moved over towards him. 'Weird? In what way?'

'I've got a pain down my left arm,' he said, 'and I feel a bit sick.'

'Oh, Dougie, let me get you a glass of water and see if I've got some paracetamol or something in my bag.'

He tried to sit up but fell back. 'I feel really dizzy,' he said. 'Give me a few minutes and I'll probably be OK.'

Tess headed for the water container and filled up a mug.

'Drink this,' she said, but as he tried to sit up he fell back again onto the pillow.

'Tess,' he said, 'I don't want to worry you unduly, but I think this might be my heart. I had a similar thing a few years back and was told to take it easy.'

'And did you?' Tess felt panic rising in her chest. A heart attack in a tent in a field in the middle of nowhere! Dear God, what was she supposed to do now?

'No, I didn't,' he replied. 'I have pills, but I've forgotten to bring them with me. Oh, God…' His voice trailed away as he clutched his chest.

Tess was now terrified. What if he died? She picked up her phone. 'I'm going to call for an ambulance.'

He didn't reply; just lay with his eyes closed, clutching his chest.

'Oh shit!' Tess realised she had no address. 'Where do I say we are? A field near Woodstock?' There must be hundreds of fields near Woodstock. She remembered it was called Parson's Meadow. That wouldn't be in the telephone book for sure. How could she describe their whereabouts?

'Dougie?'

He groaned softly but didn't answer.

'Dougie! Try to tell me – the name of the farm, anything!'

He murmured something she couldn't decipher. She knelt beside him and listened to his breathing, which sounded laboured and irregular.

This was a complete nightmare.

'Try to tell me,' she pleaded, close to tears. 'We need to get help, Dougie.'

If need be, she thought, I'll just have to say we're on a farm a few miles past Woodstock. Down a funny little lane. What lane? What farm?

He muttered something she couldn't understand. She put her ear near to his mouth. 'Say again.'

Cresswell! She was sure he said Cresswell, and she seemed to remember that from the night before. And then she remembered the farmer, because his name was Regan, and Orla's married name was Regan; she'd noted it at the time because it wasn't a very common name.

Tess had never dialled 999 before. Once she was connected to the ambulance service, she realised her voice was shaking.

'Take it easy.' The guy's voice on the other end was calm. 'OK, so you're in a tent in a field. Can you tell us a bit more? Like the name of the farm, perhaps? Or the owner?'

Tess told them everything she knew. 'How about if I walk up to the main road and look out for you?' That meant, of course, leaving Dougie on his own – but what choice did she have?

'We'll find you,' he said. 'Stay with him, keep talking to him, keep him calm. Any problems and we'll call you back.'

Tess stared down at her phone, which was still half charged, and thanked her lucky stars she'd remembered to charge it up fully before she left home. But how could they possibly be found? What if he *died*? He seemed to be asleep, but he was breathing and there was little she could do but sit beside him and wait for her phone to ring.

Nearly half an hour passed before she heard footsteps approaching. Almost weeping with relief, she jumped up and leapt outside to find a tall, bespectacled man in work clothes and wellington boots. He held out his hand. 'Ollie Regan,' he said. 'I've been contacted by the police and ambulance service, and they're on their way. Let me have a look at the poor bugger.'

Tess felt relief wash over her. Thank God she'd remembered this man's surname. She sat outside for a moment and studied the view, which hadn't changed a bit and looked just as beautiful as it had the previous day. Then she turned away and looked at the rings on the table surface, made by their overfilled wine glasses last night. But oh, how everything else had changed! Then she heard the sirens.

Ollie Regan emerged from the tent, put a hand on her shoulder and said, 'Stay here. I'll go to guide them down – they may decide to stretcher him up to the main road.'

With that he galloped away, and a few minutes passed before she heard the noise of the ambulance making its way down the lane and suddenly appearing in Parson's Meadow.

The two young paramedics were out of the front in a flash and into the tent, carrying a selection of equipment. Ollie Regan came out and said, 'They'll take him to hospital, and I imagine you'll want to accompany him?'

'Well, of course,' Tess replied. She indicated the tent. 'And what on earth am I supposed to do about dismantling all this, and loading up the trailer?'

'Don't worry about all that,' he said. 'I'll see to it. I know where he lives.' He sighed. 'He never learns, that guy.'

Tess wasn't sure what he meant, but was only relieved that he'd take over the dismantling of the tent and getting everything back to Dougie's home.

They took about ten minutes to stabilise him, inserting a drip and stretchering him out into the ambulance. Scott, the younger paramedic, held open the door for her. 'In you come!' he said. 'Bob's doing the driving.'

And off they went, sirens screaming, back through Woodstock, past Blenheim Palace and straight to the John Radcliffe Hospital in Oxford.

'He's OK,' Scott reassured her. 'He's stable. They'll sort him out, don't you worry.'

They were both so kind and lovely, which made Tess feel more fragile than ever. She wiped away a tear and followed them into the accident and emergency unit. No, she didn't know his next of kin, only that he lived in Maidenhead and sold tents. She didn't know the name of the company either. She wasn't to worry, they said, because the farmer had given them an address. Then Tess wondered at the likelihood of anyone being there, as both his daughters were in London.

'Do you want to stay?' a nurse asked Tess, who was now sitting in a small, crowded waiting room while they sorted him out.

'Well, of course I do!' Tess exclaimed. She could hardly go heading off for the station and leave him there all alone. She'd called for the ambulance after all, and he might have died otherwise. She needed to know he was well on the road to recovery before she left. She'd phone Orla and tell her of her plight, and that she possibly wouldn't be back for a few days. Then she'd try to find a phone charger and top up her phone. Hopefully she'd be allowed to see Dougie before too long, and he'd give her his daughters' addresses. He presumably had a history of heart problems. Had they made love once too often, and could *that* bring on a heart attack?

The nurse reappeared. 'Mrs Templar? No need for you to worry. He's going to be OK. We've contacted his wife, and she's on her way now.'

Tess felt faint. 'His *wife*? Do you mean his *ex*-wife?'

'No, no, we rang up his home number and spoke to her. She was nearly sick with worry, as you can imagine. She couldn't understand what he was doing in Oxford – thought he was at some sales conference in Halifax.'

Tess stood up. 'There's no need for me to wait then,' she said as calmly as she could.

'She'll probably want to thank you for calling the ambulance and getting him here. Apparently you found him in a field or something?'

'Or something,' Tess muttered. 'Don't think I'll wait though.'

She picked up her overnight bag and went off to find the station. She couldn't believe she'd been duped again. Were there no decent men left on the planet?

CHAPTER TWENTY-ONE

EASTERN PROMISE

Orla, for once, was speechless.

'A conference in Halifax!' Tess exclaimed. 'That's where he was supposed to be! Not having it off in a field in Oxfordshire! Anyway, I only need to meet one more no-good "heart" before I've reached my half dozen, and then I can claim my £150 back. And I certainly intend to do so. "Ace of Hearts", what a joke! And I'll definitely be complaining about their so-called vetting procedure.'

After leaving the hospital, Tess could barely recall finding the station in Oxford, or anything much about the journey home. She hadn't known whether to laugh or cry at her own stupidity. Paul Newman indeed! No fool like an old fool, she reminded herself.

'Well,' Orla said after a while, 'I suppose you should be flattered, in a way. I mean, you're sixty-two, and married men usually go for a young bird.'

'Not with MMM, they don't.'

'Perhaps he's with several sites, or perhaps he just likes older ladies, the two-timing bastard!'

'We had such a lovely evening,' Tess said sadly. 'He was so nice. I simply can't believe all this.'

'You're far too trusting,' Orla said. 'I never believe any of them these days. Now I think back on it, I wonder if that Paul wasn't married. But I have to say that I'm fairly certain Ricky's all right. After all, I've been to his flat often enough and I'm pretty sure he hasn't got a wife hidden away somewhere. Anyway, you saved this bloke's life, so he should be eternally grateful to you.'

'That's if I didn't bring on his heart attack in the first place.' Tess groaned. 'Then again, he did admit that he'd forgotten to take his pills with him.'

'It's getting to be a habit, looking after these dodgy blokes, like poor Barry. Anyway, stop torturing yourself!' Orla said. 'There's more fish in the sea. But I'd give a lot to know how he explains this little episode to his wife. "I just happened to be camping in Oxfordshire, and while I was having a heart attack this lady came along and called an ambulance!" Would *you* believe that?'

Tess laughed. 'Unlikely.'

'Well, there you are then. Forget it.'

Tess sighed. 'But I'm no nearer to finding an escort.'

'But you're well on the way to looking great,' Orla consoled her. 'And don't forget, Sanjeev might still phone.'

'Tess has lost over two stone!' Judy proclaimed loudly to one and all the following Tuesday morning. 'And there's still a couple of weeks to go before your wedding, aren't there, Tess?'

'Correct,' Tess said.

'Oh, how lovely, you're getting married!' one of the new members gushed.

'No!' Judy bellowed. 'Her lovely daughter's getting married, and Tess here is going to upstage the bride at this rate.'

'Well, I wouldn't go that far,' Tess said, feeling pleased. She looked around. 'Honestly, if I can do it, anyone can!'

She'd continued jogging in the few weeks since she'd returned from the cruise. At one time she'd thought that once she got near her target weight she'd give it up, but she found she was enjoying it now, and it would certainly help to maintain her shape. And her diet was definitely healthier, although not as strict as that decreed by Slim Chance. Her downfall was the wine. And just look at where too much wine was getting her: hotel bedrooms, tents and goodness knows where else if she wasn't more careful. How had she managed to reach sixty-two years without being able to spot a Lothario a mile off?

There was a round of applause for her great achievement. Tess wondered how many more times she'd attend Slim Chance to lose those last stubborn few pounds. Although the green dress fitted beautifully now, there was no leeway for gain. Another few pounds off would make her, and it, an absolute wow. She'd like a fantastic stop-'em-in-the-aisle hat too. But hats were expensive.

One more of these wretched men to go, and then she could claim back the £150. And that should cover the cost of a great hat.

She was still mulling over the problem the following morning as she and Orla were having their mid-morning coffee.

'I can't believe,' Tess said, 'that I could meet so many weird blokes.'

'*Some* of them were OK, weren't they?' Orla said.

'Not really. First there was Benedict, with the old mother and the French boyfriend. Then there was the motorbike man, James, and Wally the exercise maniac.' She thought for a moment. 'And Andy, of course, with his hotel...'

Too late she realised what she'd said.

'Andy?' asked Orla.

'Oh God!'

'Andy, with the hotel?'

'Yes, Andy with the hotel,' Tess groaned. 'I wasn't going to tell you because I felt like an idiot.'

'What, you dated him after I told you what he was like?'

'No, *before* you told me what he was like!' Tess confessed.

'So why didn't you tell me?'

'Don't ask!'

Orla snorted. 'You *did*, didn't you?

Tess said nothing.

'He seduced you, didn't he? Go on, admit it!'

'I feel so bloody stupid!'

Orla laughed. 'Was he any good?'

'I seem to remember enjoying it, but I was still in an alcoholic haze. But, Orla, you were right; he's a serial seducer.'

'That's for sure!' Orla said cheerfully. 'But I must admit, he had great charm.'

*

And then Sanjeev phoned.

Sanjeev wished to meet Tess the very next day, for afternoon tea at the Tea Plant in Richmond. She wore her dark green silk shirt and white trousers, and decided to take the train to Richmond where she knew parking could be difficult. It turned out to be quite a walk from Richmond station, but it was a lovely day and a very attractive part of the world with its smart shops, beautiful houses and elegant low-rise red-brick flats, geraniums tumbling from their balconies.

The Tea Plant was double-fronted with window displays of tea urns, samovars, oriental and antique teapots, set against a background of Eastern ladies harvesting tea leaves into panniers held in position with straps round their heads, which looked a tad tricky.

Tess was so thirsty after her walk that she went straight inside, where there was a wonderful aroma of teas and spices. Unlike a pub, she wouldn't mind one bit waiting in here on her own. But she didn't have to, because Sanjeev stood up from where he'd been sitting just inside the door and said, 'How lovely to see you again, Tess!' He was immaculate in a smart grey suit and pristine white shirt. He still reminded her of Art Malik.

'Great to see you, too!' Tess said truthfully.

'Did you manage to get parked? I would have liked to come and collect you but, in the end, I decided to come by train.' He smiled disarmingly.

'I came by train too,' Tess said.

'How very wise. Now, here's the menu... Tell me, have you ever seen a greater collection of teas?'

Tess definitely hadn't. There were pages and pages of teas that she hadn't known existed. There were teas from Assam and China and Sri Lanka and Kenya and places that Tess had never heard of, followed by further pages of fruit teas and herbal teas. Teas made from just about anything.

'This is amazing!' Tess was thoroughly confused. 'What a fantastic choice! But do you know what? I'd really love a good strong Indian tea, with hot water and lemon.'

'Those are my thoughts entirely,' he agreed, summoning the young waitress, who then listed half a dozen Indian teas. Tess settled for Assam.

'For us both, please,' said Sanjeev. 'And some of the nice biscuits.'

'Biscuits?' Oh well.

'For dipping in the tea,' he explained. 'This is one English habit that I have become very fond of.'

Tess laughed. 'I couldn't agree more.' He was worth a few calories.

'It is so kind of you to come all this way to meet me today,' Sanjeev said. 'But unfortunately, because of a shift change at the hospital, I have to be reasonably near in case I am needed. How is your work going?'

'OK thanks, although it seems a very trivial occupation compared to the life-saving work you do, Sanjeev. But yes, I've been making quite a few outfits for ladies who, shall we say, are a little on the large side and difficult to fit.'

'This is also skilled work,' he said. 'I am sure you make these ladies very happy.'

At this point the waitress deposited the tea things on the table, along with a selection of thin biscuits.

'Perhaps you would prefer cake?' he asked anxiously. 'Or perhaps some scones?'

'Oh no, no!' Tess replied as she poured the tea. 'Were you born in India, Sanjeev?'

'Oh, indeed. But my parents came to England when I was seven, so I've been here for a very long time. Nadira was born here. She was two years younger than me, so it was an ideal arrangement.'

Tess dunked her biscuit. 'You are so right about arranged marriage. The way you tell it makes complete sense.' She thought of Gerry – how she'd fallen for his looks, his penchant for power and, not least, his sex appeal. And look where *that* had got her.

Sanjeev leaned forward. 'But I have some sad news. Our friend Barry has died.'

'Oh, Sanjeev!' Tess could feel the tears welling up. 'I knew he wasn't going to get better, but that is so sad. How did you find out?'

'Well, I'd given him and Alan one of my cards and said to contact me if I could help in any way. I got the call from Alan just yesterday.'

'He was such a nice wee man.' Tess blew her nose. 'And so interesting.'

'You must not be upset,' he said gently. 'You were very kind to him, and I believe at the end it was very peaceful.'

'I suppose you get used to that sort of thing with the work you do.'

Sanjeev smiled. 'My job is to prevent people from dying, Tess. And believe it or not, I still feel incredibly sad when one of my patients slips away.'

'You don't become immune to people dying then? I often wonder how doctors and nurses avoid being emotionally involved, particularly when you build a relationship with a patient and become fond of them.'

'We're only human. But we have to keep our emotions in check. And don't forget that I lost Nadira to cancer, so I'm aware that every single death is a tragedy for someone. Now, shall we talk about something more cheerful?'

'OK, so, if you hadn't become a doctor, what else would you like to have done?'

He thought for a minute. 'I think I'd have liked to be involved in film-making. The cinema fascinates me; particularly the Bollywood films of India. I think I'd have had a go at directing films. And you?'

'I sometimes think I'd like to have studied architecture. Buildings, and houses in particular, fascinate me... but I wasn't really bright enough and there wasn't the money. My parents were quite old-fashioned; they thought that you should get a job when you left school, or do an apprenticeship in something or other. University was for the super-brainy who would become lawyers and teachers. And doctors, of course! And girls did *not* become architects in their neck of the woods.'

'That's sad.'

'Not really, because I enjoy what I do. And I'd probably have been an awful architect!'

'I'd have commissioned you to build my house, and my film sets!' Sanjeev said, laughing.

Tess was struck again by what a charming, clever man Sanjeev was, and such a refreshing change from the dreary devious 'hearts' she'd met so far. Of course that was probably because he *wasn't* a 'heart'. She was dunking her second biscuit when Sanjeev's phone rang. There followed a monosyllabic conversation, ending with, 'OK, I'm on my way.'

He leaned towards Tess as he replaced the phone in the breast pocket of his shirt. 'I am so very sorry, but I have to go.'

'I'm sorry too, Sanjeev.' And she was *very* sorry.

'This is what always happens. Please forgive me. But can we meet again, Tess? I'd really like to.'

'And so would I,' Tess said with feeling.

As it was only half past three when she got back to Milbury, Tess decided to return to the shop.

When she walked through the door, Orla looked up in surprise. 'What happened to the date?'

Tess sighed. 'He was called away just as we were getting chatting.'

Orla rolled her eyes. 'Is he really worth all the bother if he's always going to be dashing off to his work?'

'But he's so gorgeous!' Tess said.

'Well, I suppose he'd certainly be handy to have around,' said Orla. 'You can get all your ailments lined up and be diagnosed by your own personal physician, instead of having to wait for weeks for an appointment at the surgery here and then discovering that your own quack's gone on his holidays.'

'I wouldn't take advantage like that. Anyway, he's an *oncologist*, Orla.'

Orla said, 'You could have done with him over the last couple of years, couldn't you?'

'I certainly could. And he's so good-looking and charming,' Tess sighed. 'And so polite.'

'Hang on to him then. Men like that are scarcer than hens' teeth.'

'And he had an arranged marriage. Can you imagine that?'

'No, I can't, but marriage is such a gamble anyway that I guess that's as good an arrangement as any. At least you'd probably be well matched, no skeletons in the cupboard. But what if he turned out to be as ugly as sin? It's all right if he looks like your Adonis.'

When she got home that evening, there was an email waiting.

Dear Tess,

I apologise profusely for having to abandon you in the Tea Plant. Please forgive me and permit me to take you out for dinner. Would you be free on Sunday or Monday evening? And what type of food do you like? Please don't feel obliged to say vegetarian!

Kindest regards,

Sanjeev

Tess re-read the email several times. What a gentleman! And she would most definitely like to have a meal with him, and Sunday evening would be just fine. For a moment she considered giving him her home address, but then thought perhaps not yet. Maybe next time – if there was a next time, which she hoped there would be. Furthermore, one of her favourite places to eat was the excellent Indian restaurant in Milbury, so she wouldn't have far to go home if he should be called out again.

She emailed Sanjeev back to say she'd love to have dinner with him on Sunday evening and that she adored Asian food, so how about the Taj Mahal in Milbury? Not to be confused with the one in Agra, of course. She resisted the temptation to add 'ha ha'.

In return, he promised he would not be called out this time and Tess decided that, if the dinner went well, she might just invite him home for coffee. But definitely no sex, even if he was very fanciable. She still felt embarrassed at the goings-on in that tent, not to mention at the Beeches. What on earth had got into her? Alcohol, that's what had got into her. But with Sanjeev that wouldn't be a problem. And Sanjeev, she felt sure, was a man of principle with respect for women. A gentleman at long last.

Wearing her pink sleeveless shift, which she considered to be suitably demure, Tess arrived at the Taj Mahal at twenty-five minutes to eight, and there he was, in a blue open-neck shirt and white trousers, looking even more like a film star than Art Malik. He stood up, shook her hand (no kissing or lip-smacking the air), and asked her what she would like to drink. She decided a lager would be a suitable accompaniment to the curry she intended to have. Sanjeev ordered a tonic water with ice and lemon for himself.

'But please, you must have whatever you wish. Most of my colleagues drink; in fact I'd go so far as to say that some of them drink a little too much!'

'Well, I guess yours is a very stressful job,' Tess said, studying the menu.

They chose four different curries to share, two of which Tess had never tried before, plus rice, poppadoms and mango chutney. She tried to remember to sip her lager and not gulp it, as she was prone to do. He might be a good influence on her, as she sometimes felt she enjoyed her wine just a little too much. And she certainly exceeded the maximum number of units she was supposed to imbibe per week.

With difficulty, Tess managed to make her single lager last for the duration of the meal, and was about to suggest he come back to hers for a coffee when he said, 'Do you mind if we have some tea or coffee and then I leave you? I know it's quite early but I was on duty last night and only managed a couple of hours' sleep today, and I'm on again tomorrow morning.'

Tess's spirits plunged. 'Of course,' she said.

What made it even more disappointing was that she'd spent the morning vacuuming, tidying up, plumping cushions and arranging flowers in vases – just in case she decided to ask him back. She'd thought it would be nice to provide a retreat for him from the rigours of hospital life. A place he might like to return to time and time again.

They agreed on tea. It was only half past nine when they parted company and he was very concerned about her getting home safely, unaware it was a mere five minutes away. He was apologetic, yet again, about the necessity of his early night. He would be in touch soon.

As Tess sank into her armchair in her unusually pristine lounge, she wondered if and when he would be in touch. She was sure they moved in totally different social circles, and he had such a demanding profession. But she so hoped he would.

He didn't contact her the next day and, as she and Orla had a lunch break after a manically busy morning, Tess sighed and said, 'I'm wondering if he'll call me again. He seems to work round the clock.'

'Give the man a chance! Well, give him a week anyway. And in the meantime, why don't you try another "heart"? How many more do you have to go?'

'One more and I'll have met the six. And if the next one is rubbish then I'm going to try to get my money back.'

'Why shouldn't you get your money back – how are they going to know whether or not you want to see any of these guys again?'

CHAPTER TWENTY-TWO

RUSTIC REALITY

Number six was George Barratt, who lived a mere three miles away in the countryside. He was a farmer. Tess knew she had to go through with this, regardless of what he was like, to complete dates with the number of hearts she needed in order to apply for a refund from MMM.

'Farmer George!' Orla snorted.

George was looking to meet someone who liked animals, good food and country air. It all sounded very healthy. George wondered if she'd like to meet him at the local pub, aptly named the Plough, and then she might like to see his sheep and his goats and his newborn piglets.

This, Tess thought, is definitely a day for jeans and a T-shirt. Dresses were to be saved, hopefully, for a further date with Sanjeev. The Plough, which she'd driven past many times, was suitably rustic, boasting a large rusty plough positioned in front – perhaps in case some passing alien might not know what a plough was. Inside, the decor was predictably spit-and-sawdust, complete with beams adorned with various farming implements and a fair few cobwebs.

George was leaning against the bar, as he'd promised he would be, clutching a pint of bitter. He was a little taller than Tess, chubby, balding, with a careful comb-over and a pleasant open face. He was tanned but still not as attractive as his MMM photo which, of course, she'd now come to accept as being the norm. He wore an open-neck checked shirt and jeans jammed into a pair of no-nonsense wellington boots. He was Farmer Giles all right.

'You must be Tess?' he asked, which was a fair assumption as there was no one else in the bar, except four old men at a corner table playing dominoes.

'Nice to meet you, George,' she said as they shook hands. She was becoming an expert at meeting all these new men: shaking hands, smiling brightly, looking directly into their eyes. She'd read somewhere that this was the correct approach and she was certainly getting plenty of practice. There would be ample time – after they'd got through the niceties of 'have you come far?' and 'how was the traffic?' – to examine him in closer detail.

He told her he hadn't come very far because he lived just a few miles down the road. As Tess lived a few miles in the opposite direction, this all seemed very satisfactory.

Tess ordered a glass of white wine, which he insisted on paying for. A definite plus point. He told her in some detail that his wife had taken off with a vet who'd come to sort out the mastitis of one of his prize cows. There was little Tess could say to that, other than make a few sympathetic noises. He had one son living in Australia who kept nagging his father to go out there, but George wasn't keen on flying all that way and paying all that money. Anyway, who would look after the farm?

To enter into the spirit of the thing, Tess decided to have a ploughman's lunch, which consisted of the usual chunks of bread and cheese, along with a pickled egg and chutney. She'd only had some fruit for breakfast, so she reckoned she could probably get away with eating half the bread and half the cheese. She'd eat it very slowly – Judy told them every week that it takes about twenty minutes for the brain to inform the belly that it's had quite enough, so the half should do it. She paid for her own meal and George didn't argue. She always did offer to pay for her own whatever-it-was, but the majority of 'hearts' insisted that she put her purse away. George did not insist that she put her purse away. Were farmers supposed to be hard up these days? She supposed it depended on the farmer.

Like most men, he preferred talking to listening. He talked about his cattle, the price of animal feed, the astronomical cost of vets, the lack of subsidies, and the general disinterest of the government in his numerous problems. Tess felt her eyes glaze over a couple of times and had almost dropped off at one point when he said, 'Do you fancy coming back to my place for a cup of tea?'

She jumped. 'Tea?'

'Yes, or coffee if you prefer.'

Well, why not? she thought.

'You can follow me,' he said, as they came out of the pub and he headed towards an ancient mud-splattered Land Rover. As Tess drove up behind, the Land Rover came to life, belching clouds of black exhaust fumes. Even with her windows closed, Tess was coughing as the fumes found their way into her car. Couldn't he even afford a new exhaust? As she followed along, she tried to imagine him in a morning suit. She'd probably end up having to pay for the hire.

And although he wasn't bad-looking, he certainly wouldn't be getting the admiring glances that Sanjeev would.

He led her up a dusty lane, past a wooden sign proclaiming 'Stonecroft Farm' which, Tess reckoned, would be a sea of mud in the winter, and arrived at a farmhouse surrounded by a collection of ramshackle buildings, two tractors and two hysterically barking collies. She parked behind him and got out cautiously, none too sure of the canine welcome. The dogs jumped all over George, tails furiously wagging, before turning their attention to this visitor, almost knocking her over in their enthusiasm.

George grabbed both dogs by their collars and, indicating the one on his right, said, 'This one's Sadie, and this one here's her son, Bobby.' He held on to them while they quietened, and Tess stroked their heads. They were lovely dogs, if a little dirty. In fact, they were filthy. He then led the way to the farmhouse door, which badly needed a coat of paint, and into a hallway jam-packed with jackets, caps, odd socks, boots, piles of old newspapers and boxes of empty beer bottles, all covered in a generous coating of dust.

'Keep meaning to have a tidy up in here,' said George. 'But there should be some wellies to fit you, if you fancy having a look around after we've had some tea.'

He then pushed open another large heavy door into an enormous kitchen, where an ancient Aga presided amongst a jumble of dressers and cupboards randomly placed round the walls, with a long wooden table down the centre. As far as Tess could see, there wasn't a square inch of space on any of the surfaces. There were stray cups, plates, papers, hammers, nails, boxes, bags, some unidentifiable objects and two large cats. The slate floor was navigable, with care, through a selection of dog and cat bowls and stray boots. It was hot, stuffy and smelly.

'Sorry it's in a little bit of a mess,' he said cheerfully. 'You don't bother much when you're on your own, do you? Needs a woman's touch.'

Tess avoided eye contact. Not *my* touch, she thought. Did anyone ever tidy up or clean in here? she wondered. And where would you start? One of the dogs brought a much-chewed rubber ball to Tess, and looked up at her hopefully, tail wagging.

'He wants you to throw it,' George explained.

'I can't very well throw it in here,' Tess said, patting the dog's head and trying to calculate how many objects you could hit by just rolling it along the floor.

George located the kettle, elbowed his way through the dirty dishes in and around the old butler sink, filled it with water and stuck it on the Aga. At that moment, there was a rapping at the door and a cacophony of barking from the dogs.

'That'll be the vet, come to see Mabel,' he said.

Mabel? Surely not Mabel with the buttocks from Slim Chance? No, Mabel was his prize Jersey cow, who'd recently given birth and was now beset with problems.

'I shouldn't be long,' he said, heading back towards the door, both dogs at his heels leaping and barking with excitement. 'Could you make us a cup of tea? Kettle's on, teapot's around somewhere, and tea's in that red box over there.'

With that, he and the dogs were gone. The door banged shut and Tess looked round at the wall-to-wall chaos. She made her way cautiously towards the window, pulled back the greasy half-drawn curtain, and wrestled with the window latch for a minute before finally forcing it open. Warm, clean summer air rushed in. Tess took a deep breath and went in search of a teapot and some mugs, none of which were immediately apparent. The sink was full of dirty crockery and there probably was a teapot buried underneath in the murky depths. There was nothing for it; she'd have to clear the sink.

At least there was hot water, and she eventually found a near-empty bottle of Fairy Liquid hidden behind a half-full bottle of West Country cider. Some of these dishes appeared to have been in there for days; plates encrusted with scraps of food and mugs stained black with tannin. Tess shuddered. No chance of finding any Marigolds round here, so she plunged her hands into the hot soapy water and commenced the mammoth task of washing up. There was what appeared to be a scrubbing brush on the water-stained wooden draining board, and Tess used it to ease off some of the detritus from the crockery.

As the kettle began to sing on the stove, Tess stopped short. She hadn't heard that sound in years! She was immediately transported back to her childhood and to her mother's immaculate kitchen. But you never heard electric kettles singing, and she couldn't remember the last time she'd placed a kettle on a hob.

Some of the dishes, as they emerged, were surprisingly delicate and pretty. Probably a throwback to when his wife was around. Had the poor woman looked round this mish-mash of a kitchen and headed off gratefully to the vet's minimalist stainless steel one? And surely it couldn't be the same vet who was now outside tending to Mabel?

Tess washed, rinsed and extracted from the sink seven mugs, four plates, five bowls, masses of cutlery and, finally, a large brown teapot. Drying was out of the question in the absence of any kind of towel, so she hoped that the fresh air now filtering in might do the job eventually. The teapot would have to stay wet. The red box that housed the teabags had once contained somebody-or-other's ginger biscuits, but most of the writing had worn off over the years. She wondered how long George was likely to be and whether she should make the tea now or wait for a bit. She decided to wait and looked round for something to sit on. The Windsor chair beside the Aga was occupied by an enormous ginger cat, who watched her every move. It would not be a good idea to attempt to move that cat, she decided. Then Tess pulled out a chair from the table, removed several copies of *Farmers Weekly* from the seat, and sat down. The ginger cat continued to stare at her, while the tabby cat slept peacefully on what appeared to be a pile of old socks. She looked round at the animals' food and water bowls, and decided that they too were entitled to a modicum of hygiene. She gathered the four up, emptied what little remained in them, returned to the sink and proceeded to scrub them all. She filled two with clean water and returned them to the floor, leaving the other two to drain.

'You should be thanking me,' she muttered to the ginger cat, who was still staring at her. He didn't look particularly appreciative, just yawned, stretched and continued to study her. Then she heard voices outside the door, indicating that George and the vet had finished with Mabel, and that she should make the tea. She was aware of a flash of lightning and a rumble of thunder in the distance, and a few drops of rain finding their way in through the window.

A few minutes later, George strode in.

'Sorry about that,' he said, removing his jacket and slinging it on top of some others languishing over the back of a chair. There was another flash, and then a crash of thunder, which seemed to be directly overhead, and the heavens opened, storm clouds gathering and darkening the room. Tess hoped she hadn't left her car windows open.

'Thanks for making the tea.' George removed the ginger cat from the Windsor chair and plonked himself down. 'And for doing the washing-up,' he added, eyeing the sink.

'No problem,' Tess said airily, pouring the tea into two still-damp mugs. 'Milk? Sugar?'

He indicated the fridge. 'Milk and three sugars, please.'

Tess was beginning to wonder who was supposed to be entertaining whom. She opened the fridge door to find every shelf heaving under the weight of cans of cider and beer. There was, however, a supermarket carton of milk, which plainly had not originated from Mabel.

'Sugar's on the table,' he said, indicating an open bag of Tate & Lyle with a spoon rammed into it vertically. Tess added the milk and sugar to his tea, stirred it and handed it to him. He thanked her but made no other comment, so she reckoned this was what he expected of his female visitors.

The rain was now hammering down relentlessly.

'When this eases off a bit,' said George, gulping his tea, 'I'll show you round the farm.'

'Well, that would be very nice, George,' Tess said, 'but I really should be going soon. I have a lot of work to do.'

'Work?' He took another gulp.

'Yes, I told you I was a dressmaker.'

'So you did. Not sure I'd call that *work* exactly.'

Tess bristled. 'Call it what you like, George – it gives me a living, pays the bills, runs the car.'

'OK, OK, keep your hair on! Didn't mean to upset you,' he said, standing up. 'Any more tea in the pot?'

'Help yourself,' Tess said without moving. What a boorish, chauvinist pig! she thought. Rain or no rain, I'm not staying here.

'Fancy staying for a bit of supper?' He refilled his mug without offering her any more.

'Thank you, but no.' Had it not registered in his dull brain that she'd said she had to work? She imagined herself doing all the cooking, struggling with the Aga, and rounding off the evening with a heavy load of washing-up, which was almost certainly what he had in mind. Was it likely that he'd ever find a woman who'd happily don an apron and sort out both him and his shambolic house? Tess shuddered to think what the rest of it might be like, but she had no intention of ever finding out.

She stood up and grabbed her shoulder bag. 'I'll be off now, George. It's been really interesting meeting you.' How many times had she said that to these hapless 'hearts'? But this, for sure, was the grand finale.

'Still coming down in stair rods,' he remarked, crossing to the window. 'Don't know why you opened this.' He pulled the window shut.

Tess got to the door, wondering if he might at least escort her to the car. He got as far as the hallway, muttering, 'There must be an umbrella somewhere.' He rummaged around for a few minutes, lifting up coats and jackets and boxes. 'Could have sworn there was one in here.'

'Don't worry,' Tess said, pushing open the outer door. She could see her car parked behind his, about fifty yards away. 'I'll make a run for it.'

'Mind how you go then!' he said cheerily. 'I'll email you. You might fancy coming over for supper next week.'

In the short time it took Tess to reach her car, she was absolutely soaked. She glanced back at the door but he'd already disappeared inside. No question of accompanying her to the car or guiding her out of her parking spot. Fortunately she hadn't left any windows open, but she felt cold and extremely wet as she slithered damply into the driving seat. She switched on the engine, engaged the windscreen wipers at top speed, and proceeded to do some tricky manoeuvres in an effort to turn the car around.

Finally she exited Stonecroft Farm down the lane, which had already reverted to a sea of mud.

After a long soak in the bath, Tess got into her dressing gown, poured herself a large glass of Merlot, and sank into a chair with her laptop. The rain was still hammering against the windows and was most likely on for the night.

She ploughed her way through her emails, deleting most of them, before finding one from Sanjeev, who'd been visiting one of his sons in Norwich, but was now back in London and wondered if she might be free next Friday, when they could perhaps spend a day at the coast together, weather permitting? At least, she thought,

I seem to be able to attract one decent man. But what would Orla say tomorrow when she had to admit that 'heart' number six had also been a non-starter?

'Do you sometimes wonder if you're being just a teeny-weeny bit too fussy?' Orla was sitting down after a long hard morning of measuring and fitting.

'I don't think so,' Tess replied. 'And don't forget *you've* been exceptionally lucky.'

And she had too. Orla and Paul had got on well for quite some time, and at least she'd got her plumbing sorted out so she'd got something to show for it. And now there was Ricky, he of long-distance haulage fame, and he too had been on the go for some time. Of course, Orla had had to adapt accordingly, which meant she pretended to love watching *Match of the Day* and being passionate about Chelsea. She'd even accompanied him to a Chelsea match! Until now, Orla's interest in Chelsea had been restricted to posh shops and buns. But suddenly Orla was an expert on the Premier League, moaning about the idiocy of the goalkeeper during the match with West Ham, or the player sent off during the Manchester United game.

The thing about Ricky was that he was constantly away. Perhaps absence made the heart grow fonder. And his return was frequently delayed, due to various problems such as dock strikes, mechanical faults, loads not ready to be loaded, and so on. Tess occasionally wondered about this. Back in the days of yore, when only sailors travelled for a living, they were known to have a girl in every port.

Hull, Huddersfield and Harwich might not have quite the same kudos as Haifa, Hong Kong and Honolulu, but the principle was very much the same.

Maybe, Tess thought, I *am* too picky. Maybe Orla has the right idea, accepting whatever comes her way without complaint. But try as she might, Tess could not imagine any of the guys she'd met becoming a long-term prospect, or even a short-term one for that matter. Certainly none of them was likely to impress Gerry and Ursula at the wedding. None, that is, except Sanjeev. She'd gladly have Sanjeev escort her up and down the aisle, or anywhere else for that matter. And now he was suggesting a day at the seaside! Bognor? Brighton? Bournemouth? What did it matter? Sea, sun, sand and Sanjeev! Friday – hey ho!

CHAPTER TWENTY-THREE

SEA BREEZES

When Tess woke up on Friday morning the rain was lashing with fury against her bedroom window, and there was a definite chill in the air. She looked mournfully at the T-shirt and cotton trousers she'd planned to wear. Perhaps the weather would improve? It was, after all, only seven thirty, and everything could change within the next couple of hours. However, according to the cheerful weather forecaster on the TV, this weather was set for most of the day, the unseasonal Atlantic gales driving the rain horizontally into every nook and cranny. He looked amused, standing there in a nice warm studio, as well he might.

Perhaps Sanjeev would postpone the outing? Perhaps they could settle instead for a nice cosy pub and then a movie. Perhaps, perhaps. Tess found a warm sweater to wear over her T-shirt and swapped the cotton trousers for jeans. That blue, blue Aegean was but a memory.

She fed Dylan and made herself some porridge. Just over a week to go to the wedding! Surely summer would return by then, as she hadn't planned to wear any kind of jacket or coat over the beautiful emerald dress. Then she fiddled with her hair, knowing full well it would be a wasted effort if she had to squash it all day under a hood. And she'd also planned to wear sandals, so that was another no-no. She'd have to wear the trainers. This was *not* the look she'd been planning.

Sanjeev hadn't been to her house before, and she had no idea what he might be driving. When he arrived promptly at half past nine he was wearing a long waterproof over his jeans, with sturdy boots.

'This is nice,' he said, looking round Tess's lounge. 'Very homely.'

Good, she thought; perhaps he'll want to come here often to unwind.

'But what a day!' he added.

'Are we still planning on going to the seaside?' Tess asked.

'Of course!' Sanjeev replied. 'I need to get some good clean sea air into my London lungs!'

'Oh yes, absolutely,' Tess said, trying to sound enthusiastic.

'I thought, perhaps Brighton?'

'Fine.' Tess thought of the Lanes, the shops and the great restaurants. 'Would you like a coffee before we go?'

He glanced at his watch. 'That's kind of you, but would you mind if we get on our way? Perhaps we can stop for a coffee en route.'

Tess put on her hooded raincoat and followed him out to his smart car. Just as well she wasn't planning any major shopping, as there wouldn't be a great deal of space in Sanjeev's small Mercedes.

'It's small,' Sanjeev said as they strapped themselves in, 'but ideal for London. Easy to park.'

Off they went, windscreen wipers at full speed, de-misters on, sloshing their way through the deep puddles that had already formed.

'Perhaps we should have postponed this?' Tess said, peering through the windscreen.

Sanjeev laughed. 'But how can you rely on British weather? It could be worse tomorrow!'

'Could it?' She gazed out at shoppers battling against the elements, umbrellas blown inside out, huddling in doorways.

They didn't stop for coffee or anything else until they got to an equally rainswept Brighton just over an hour later. They took the best part of another half hour trying to find somewhere to park, while Tess continued to dream of a cosy pub and a good movie.

'Right!' said Sanjeev as they finally found a space, 'make sure you're well buttoned and belted up – Brighton beach, here we come!'

Was he *kidding*? No, he wasn't. He took her hand and led her down a narrow street where, at the end, she could see the raging grey sea.

'Are you *sure* this is a good idea?' Tess asked, struggling to keep her hood on. Why had she bothered with her hair? Or her make-up, as the rain lashed against her face.

Sanjeev laughed. 'Of course! We have come all this way to the seaside, so we must see the sea!'

'We must?'

'Tess, we are British. This is British summer weather! We can't let some rain stop us from getting the sea air. I want to feel the spray, taste the salt, blow the dust of London away!'

As he spoke, a truck went by and doused them liberally with water from a giant puddle.

'I've just felt the spray,' Tess muttered, her right leg now soaked by wet denim.

They reached the deserted seafront. 'Let's turn right,' he said brightly, 'into the storm. Get the worst over with first, and then it'll be behind us on the way back.'

They were the only people on the beach and for a brief moment she wondered if he might be joking, but he wasn't. They struggled along the pebbles against the rain and the wind, hand in hand, water streaming down their fronts. I should have worn that waterproof mascara I bought for the wedding, Tess thought.

'Not like Greece, is it?' he laughed.

'No, it damned well isn't,' she said, wiping her eyes so she could see where she was going. They battled on a little further before she said, 'I don't know about you, Sanjeev, but I've had more than enough!'

'OK, OK,' he said, chuckling. 'Let's turn round. It'll be easier going back.'

It was, and now her back was soaked as well as her front. Tess began to see the funny side of it.

'It's due to clear up later,' Sanjeev said, 'but look, fish and chips!' They'd got back to where they started. 'I've just seen a sign over there.' He pointed up a lane opposite.

'Aren't you vegetarian?' Tess asked, visions of a nice glass of Merlot in a characterful pub rapidly dissipating.

'Yes, but I do eat fish,' he replied, steering her across the road and dodging the traffic.

The fish and chip shop was called Wanda's. The sign on the counter, alongside the salt shakers and vinegar bottles, said 'The fish isn't called Wanda but the fish fryer is!' Behind, with an arrow pointing to some tables and chairs, was another sign, which said 'Wanda in for Waitress Service!'

So in they wandered, Tess intent on finding a toilet to inspect her ruined hair and make-up. She stared at her dishevelled locks and panda eyes in the mirror, and tried to do some repairs. She finally emerged to find Sanjeev sitting at a table near the steamed-up window. It was warm, with a smell of fried food and wet clothes.

He grinned at her as she sat down. 'I know this doesn't exactly compete with the White Rose restaurant,' he said, 'but I just thought it might be fun to have a typical day's outing to the seaside, British style.'

'Hope you weren't planning on a visit to the funfair after this,' Tess joked, but nevertheless was aware that he just might be.

'No, even I don't fancy the Big Dipper in this weather! Ah, here's the waitress – shall we have a pot of tea?'

Tess studied the menu. The place wasn't licensed, so no Merlot. 'Yes, tea's fine,' she said.

They both ordered haddock and chips. Did they want mushy peas? Tess thought of Orla's feast on the way back from Birmingham. And a pickled onion? Pickled egg? Yes, yes, yes!

'Such sophistication!' laughed Sanjeev. 'Then, looking into her eyes, he said, 'You don't mind coming here, do you?'

'No, of course I don't mind,' Tess said truthfully. She was beginning to find the whole thing charming in a strange sort of way; almost like a teenager's romantic antics.

'Then I'll just need to find some candy-floss to round off the day,' he said.

'Are you serious, Sanjeev?'

'No, I just wanted to see your face!'

They both exploded with laughter.

The fish and chips were delicious; Wanda had excelled herself.

'How are the wedding plans coming along?' he asked out of the blue.

'Oh, fine, I think. Well, they'd better be, because the wedding's only eight days away. But everything's booked, I've finished Amber's dress and also Ellie's – she's my little granddaughter, who's going to be a flower girl.'

'And have you had time to buy yourself something to wear?' he asked with a smile.

'Yes. I've found a lovely dress.' Tess thought for a moment. 'But I've still to find a *hat*!'

'Have you found a date yet?'

Tess sighed. 'No, I haven't, but I've decided not to bother. I'm quite happy on my own.'

'Are you sure? I'd be delighted to do the honours if you change your mind and can't find anyone more suitable.'

'You *would*? *You?*'

'What's wrong with me?'

'Nothing, nothing at all! Oh my God, Sanjeev, that would be terrific! Are you really serious?'

'Of course I am! Let me make a note of the date. Goodness only knows I've put in enough overtime, so they can't deny me a day off.'

'I can't thank you enough!' Tess hoped she didn't sound too desperately grateful. But suddenly, bells were ringing, lights were flashing, fireworks were exploding in her head! This tall, handsome, successful man! She'd tell Gerry and Ursula that they'd met on a *cruise*, that he was a consultant and had gone to a great deal of trouble to get a day off from the Royal Marsden. Put that in your pipes and smoke it, Gerry and Arsula! she thought.

Tess no longer cared about the rain, the wind, the wet clothes, her ruined hair, the spilt vinegar on the Formica table. When they left Wanda's, Tess had a peek into several shops before Sanjeev said, 'Do you mind if we go back soon?'

It was only three o'clock and she'd been going to suggest a visit to the Royal Pavilion.

'There's a few calls I need to make this evening,' he said, 'before I have to attend a fundraising do at the Savoy. Not that I'll be eating much!' He patted his tummy.

'No, no, that's fine,' Tess said. She was rapidly finding out that his work would always dominate. That was the way he was.

The wind had died down, the rain had lessened and, by the time they got back to Milbury, the sun had come out. All was fast becoming right with the world, Tess thought. Wait till I tell Orla!

'Sanjeev's going to escort me to the wedding,' Tess said, 'and I didn't have to ask him, he actually offered.'

Orla rolled her eyes. 'Last I heard, you were going to show the world how independent you were. Who needs a man, you said, in this day and age?'

'Well, I've changed my mind.'

'Has he kissed you yet?' Orla asked. 'I mean, *really* kissed you, not a peck on the cheek.'

'Not really, no, but he's not gay or anything. We've just had our dates cut short for one reason or another.'

'And do you mind?' Orla persisted.

'Mind what?'

'Mind that he hasn't snogged you, had a little grope or something.'

'*Orla!*'

'Because it doesn't seem normal to me.'

'Well, it's fine by me, Orla. He's just devoted to his work.'

'And he always will be, by the sound of it. He's the dedicated type, so let's hope some emergency doesn't keep him from being at the wedding.'

'Of course it won't. He said they owe him time off.'

'So, when are you seeing him again?'

'Probably not before the wedding now, but he's going to phone.'

'Hmm,' said Orla. 'Do you think you could fall in love with him?'

'I don't know. But he's such a nice man…'

'I *do* know,' retorted Orla. 'You're not in love with him, you're just attracted by his looks and his profession.'

'Love comes in time,' Tess quoted, trying to remember what Sanjeev had said. Something about respect and shared interests.

'Not for you it doesn't,' Orla went on. 'I know you better than anyone, and I'm telling you that if you were in love with him you'd know by now.'

'Rubbish!' said Tess.

'You mark my words. But he'll make a very nice escort for the wedding. Now, what are you going to do about getting your money back from MMM?'

'Funny you should ask. I'm composing an email at the moment and here's the draft of what I've written. What do you think?'

Tess passed Orla a sheet of paper.

I am writing to claim back my £150 MMM Hearts Club membership fee. I have met six males, as listed below, none of which has resulted in a relationship. Furthermore, they were plainly not all vetted for their eligibility, as you advertise. They are:

Benedict Leblanc – who is in a homosexual relationship. I was dated to pacify his mother.

James Jarvis – eligible but not compatible.

Andrew Barrymore – collects several women a week from MMM purely for sex.

Walter Watson – eligible but not compatible.

Douglas Morrison – after an overnight camping trip he had a heart attack and I discovered he was a married man.

George Barratt – eligible but not compatible.

There was also a William Appleton of the so-called Appleton Catering Services. This date I cancelled, having discovered that not only did he have a wife, but also the 'catering empire' describe in his MMM profile consisted of one shabby hamburger van.

Bearing in mind that at least three of these men were plainly not vetted by you, and that I have not found my 'Ace of Hearts', I expect my £150 to be reimbursed as soon as possible.

Orla snorted. 'My God, you did meet a weird bunch, didn't you? Well, good luck with that, but I expect they'll have some excuse lined up to wriggle out of paying.'

'I shall keep at them until they do pay,' Tess said firmly. 'I need that money to cover the cost of a hat.'

'*What!* You haven't bought a hat yet? The wedding's on Saturday!'

'I'll buy one in Kingston tomorrow.'

'What colour have you finally decided on?'

'I haven't. I'll find something.'

The following morning Tess sent off the email to MMM, then took a photograph on her phone of the emerald green dress and set off for Kingston.

There were big hats, little hats, frothy hats, frilly hats, feathery hats and fascinators. None of them cut the mustard with Tess, until she was almost ready to go home and then, in a tiny boutique she'd never spotted before, there was The Hat. It was wide brimmed and frothy, and made of silks and ribbons in emerald green and turquoise. She hadn't even considered turquoise as a colour that could be coordinated with emerald green, but it looked amazing. And different. And £125.

'I'd never have considered these colours together,' she told the saleslady, holding the phone next to the hat.

'Well, you can see for yourself how stunning the combination is,' was the reply. 'And I have a bag too!'

The bag was small and made of narrow leather strips in exactly the same colours. It had a long gold chain, so she could wear it over her shoulder, and it would match the gold sandals she planned to wear.

'It's been reduced to just £50.' *Just* £50, was she kidding? Tess was now spending £175, but never mind – the outfit would be perfect because this hat and bag were stunning, the dress was stunning and her escort was stunning. She'd lost nearly two and a half stone and she had a suntan. It had taken months of hard work. And, OK, she hadn't met a soulmate, but deep down she hadn't really expected to. And perhaps her friendship with Sanjeev would develop into something special.

When she got home with her purchases she checked her emails. And there it was:

Dear Mrs Templar,

Thank you for your communication, and we are sorry you were unable to find a suitable partner in our Hearts Club.

However, the rules specifically state that, after one date you must decide **there and then** *not to progress the relationship further. You yourself have stated that you camped overnight with Mr Douglas Morrison.*

We regret, therefore, that we are unable to refund your money.

Yours sincerely,
The MMM Team

Tess fumed. How dare they try to get out of repaying her! Yes, she had seen one or two of these men more than once, but MMM's vetting procedures were dodgy; there was no denying that! She was going to win this battle, not least because of all the money she'd spent this afternoon. They might not be able to supply a suitable man, but they sure as hell were going to pay for the hat and the bag. She was not going to let the matter rest there.

CHAPTER TWENTY-FOUR

FINALISATION

Amber's dress fitted her beautifully. As she swanned backwards and forwards in front of her mother's full-length mirror, she said, 'Mum, you're a genius!'

Tess had a lump in her throat at the sight of her daughter looking so lovely. Amber's auburn hair would be worn up, and adorned with a band of cream roses – some real, some silk – and she'd carry a posy of the real ones, all supplied and put in place by the Chelsea florist at vast expense.

'Now, let's have a look at your outfit again,' Amber said.

'Oh, my hair's a mess and I—'

'Never mind your hair,' Amber interrupted, 'I have a great imagination.' She stepped carefully out of the dress. 'I'll pop down and put on the kettle while you get into all your gear, OK?'

Tess was due to have her hair trimmed, styled, highlighted and lowlighted the day before the wedding, and now it looked messy and the colour had faded. There was nothing she could do about it at the moment, so she put on the dress, the hat and the sandals, and slung the bag over her shoulder before making her way downstairs.

Amber turned round from where she'd been gazing out of the kitchen window.

'Mum, you look *sensational*!'

'Well, not *too* bad, am I? It's all cost a small fortune, but I must say you're worth it!'

'Seriously, you look fabulous! You'll put the Arse in the shade without a doubt! And I don't know why we giggled at the thought of you meeting a man. I should think they'll be falling over themselves to be introduced!'

'No need to go over the top, Amber. Anyway, I'm bringing a plus one.'

'You *are*?'

'I am.'

'Who's this, Mum?'

'I met him on the Greek cruise. He's called Sanjeev. He's Asian, tall and good-looking.'

'Blimey, Mum, this is all a bit sudden! And what does your good-looking Asian do?'

'He's a doctor. An oncologist.'

Amber's jaw dropped.

What did she expect him to be? Tess wondered. The owner of the local Indian takeaway?

'Wow! That's a turn-up for the books!'

'Isn't it just! But you'd better warn Peter and your father, because I'm not sure how that will affect the seating arrangements.'

Amber was still staring at her mother. 'Is this guy serious? About you, I mean?'

'I shouldn't think so,' Tess replied airily. 'We're just good friends.'

'But how do you feel about *him*?'

'He's nice, but there's no great romance or anything.' Chance would be a fine thing, she thought.

'Well, well!' Amber was draining her mug of tea.

I bet she can't wait to spread the news, Tess thought, smiling to herself.

'You know what, Mum? I've done you a favour by getting married. It's got you losing all that weight and spending some money on yourself. And you've obviously become more attractive to the opposite sex. So, good for you!'

For a brief moment, Tess wondered if she should tell Amber about MMM and the disastrous dates. No doubt Amber would think it hilarious, but might also judge it to be the action of a desperate woman.

'I think that, as far as the seating's concerned,' Amber went on, 'we will of course have you at the top table but, er, what's-his-name…'

'Sanjeev.'

'Sanjeev can sit at the next one down with Matt and Lisa. Only because nobody knows him and, if we sat him at the top table next to you, everyone would think you were getting married to him or something.'

Or something, Tess thought.

'Anyway, who knows if Lisa will be there? She's already overdue,' Amber added.

*

When Tess had paid her final visit to Slim Chance on the Tuesday, Judy had awarded her the coveted Gold Star Certificate in honour of attaining her target weight: eleven stone and nine pounds.

'Tess is an example to us all,' Judy preached to the gathered slimmers, after the applause had died down. 'If she can do it, you can do it! Give them a few hints, Tess!'

Tess decided to be honest. She cleared her throat. 'It helps if you have a really good reason; a target for a specific date, for instance. My target was my daughter's wedding, which is next Saturday. Apart from obviously wanting to look good on the day, I had the added incentive of competing with my ex-husband's new wife, who's younger, better looking and slimmer than me.'

There were sighs of sympathy.

'I couldn't do anything much about being younger or better looking, but I could lose two and a half stone. And, do you know what? Everyone seems to think I appear younger and better looking as a result!'

Thunderous applause erupted.

'But,' continued Tess over the clapping, 'it's made me realise that I've really done this for myself, so I can hold my head up high and know I'm looking as good as I can. And I intend to stay this way; the moment I put a few pounds back on I'll be straight back here!'

More applause, some cheering and a hug from Judy followed. They really were a very nice bunch of women. Tess laughed, gave a little bow and returned to her seat.

'Fancy a drink?' Shirley, who'd arrived late, asked. 'There's something I'd like to tell you.'

'I'd love one,' Tess replied. 'And I'm desperate to know how your romance is going!'

It was another beautiful day and they sat in the garden of the Wily Fox with their glasses of wine.

'Tell me all!' Tess said.

'Charlie's asked me to marry him,' Shirley said.

'Oh, Shirley! How fantastic! Have you said yes?'

'I have!'

'Oh my God, we should be drinking champers!'

Shirley laughed. 'Come over to my place next week and we'll do just that!'

'Congratulations! This is *such* lovely news!'

Shirley told her how Charlie had whisked her off to Paris for a weekend, then proposed to her, on bended knee, right in front of the Eiffel Tower. How could she refuse?

'Now, how about you, Tess?'

Tess told her about the final few 'hearts', about the cruise and about Sanjeev.

'He sounds really nice,' Shirley said. 'And who knows, maybe accompanying you to the wedding will direct his own thoughts in that direction.'

Tess shrugged. 'I'm not honestly sure if I feel that way about him or not. But do you know what? It doesn't matter any more. I don't need a man in my life. I thought I did, but now I don't.'

Shirley arched an eyebrow. 'These things usually happen when you aren't looking for them.'

'I'll take your word for that.'

Two days to go. The wind and rain had moved on to central Europe, and there was now a heatwave: such were the vagaries of the British weather. Tomorrow Tess would get her hair done and get herself ready for the big day. For now, it was time to contact MMM again.

With reference to your email earlier this week, I concede that I did see one of those so-called 'hearts' on more than one occasion. However, as at least three of the six 'hearts' I met were plainly not checked by you, this has caused me considerable distress as well as wasting my time. I paid £150 because that was supposed to guarantee my contacts would be vetted. You have clearly not kept your side of this agreement and so, again, I am requesting the return of my money.

In the event that my account is not credited with this money within the next seven days, I shall send copies of all our correspondence to the national press, in an attempt to save other women from wasting their money on your less than reputable agency.

Yours sincerely,

T. Templar

*

At 11 p.m. on the Friday night, the telephone rang just as Tess was trying to get to sleep. Who could be ringing so late? Her heart thumping, Tess picked up the phone. Had Amber changed her mind?

'Sanjeev!'

'I am so sorry to phone you so late, Tess, but I have a problem,' Sanjeev said.

'A problem? What sort of problem?'

'I've just had a call from my son in Norwich. His little girl, who's only five, broke her arm in two places yesterday, and she's spent all last evening in hospital having it set. Now she's home and calling for her grandpa. I'm afraid I rather spoil her, but she's such a lovely little girl. And now they want me to go up there tomorrow to console her, and I'm afraid I must. I'm so sorry, Tess.'

Tess was still trying to process the information. '*Tomorrow?* Does that mean you'll have to leave the wedding early?'

'No, Tess, it means that I won't be able to come at all. I'm going to drive up there first thing in the morning. I realise I'm letting you down but you can see my dilemma, can't you?'

Tess was now wide awake. 'I am so sorry about your poor little granddaughter. But how about coming just to the ceremony, but not the reception, or—'

'I'm sorry, Tess. By the time the wedding begins I shall be up there. And you did say that you were prepared to go on your own. Please try to understand. I promise to phone when I get back.'

'But, Sanjeev, it's only a fractured arm! I mean, it's not life or death or anything…'

'Perhaps not, but she's so little and being so brave, and just wants me to be there. This is very important to me, Tess. There is no way I could enjoy the wedding knowing that she wants her grandpa so much.'

Tess could tell by the tone of his voice that he'd said his piece, made his apologies, and the matter was now closed.

She sighed. 'Fine, Sanjeev, I hope all goes well with your grand-daughter. And drive carefully.'

'I will, and I knew you'd understand,' he said.

Did she understand? Only to a point. Yes, of course she'd be upset if Ellie broke something, but surely a few hours or even a day wouldn't make that much difference? Plainly, Sanjeev's family, as well as his work, were very important to him and she'd better get used to it. She wouldn't have been able to enjoy the wedding anyway with him being there on sufferance.

Poor Sanjeev, poor granddaughter, poor me, she thought. So, going on my own again. They'll probably think I made him up, that he was a mere figment of my imagination, wishful thinking on my part. Poor old Mum, on her own as usual.

Sanjeev was a good man, but probably not for her. As he'd reminded her, she'd been quite prepared to go to this wedding on her own, and that's what she was going to do – with her head, under that glorious hat, held high. Now she must try to get some sleep.

CHAPTER TWENTY-FIVE

ONE FINE DAY

Afterwards she would always remember that, for the first part of that momentous day, all she said was 'Thank you!' and 'Norwich, family crisis' in reply to 'You look wonderful/slim/great' and 'So, where's this *man*?'

In spite of the fact that she'd slept badly and fitfully, Tess was relieved to see herself looking reasonably bright-eyed in the morning. Probably feverish excitement, she told herself. She still hadn't lost the final two pounds, but never mind. And later, being told how good she looked did lessen the embarrassment of explaining where *the man* was. In the end, Sanjeev's absence was of minor importance, because it turned out to be a day to remember for completely unexpected reasons.

Matt, Lisa and Ellie arrived at midday to pick her up, along with Orla. When she told Orla about Sanjeev, Orla said that all men were unreliable bastards and who needed them anyway? Orla looked good in a Curvaceous special, a pale blue silk two-piece which minimised her generous measurements. 'We don't look too bad for a couple of old bats,' she said to Tess.

'Wow! Don't you look great!' Lisa exclaimed as they got into the car. Lisa, very overdue, was bursting out of a royal blue number, and Ellie was jumping up and down with excitement at being the flower girl.

Matt was driving and, as they left Temple Terrace, he said, 'Have you heard about Dad?'

'Have I heard what?' Tess asked, giving Ellie a hug.

'That Ursula has taken off.'

'What do you mean, taken off?' Tess asked.

'She's moved out. *Gone.*'

'You're kidding!' Tess could hardly believe her ears.

'Nope, I'm not. She moved out a couple of days ago, apparently.'

'Good Lord!' Tess turned to Orla. 'Did you hear *that*?'

'I *told* you not to bother slimming just to compete with that bitch, didn't I?' Orla said.

Tess was still absorbing the news.

'So it's you and Dad together at the top table,' Matt continued with a grin. 'Think you can look happy about it? And he'll be sitting next to you after he's walked Amber up the aisle, of course.'

'Problem solved!' said Orla. 'You've got an escort after all! Just as well Sanjeev couldn't make it!'

Tess was beginning to feel dizzy; this was not at all how she'd imagined the day was going to be. She was disappointed too that Barbara hadn't been able to make it. 'I'll come to visit you all afterwards,' she said in her email. She'd had an important engagement in Monaco, she'd said. More important, obviously, than her only niece's wedding. What a strange woman she was!

On arrival at the church Tess, Matt and Orla made their way to the front pew, Tess smiling and chatting with people she knew as she headed down the aisle. Lisa had stayed at the entrance with Ellie to await the arrival of the bride.

Peter grinned nervously at Tess, as he stood with his brother at the altar. Peter's brother had a vast repertoire of smutty jokes apparently, and he appeared to be relating some of these quietly now to Peter, who was snorting with suppressed laughter. It was a tricky time, Tess thought. Did you stand quietly, nervously tugging your tie and looking solemn, or did you snigger away like these two overgrown schoolboys?

The vicar appeared, the snorting stopped, and the organist sprang to life with a jerky rendition of the 'Grand March' from *Aida*, which Amber had insisted upon. 'A bit over the top, but at least it won't be dull,' was how she'd described her choice. Now Amber began her own grand march up the aisle on Gerry's arm. She looked radiant, and Tess felt tears forming as she gazed at her. And there was Ellie, following behind with her little posy and a nervous smile, plainly enjoying the oohs and aahs. I'm *so* lucky, Tess thought, looking at her son and his very pregnant wife, and at her daughter and her granddaughter. And her soon-to-be son-in-law. I should *never* complain about anything.

Tess waited until the vicar began to speak, and then held her hand out to Ellie to join them.

'Was I OK?' Ellie whispered.

'More than OK, Ellie,' Tess whispered back. 'You were fantastic, and you look lovely!'

'Fantastic!' agreed Lisa, cuddling her daughter.

After Gerry had given his daughter to be married, he sat down next to Tess and they gave each other a polite smile. A little later, as the newly married Amber and Peter headed back down the aisle, Ellie got into position behind them, followed closely by Tess and Peter's father, and Gerry with Peter's mother, followed by the other close relatives. Then came the photographs: an interminable half hour of grouping and regrouping, Tess and Gerry standing together with fixed smiles.

It was a ten-minute ride to Ashley Grange, where the reception would be held, in the wedding car laid on to transport the bride's family, Tess and Gerry sitting side by side.

'Didn't expect to see you here on your own,' Tess murmured.

'The bitch took off a couple of days ago,' Gerry replied. 'Anyway, rumour had it that you were bringing along some bloke or other.'

'Yes, well, he had a family emergency,' Tess repeated for the umpteenth time.

'So I guess it's you and me back together for the day,' he said.

'Looks like it; for today,' sighed Tess, intending to lose him as soon as she could politely do so, although obviously they'd have to sit through lunch together.

Gerry was studying her intently. 'I must say, Tess, you look stunning!'

'Thank you, Gerry.'

'Just like old times, eh? You and me together like this?'

'Not quite like old times, Gerry,' Tess said. Dear Lord, she thought, is he coming *on* to me? And Ursula's hardly out of the door! And I feel nothing for him now, other than that he's the father of my children.

Gerry was courteous and attentive to such an extreme that Tess had a job to get away from him on arrival at Ashley Grange. She kissed and congratulated Amber and Peter, grabbed a glass of champagne, and circulated amongst the guests she knew. As for the half she'd never set eyes on before, they were a type: the men balding, affluent-looking, expensively suited to conceal their paunches; the wives all shapes and sizes, but mainly outsize. Tess wondered if there was any way to discreetly distribute some of her business cards. There was also an excess of salmon pink, which must be this year's wedding colour, and the usual assortment of pastel shades and enormous hats.

Gerry was back at her side. 'Who are these people, Gerry? I don't recall seeing them before.'

He cleared his throat. 'Well, no – there are a few business contacts of mine here, Tess. You know how it is – some awfully useful chaps. You see Selwyn Hornby-Jones over there? You wouldn't believe how big he is in advertising, and he's put a lot of money my way. Great dinner at the Grosvenor House a couple of nights ago.' He moved away. 'Hello, Selwyn old chap! So glad you could make it…'

Tess tried to remember if he'd always been such a sycophant. She found herself next to Ivor, Peter's father. 'Don't know who half these people are, do you?' he asked. So she wasn't the only one who'd noticed. They chatted for a moment and then Tess spotted Orla talking with a tall, thin chinless man. He appeared to be doing most of the conversing and Orla had the look of a woman desperate to escape.

'Mrs Regan!' Tess said, grabbing Orla by the elbow. 'I've been looking for you! Do excuse us…' she added to the chinless one.

'Thought you needed rescuing,' she murmured when they were out of earshot.

'Too right!' said Orla, draining her glass. 'Talk about boring! He could bore an oil well, that one. I think we both need more fizz.'

'You're right,' said Tess, looking at her empty glass. 'You know what? I've really never liked weddings.'

'You're always saying that,' said Orla, holding out her glass for a refill. 'And yet you've been preparing for this one for bloody *months*! If you'd stayed the way you were you'd still have looked better than half these women, and there's no Ursula either. And you've had to meet up with all those awful blokes, and for *what*? You've still had to come on your own, but at least you've an escort now, even if it is only Gerry.'

'I can't argue with any of that, Orla. But you must realise I've done all the dieting and exercising for *myself*. I feel happier, I look better, I feel better and I *know* I'm healthier. I do *not* need any man in my life, and certainly not Gerry again.'

At that moment Amber came along and said, 'I can't tell you how many people have admired my dress, Mum, and Ellie's too. They've all asked me where I got it from and I've told them it's my brilliant mum, and now they all want to know who you are and where the shop is.'

'It just so happens,' said Orla, 'that I have a bag full of cards right here. I'll find a quiet corner somewhere and write on the backs of them "makers of the bride's dress", and then scatter them around any available surface.'

'Brilliant idea,' Tess agreed. 'If Gerry can use his daughter's wedding to bolster his business, why shouldn't we?'

*

And so began the wedding lunch, with Tess and Gerry sitting next to the bride, with Peter's parents and brother balancing the other side. The other tables were round, and seated eight people apiece. They were all beautifully set with linen tablecloths, fine crystal and silver, and stunning cream rose arrangements. The wine and champagne flowed, the food was delicious, and the speeches were long and predictable. When Gerry's turn came he got to his feet and said how delighted he was that his beautiful daughter had finally decided to legalise her relationship, and what a very fine man Peter was; he couldn't wish for a finer son-in-law. And so on and so on. And of course, he was so pleased to see so many of his business associates here. Furthermore, he wished to pay tribute to his lovely wife – oops! *Ex*-wife! Cue a ripple of embarrassed laughter.

When he finally sat down, Tess asked pleasantly, 'So what exactly happened with Ursula?'

'She wanted her freedom,' Gerry replied with a sigh. 'Things haven't been right for months.'

Tess was tempted to say 'divine retribution', but didn't.

'I suppose you think it serves me right,' he said, having obviously guessed correctly.

Tess smiled but said nothing.

The best man's speech went on and on: some dodgy jokes, some raucous laughter.

'Finally,' he said, 'we have a poem to love, written by the great Lord Byron, which will now be read by that well-known actor, Simon Sparrow!'

Who on earth is Simon Sparrow? Tess wondered.

Simon Sparrow was seated at one of the round tables and was obscured from her sight by a large pillar. But she could see him now. He looked vaguely familiar; had she seen him in *Holby City* or something? Tess sat rooted to the spot as this tall, very attractive grey-haired man stood up, cleared his throat and, in a deep expressive voice, recited Lord Byron's 'All for Love'.

'*O talk not to me of a name great in story; The days of our youth are the days of our glory...*' he began, and Tess, mesmerised and spellbound, couldn't take her eyes off him. She began to wonder if she was being hypnotised.

'*...Than to see the bright eyes of the dear one discover, She thought that I was not unworthy to love her...*'

He was a beautiful man. *Beautiful.* But who the hell was he? That voice! Coffee brown, smooth textured, and yet had a suggestion of roughness, like a fine emery board. Tess only knew she could listen to him forever.

'*...When it sparkled o'er aught that was bright in my story, I knew it was love and I felt it was glory.*'

He gave a little bow and sat down again to some enthusiastic applause.

'Who was *that*?' Tess asked no one in particular.

'No idea,' said Gerry dismissively.

'A friend of Peter's dad's,' said Amber on her other side. 'And didn't he read it beautifully?'

'Oh, he did!' Tess cursed the pillar because now she couldn't see him. But she could see several women at his table, and wondered which one might be his wife. He was bound to have a wife. She had to know. She'd find out when everyone got up to circulate again. What excuse could she make to meet him?

As if reading her thoughts, Amber whispered, 'I'll find out if he's married.'

'Can't say I care much for poetry myself,' droned Gerry. 'Awfully slushy, most of it. But at least that rhymed, which is more than some of that modern stuff does.' He looked fondly at Tess. 'Only seems like yesterday when I fished you out of that puddle!'

'No, Gerry, it seems like what it was – a *very* long time ago,' Tess replied truthfully, noting that Amber and Peter were now getting up from the table.

Amber smoothed down her dress. 'Come to the loo with me, Mum.'

Everyone was now standing up and moving around. Tess looked in vain for Simon Sparrow. Had he made a quick getaway? Surely not.

As they washed their hands and surveyed each other in the cloakroom mirror, Amber said, 'Simon Sparrow is an actor, and a great friend of Ivor's. Apparently he's divorced, Mum, but he does have a lady-friend. Peter thinks it's the one in the floral dress with the big pink hat.'

'Not that it matters to *me*,' said Tess.

'*Of course* not, Mum,' said Amber.

As she re-joined the guests, who were now spilling out onto the lawn again, Tess looked round for the wearer of a pink hat. Come to think of it, who *wasn't* wearing a pink hat? They seemed to be everywhere. She needed another glass of champers and then she'd look thoroughly. Presumably they'd be together and the pink hat might be easy to spot.

At least she'd managed to lose Gerry, who was now deep in conversation with a couple of city types. Coffee and tea were being served in the lounge, prior to the evening disco, and several of the ladies were sitting down balancing teacups, including one in a dress of multicoloured flowers – were they supposed to be peonies? – and a large pink hat. She was an attractive dark-haired woman and, on the assumption that this was possibly the lady-friend, there was a chance that Simon Sparrow might just be on his own somewhere.

Tess got waylaid several times as she made her way out onto the lawn and down to the riverbank. Perhaps he'd gone. And she'd never see him again. Oh God, no. But it was a beautiful day, and she strolled along by the water to a quieter part of the garden, towards the tennis courts.

And then she saw him. On a sunbed, in the shade, fast asleep.

Tess wandered over and cleared her throat, but he continued sleeping. She studied him. He'd been very dark – she could tell by the black strands still on the top of his head – but his neatly cut hair was almost all grey now. Tanned, with long dark lashes, he had an aquiline nose and full lips, and she was pleased to see he slept quietly with his mouth closed. He'd removed the jacket of his expensive grey suit, and slung it over the back of the chair. Tess could see the label: a Savile Row tailor. She might have guessed. His ankles were crossed neatly to display some black silk socks and shiny black shoes. They had to be Italian.

'How many marks out of ten?'

Tess jumped at the sound of his voice. 'Oh,' she said, flustered, 'I was just admiring your shoes.' He had beautiful hazel eyes.

'They should rate ten out of ten,' he said, sitting up. 'They cost me a fortune in Milan last year.'

'They're very elegant,' Tess said, cursing herself for not being able to think of anything more original.

'Well, if it isn't the *mother of the bride*!' he exclaimed, suddenly getting to his feet. 'I'm Simon Sparrow. I wasn't able to see you properly because there was a pillar in the way. I could only see your husband. And you are…?'

'I'm Tess, and he's *not* my husband,' she said, then added, 'although obviously he *was*, a long time ago.' She held out her hand, which he immediately grasped. She liked his firm handshake.

'Oh, good! No need for you to go rushing back then. And I must say you look very lovely, Tess.'

'Thank you, Simon. Now, tell me, where have I heard your name before?'

'I was born the same year as my dear mother fell in love with Dirk Bogarde in the film *Doctor in the House*. He played Dr Simon Sparrow in the film, and our surname was Sparrow, so there it was! I got teased mercilessly at school, but even so I think that was the reason I wanted to become an actor. Probably before your time, Tess.'

'Not at all – I loved that film!' Strangely enough, she didn't think he looked anything like Dirk Bogarde. He was unique.

'Let's find a quiet place to sit together,' he said, taking her by the elbow and heading further away from the wedding party. 'Ah, here we are…' He'd spied two seats beneath a weeping willow, which stroked the lawn with its abundant branches and hid them from sight.

Tess's heart was thumping. This was crazy.

'Haven't you a wife back there somewhere?' Tess asked, hoping Amber's information was accurate.

'Wife? Good Lord, no! Just Cynthia, who's an old friend who steps in when I need a lady on my arm for a special occasion – and she's used to me disappearing.' He smiled at her disarmingly. 'Thing is, Tess, I'm not awfully keen on weddings.'

Tess laughed. 'That makes two of us!'

'Let's you and I just pop along to the registry office then, shall we?' He was smiling but watching her closely. What a joker!

'Great idea!' Tess replied. *Of course* he was joking.

'But I should really know more about you first. Tell me about yourself, Tess.'

She told him about Amber, about Matt and Lisa – who was about to pop – and about Ellie, Orla, Curvaceous and the fat ladies, which he found most amusing. 'And I believe you're an actor? You have a very distinctive voice, and I loved listening to you reciting that poem.'

'Thank you. It's useful for voiceovers. Sadly, acting parts are few and far between these days, although I had a supporting role in a film they've been making in Hungary, and only got back last night, which is why I'm a little knackered. Now I have a six-month contract to appear in a soap on TV, starting in October, which takes me to April. After that it's anyone's guess. It's a precarious business, and I should really be thinking about doing a proper job now I've nearly reached retirement age.' He winked.

'It sounds very exciting to me,' Tess said. 'Far more interesting than measuring up a load of generously proportioned ladies and then spending hours at the sewing machine.'

'Put that way,' he said, 'you might be right!'

She liked the way his eyes crinkled at the corners. She liked everything about him.

'Tell me,' he said, 'how you manage to stay so slim?'

'How much time have you got?' Tess laughed. If only he knew!

'Not as much as I'd like,' he said, 'because Cynthia wants to be home by six for something or other. However…' He looked deeply into her eyes, and Tess's heart did some further somersaults. 'We should really have a few dates before *our* wedding, shouldn't we? Would you be free for dinner next week?'

Tess found her voice with difficulty. 'Oh yes,' she croaked.

'Good. How about Tuesday?'

'Tuesday would be fine.' As would Sunday, Monday, Wednesday, Thursday, Friday or Saturday.

'Then I need to know where you live,' he said, getting out his phone.

'I live in Milbury,' Tess said. 'It's near—'

'I know where Milbury is,' he said. 'My sister lives there. Not for much longer though; she's about to get married again too.'

'Her name wouldn't be Shirley, would it?'

'It would. How did you know *that*?'

Shirley, his sister! Of course; she'd said something about her brother being an actor, but Tess had paid scant attention. Now, as she gave him her address and phone number, she remembered he'd said a few minutes ago that Shirley was getting married again *too*. *Too!*

'I shall look forward to Tuesday,' he said.

'So will I.' He could have no idea just how much she *was* looking forward to it. This was a crazy day and a crazy conversation, but she was throwing caution to the wind. Everything felt right. One hundred per cent.

As they headed back towards the wedding guests, he apologised for being about to leave and then said, 'I think there's some excitement going on over there among your guests.'

There was, in fact, chaos. Tess left him reluctantly and rushed inside to see what was going on and what the fuss was all about. The fuss was about Lisa, whose waters had broken, and who was having contractions every few minutes. Matt was talking frantically on his phone, and Amber was trying to pacify a screaming Ellie.

'It's OK, darling, the ambulance is on the way,' Matt said, putting his arm round the shoulders of a doubled-up, panting Lisa.

'That's not all that's on its way!' yelled Lisa.

Someone had contacted the manager, who insisted that Lisa be taken to a vacant first-floor bedroom where a frantic maid was fitting a waterproof mattress cover. 'This is a first,' the maid muttered to Tess, who, along with Matt, was trying to calm Lisa.

In the middle of the chaos, Gerry arrived. 'I've been looking for you,' he said accusingly to Tess. 'Where did you disappear to?'

She ignored him. 'Will that ambulance *ever* get here?' she said.

'Do you suppose they'll charge us for the mess she made on the carpet?' Gerry asked.

The ambulance arrived just as Lisa was giving her final push.

Joshua Matthew Templar, all eight pounds five ounces of him, was born in Room 107 of Ashley Grange at 5.46 p.m.

CHAPTER TWENTY-SIX

ANOTHER FINE DAY

'Great wedding!' said Orla, when Tess delivered a dress to the shop on Monday morning. 'Best entertainment I've had in years – beats a disco any day of the week!'

Tess grinned. 'Poor Lisa! Never mind, I have a gorgeous little grandson and I've met a gorgeous big man!'

'Oh yeah? Well, Ricky got back from a long trip yesterday and do you know what? I think I might be in love with him.'

'I was just going to tell you the same thing,' Tess said.

'What? That you're in love with Ricky, too?'

'Don't be daft! But I *am* in love!'

'What – you've fallen for Gerry all over again?'

'Not likely! I'm in love with Simon Sparrow!'

'That dishy actor who read the poem? I didn't see you two together.'

'That's because we were under a weeping willow. He's *gorgeous*!' Tess gave Orla a brief account of what had transpired. 'And I'm going to marry him.'

Orla put her hand to her heart. 'You're nuts!'

'Probably,' Tess agreed.

'I mean, you hardly know the man! He's bound to be dramatic, he's an actor!'

'I think we both knew straight away,' Tess said dreamily.

'I've never heard anything quite so daft in my whole life,' Orla ranted on. 'You're talking like a lovesick teenager! You're both in your sixties, for God's sake!'

'All the more reason not to waste any time,' Tess said. 'I could murder a cup of tea. Shall we put the kettle on?'

She decided to check her emails while she waited for the kettle to boil, aware that Orla was still gaping at her in astonishment. And there it was!

Dear Mrs Templar,

Further to our recent correspondence we have agreed, in these special circumstances, to make an exception for your particular case, and we have therefore credited your account with the sum of one hundred and fifty pounds.

Yours sincerely,

MMM

All in all, it had been a very good weekend.

Two days later, Orla phoned. 'How did it go last night?' she asked. 'The big romantic date?'

'Exactly as I hoped it would,' Tess replied. 'We only wish we'd met forty years ago! But never mind, we've found each other now!'

Orla gave one of her famous snorts. 'Silver Singles become Silver Doubles? I'll believe that when I see it!'

*

She'd been incredibly nervous as she waited for Simon Sparrow to collect her. Had she dreamed it all? Was it possible you could fall in love just like *that*? It was the stuff of romantic books and movies, and things like that did *not* happen to Tess Templar. Probably he'd changed his mind. They'd both had lots of champagne, so it had most likely been the champagne talking.

Her heart had lurched when he'd arrived at her door.

'Tess,' he'd said. That was all. That and the enormous bouquet of red roses.

'Simon,' she'd said, wondering if she could stop shaking and think of something intelligent to say as well as 'Thank you for the flowers.'

'I haven't changed my mind,' he said. 'Have you?'

'No, neither have I,' Tess said, her heart still hammering.

And so they'd set off in his yellow Triumph Stag.

'I've booked at Giovanni's,' he said. 'I did try Pelligrini's but they were full.'

'I'd much prefer Giovanni's,' Tess said, with fleeting memories of Benedict.

'Good,' Simon said. 'We have much to discuss.'

'Indeed we have,' Tess agreed.

*

'And we had a wonderful evening,' she said to Orla. 'I've never been so sure of anything in my life. I really, *really* love him.'

'What did I tell you?' Orla said. 'When you fall in love, you fall hook, line and sinker. And you're planning to marry him?'

'Yes, I'm going to marry him.'

'We should celebrate,' Orla said. 'Do you fancy lunch today at Boulters?'

'Good idea,' agreed Tess. 'Just one helping though.'

A Letter from Dee

Dear reader,

Thank you so much for reading *The Silver Ladies of Penny Lane* and I hope you enjoyed Tess's mission to find the man of her dreams; not an easy task at any age, far less in your sixties!

I hope I haven't put anyone off using internet dating services because I'm sure there are lots of lovely guys out there but, you'll appreciate, I had to use some artistic licence! If you want to keep up with Tess or similar publications you can sign up to the following link:

www.bookouture.com/dee-macdonald

Your email address will never be shared and you can unsubscribe at any time.

And, if you did enjoy Tess's story I'd appreciate it if you could write a review because I do love to know what my readers think and your feedback, as always, is invaluable.

You can get in touch via Facebook and Twitter.

Dee x

 AuthorDeeMacDonald

 @DMacDonaldAuth

Acknowledgements

Firstly, thanks again to my brilliant editor at Bookouture, Natasha Harding, whose advice and encouragement is invaluable, and whose faith in me is a constant source of amazement.

And thanks to all the amazing team at Bookouture: Kim Nash, Noelle Holten, Alex Crow, Jules Macadam, Ellen Gleeson, Alexandra Holmes and my cover designer Ami Smithson.

As always, apologies to anyone I've unwittingly omitted.

A big thank you to my lovely agent, Amanda Preston, at LBA Books, and to my husband, Stan, for enduring, without complaint, my hours on the laptop. I'm also grateful to my friend, Margaret, who gave me the idea for this story, and to Rosemary Brown, my clever friend and critic, whose eagle eye rarely misses a stray punctuation mark, misspelling or grammatical howler.

Where would I be without you all!

Printed in Great Britain
by Amazon

38268028R00187